SUPER U: RISING STORM

Alex Silver

CONTENTS

Copyright

Cover Design by Samantha Santana, AMAI Designs

Proofreading by Rae Waller

ISBN: 978-1-7776786-7-8

BLURB

I've got a secret. Two, actually. I'm not that powerful. My best friend Gerald, though, he's got enough superpowers to fill the role of two heroes. His abilities are so strong, he can even make everyone believe I'm destined to be more than a sidekick. My other secret? I love him.

My crush is getting harder to hide now that we're headed off to superhero university together. With Gerald as my roommate, it's only a matter of time before he figures out how I feel. And from there, our other secrets will inevitably unravel, too. Including what truly happened the night we stumbled on a League of Villains meeting.

I never counted on the League ruining my plans to enjoy the university experience with my bestie. Or the nemesis who haunts my nightmares turning his telepathy on the city I grew up expecting to protect with my powers. One thing's for sure, superhero school isn't for the faint of heart.

Super U: Rising Storm is an M/X superhero slow-burn best friends to lovers romance. It is part of a multi-author shared universe following the university adventures of superheroes in training. Gerald is a trans man who commands the wind and electricity. Ignatius is his non-binary and autistic best friend, who controls electric sparks. Read now to watch them turn their spark into a storm.

PROLOGUE

Iggy

"**A**re you sure about this?" I already know Gerald is going to talk me around. He's my best friend, and I'd follow him to way more dangerous places than my pop's basement villain lair.

"Yeah, come on, your pop has everything we need in his lab." Gerald hops up from where we're studying in my family's dining room. His unattended pencil rolls away, clattering to the floor.

"Which we aren't allowed to use without permission," I remind him. I stand to retrieve the pencil—not because I'm going along with Ger's schemes. Nope. Not at all.

"We have to turn in our science fair project proposal by tomorrow, Ig." Gerald intercepts me before I get to the pencil. He turns me toward the basement by the shoulders. Our folks are all outside on the patio talking and enjoying the evening, so it's not like they're going to conveniently stop us. I glance longingly in their direction, anyway. I dislike breaking rules, but I hate disappointing Gerald even more.

"Well, yeah. But I thought we agreed on making an electric circuit?" I wiggle my fingers to remind him of my sparks.

"That was before I knew we could make a cannon, Ignatius. A freaking cannon, for potatoes." He squeezes his grip on my shoulders tighter and talks too close to my face. I'd hate that sort of manhandling from anyone else, but with Ger, I don't mind as much. I still can't meet his gaze and the visceral sensation of his eyes boring into me as he pleads makes me squirm.

"Isn't that dangerous?" I ask, partly to distract myself from my discomfort. Gerald seems to notice, as he backs off on the intense face-to-face.

"It's perfectly safe if we follow the plans." He turns toward his goal, and I fall into step beside him even as I continue to argue.

"That you found online?" I'm still skeptical.

Gerald waves away my concerns. "Look, there are hundreds of videos online of teens making these things. Kids younger than us. It's safe, Ig. I promise."

"Is it very loud?" I rub at my ears, preemptively blocking out the imagined noise.

"Not very." Gerald shrugs. He opens the basement door and flicks on the lights. "We can test it out before the fair, to be sure it won't bother you."

"Where?"

"I know a spot. Don't you worry."

Famous last words. It might have changed everything for us, if I told Gerald no that day. I'm not good at denying my best friend anything, though. Most of the time, I don't even want to. Gerald knew I'd go along with his plans before he even asked. I always do. He is already down the stairs and halfway to the hidden catch that unlocks the door to Foxy's lair.

"Okay, I guess we can borrow the lab to see if Pop has what we need." I relent as the door slides open to reveal a technomancer's dream work space. That's my pop, nobody's hero. He calls himself a freelancer, but most people say that's just a nicer name for unaffiliated supervillains. Either way, his lab has some impressive toys, and it's always fun when he lets Gerald and me borrow them.

***

A few weeks later, our potato cannon is ready for testing. True to his word, Ger finds a secluded overgrown lot near an abandoned industrial building that backs onto some woods and a park for our experiment.

Our science teacher is making us film the cannon in action and then calculate the force and velocity of our projectiles to present alongside the video clip. So we can use it for our science fair entry, but we can't actually bring an imitation weapon to school. The verdict from our teacher disappointed Gerald, but I figure doing this with just the two of us rather than in the crowded schoolyard makes more sense.

I stand back to record everything on my phone, noise-canceling headphones firmly over my ears to block out the sounds of the cannon firing. Gerald sets everything else up for the experiment. Armed with our science project, several cans of aerosols so we can compare their efficacy as combustion fuel, and a five kilo bag of potatoes, we get to work.

The first shot falls short. Not very impressive. So Gerald loads the next potato down the barrel. He increases the amount of fuel he sprays into the combustion chamber, and launches the next potato right into the side of the empty building.

It lands with a wet splat. The third shot shatters an old window and flies right inside… only to be chased back outside by Vespula.

Gerald drops the potato cannon and we both flatten ourselves onto our bellies in the tall grass at her unexpected appearance. I recognize her yellow and black banded super suit from footage of Balantin defending the city. Vespula is a nasty-tempered villain, like the wasp she takes her name from. Her power is flight, and she wields poisoned darts treated with a mild paralytic agent.

She likes to say her sting is worse than her bite. Whatever that means. We're in trouble when she spots us. And then more villains pour out of the building through the door and we're really screwed. I recognize most of them, and to a supe, they are part of Toronto's League of Villains. As I scan the building, some intrepid henchperson has tagged the wall near the door with their telltale double fangs logo in neon green spray paint.

"We should go," I hiss at Gerald. He doesn't seem to hear me, too focused on the supes leaving the warehouse.

The League's impromptu guild has been courting Pop to join them for longer than I've been alive. And while supes keep up the polite fiction of not knowing each other's secret identities, they all know each other. They all get their education together. And at least one villain attending this secret meeting has probably eaten at my family's table and will recognize me. Not Vespula. I only know her by reputation, but someone.

Until this year, they might have left me alone. Most of them have the sense not to interfere with other supes' families. Targeting me would only escalate. Except, this year my powers came in, and right now, there is no hiding that I'm one of them. A supe. The stress of the situation has electric charges running over my hands and arms in ticklish streaks that make me rub at the skin to dispel the charge. I hate the light ticklish brushes that make my skin go all squirmy.

"Ger..." I reach over to tug at his sleeve with my less charged hand. I have little control over my sparks when I get worked up, but they're still a part of me, and no part of me would ever hurt my best friend. The sparks don't leap to him. Too bad Gerald isn't backing down or showing any sign he intends to run. I won't leave him behind, but this is bad. Very bad.

"It's a League meeting," Gerald breathes. And even though I've made a science of studying him these past several years, I can't read the emotion in his breathy whisper. Awe? Terror? Ridiculous testosterone fueled bravado? Who knows.

"See anything?" a gruff, familiar voice barks. I can't quite place it, but it fills me with raw terror. I push one side of my headphones off my ear so that I can hear better.

"Probably kids vandalizing the place. I bet they're long gone after they broke the window," another voice opines.

"We should check, to be sure." Vespula flies a little higher and I shrink further into the weedy overgrown field in a vain effort at stealth. The breeze around us kicks up, like it does whenever Ger gets agitated these days. He's been improving his control, but this is a stressful moment. I can hardly judge his slip when sparks are still dancing along my hands and up my arms.

Something brushes against my mind, like spider silk. I shudder, realizing why he sounded so familiar when he spoke. That's Teller. As in, he tells people what to do, and they are powerless to resist him. He's a telepath and the current leader of the League here in the GTA. His presence is bad news. It was his voice that froze me in place. The memory of him pawing through my mind still fuels my worst nightmares.

Tonight keeps going from bad to worse. This must be an official League meeting. Meaning they are planning something. Something big from the number of villains milling around the exit. And Gerald knows it too, which means any chance of convincing him to slip away quietly has evaporated.

"Come on out, little rabbits, I recognize those bright young minds," Teller calls into the gloomy twilight. Even if he and his cronies can't see us clearly, he touched our minds. In my heart, I know we're powerless against him. It's not a command, not yet, since I don't feel the compulsion to obey. Using his power like that, to force compliance, is too taxing to pull out for a couple of stray kids who stumbled on his meeting. Not if he can lure us to him without it; he and his band of evildoers have the upper hand and we all know it. I wish I could turn on some music and blot everything out, but I need to hear them coming for us, so that isn't an option.

Ger and I aren't walking away without a fight. Not when we would be the perfect leverage to get my pop to throw in with the League for whatever they're planning. Or to pressure my moddy, one of the more powerful heroes employed by Toronto's Hero Brigade, into looking the other way when the city calls on them to act against the League. Not to mention Gerald's parents; compromising a well-placed sidekick can make the difference between success and failure for the League's nefarious deeds.

I want to flee more than anything, but Gerald

will never go for that. This is the chance to prove ourselves as heroes that my best friend has been dreaming of since his powers came in last year. To no one's surprise, he's an elemental, like all three of his parents and most of his sisters.

His specialty is wind. The part that no one but the two of us knows about is that even before my electric powers came in, he's been able to manipulate electricity, too. And when my powers stopped developing at a level that would barely crack sidekick classification on a test, Ger stepped in to make me seem stronger. So I could live up to my parents' hopes for me. I've always hated disappointing them. We've been playing out that lie for months now. Long enough that when I reach for my powers, I more than half-expect that Ger will be there to complete the intended action.

I'm not reaching for my powers right now. The phone is still recording for all the good that will do, but I focus all my attention on not being hunted down by the pack of villains standing less than fifty meters away from us when the lightning strikes their meeting place. It forks into blinding prongs and hits the building at multiple key points. For a moment, all I can see is Gerald's silhouette back-lit against the blinding flash of blue-white light. My meager sparks react to the huge discharge so nearby and I hastily stuff my phone into my pocket before I can short it out—again—with the static dancing on my skin.

Under any other circumstances, Gerald's supe pose might make me laugh. But tonight, it carries a certain gravitas. When the afterimage clears, smoke is coiling up from the building, and the villains are a roiling knot of chaos. Gerald grabs my arm and drags me closer. Both of us crouch low to take advantage of the late hour and the ominous storm clouds gathering above us, making it hard to see anything. Hopefully that means they won't see us and we can still slip away. A vain hope for me to cling to, since we're headed in the wrong direction for that. The villains' voices carry to us on Ger's artificial wind.

"Get back in there and grab the plans, you numbskulls! Whose bright idea was it to leave the prisoner unguarded, anyway? Don't you realize how important he is to our plans?"

"But, Tell, it's on fire!" a minion protests, a big broad one who I vaguely recognize as Blot. Blot yelps as Teller turns his powers of coercion on the hapless henchperson.

"Someone get in there and grab the plans and Dr. Lewis," Teller commands. I shiver, feeling the tug of his coercion at the edges of my mind, even though it's being directed at someone else. I twitch the pad of my headphones back over my ear; blocking out his voice helps to block out his powers. Again, I wish I could tune him out entirely.

"But the fire…" Blot complains, even as the big man reenters the burning building, his feet carrying out the order despite himself. Blot isn't a supervillain. He's one of Vespula's henchmen. One who clearly hasn't been around Teller much, if he's unused to having the man's power turned against him. Teller isn't shy about getting his way.

"That's what your super suit is for, Blot, to protect you from such mundane concerns! Vespula, go seize the meddling children, they're at the edge of the woods to the north of here."

Great. We're about to get darted. It won't kill us. We're more useful to the League alive than dead, but I saw how miserable the paralytic Vespula uses made Moddy after they stopped Vespula from robbing a store last summer.

"Did you hear that?" I ask, silently pleading with Gerald to make this better, because I can't think beyond the cold rush of terror at having the League come after us.

"I sure did, come on." Gerald grabs my hand, but instead of changing course to run away, like I'd half-hoped, Gerald drags me toward the burning building. Blot might wear a flame-resistant super suit, but we sure don't have that layer of protection. This is bad. Bad, bad, bad.

Gerald is fast, though. He can use the wind to propel himself forward. And when we're touching, that burst of speed applies to me as well. Some really powerful wind manipulators can even use it to fly. I don't think Ger has tried that yet. The thought of him going airborne makes me sick with fear for him. Like the queasy ache in my gut right now from all the smoke and chaos pressing in around us.

Gerald weaves through the panicking villains and right into the burning warehouse. Someone is yelling, cursing up a storm near the back, where the smoke is thickest. I can just make out Blot's broad shoulders, wreathed in the smoke and flames between us and the screaming man. Dr. Lewis? The name isn't familiar. I don't think he's a supe at all, let alone part of the League. A hostage? Teller called him a prisoner. If there is a civilian in the burning building, then we owe him our help, especially since our powers started the blaze.

"We have to get the doctor out of here. Come on, Ig." Gerald echoes my thoughts. I don't resist as he continues to pull me along with him on his headlong dash into danger. A bubble of fresh air surrounds us, pushing through the heat haze of the burning building. It is terrifying. I cling to

Gerald, knowing that letting go is all but a death sentence. I don't think I could walk out through the hungry flames licking at every surface around us. They roar, angry and loud in my ears, even through my noise-canceling headphones.

Gerald is the only force pulling me forward. Blot gets to the doctor first. The man remains where the villains left him manacled to a chair, cursing ever more vociferously as the heat scalds his wrists. Instead of releasing the captive, Blot focuses on gathering up the smoldering papers from the table. A glance at them reminds me of the schematics Pop keeps for his tech. I catch the words "augmentation ray" near the top of the page.

Gerald gestures, sending a blast of wind to blow back the heat and snatch up the papers. The surrounding flames burn higher at the added oxygen, but Gerald pushes away the heat and smoke from around us. Blot clings to most of the papers, still in the grips of Teller's compulsion to rescue them. Gerald ends up scrabbling with him over the documents. While he's busy with that, I go to the frightened doctor.

"Get me out of here!" he wails, thrashing at his bindings. I crouch behind the chair, ignoring the terror of the flames by focusing in on the restraints. Metal cuffs. Shit, I might have gone through a phase where I wanted to pick locks, but it never really stuck. That's something I resolve to fix if we get out of this alive. The metal is hot to the touch and getting hotter, despite Gerald's best efforts at shielding us. It's getting harder to breathe and I couldn't carry the bound doctor out of here on a good day, let alone with smoke and heat searing my lungs. Then I see the unobtrusive biometric pad. It's an electronic lock. At least on some level. I reach for the sparks and push them at the circuitry, hoping that frying the thing will make it pop open. I poke at the mechanism until a barely audible whir sounds. The cuff pops open. I repeat the process on the three remaining cuffs holding his other limbs to the sturdy chair. As soon as he's free, the doctor staggers to his feet.

I grab his arm to keep him from stumbling off into the burning building. If we go out the way we came in, we'll just deliver ourselves back to the League, too weak to fight. There are sirens blaring in the distance, but I don't know if they'll reach us in time.

"Gerald!" I call for him. He and Blot are still struggling over the singed and smoking papers. I cough. It's so hot and I don't know if we even *can* get out at this point.

Gerald glances over to assess the situation, and gives up on saving the papers. Instead, he takes a moment to study the topmost page, then propels them into the flames with another gust of heated air.

Blot yowls and chases after them, to no avail. He only stops when the paper is burnt to irretrievable ash. Teller's compulsion made him heedless to the flames, but now that the command is impossible to obey it breaks. He stumbles dazedly for the exit, hacking and coughing. I hope he makes it out, but I can't focus on him. Not when we're in just as dire a situation, trapped near the back wall in a bubble of relative safety thanks to Gerald's powers.

Gerald comes to me. There's a whoosh of cool air as he reinforces the protective bubble around me, the rescued doctor, and himself. It stokes the flames, but it's easier to breathe and the heat no longer feels like it's going to burn me. Not yet, anyway. I know Ger is powerful, but I'm not sure that he can hold this air pocket around all three of us indefinitely while the building continues to burn.

"This way." He takes the non-powered doctor's other arm and the two of us drag our rescued NP toward the nearest wall. Gerald smashes out a window, using the wind to sweep away any remaining shards of glass, and then another burst to boost me up and out. Together we help the doctor through the gap, and then Gerald leaps after us. The three of us stagger away from the engulfed building, the cool night air a sharp contrast to the super-heated atmosphere of the blaze.

We didn't die. And the sirens are getting closer. Before I pass out from the smoke and terror that has me trembling, I see Balantin and Squirt in their colorful super suits, racing to the rescue ahead of the firefighters. Moddy is here to save the day. The rest of the night passes in a blur of overstimulation and trying not to stim too obviously and draw even more attention to myself.

Once we're safe, they make us tell the Hero Brigade everything. Except I lie. To protect Ger from the repercussions of what we did and to protect the powers he's kept hidden. I say it was my lightning that started the fire. Fear and adrenaline boosted my mediocre talent to hero levels of power.

I'm still in the grace period of a new supe, when even catastrophic failures at controlling one's powers are more easily forgiven. Gerald isn't. He's had his wind powers for over a year. The electrical ones came in not long after, though he hid them, since it is exceedingly rare for anyone to have multiple distinct powers.

Gerald doesn't contradict my claims that it was my powers that saved us and the doctor from the League's nefarious purposes. He swears to my lies, to protect me from anyone finding out how weak I really am and from the consequences of lying to the Brigade.

The Brigade took my recording of our science project, too. Once they got it, someone leaked the footage to the press, and the story took off like wildfire. I didn't get Gerald in the frame as the lightning struck.

Everyone believes my sparks started the fire as a distraction to free the doctor. We told the truth about Gerald manipulating the wind to allow us to stage our daring rescue, at least.

My family has to pay a fine over the property damage, but it's nominal since the blaze stayed contained. So that cements both of our statuses as hero class supes and traps us in our lie.

CHAPTER 1

Iggy

"You don't have to keep lying for me," I whisper into the phone, paranoid that someone will overhear me. Ridiculous, since I'm alone in my bedroom, pacing back and forth with excess energy.

No one is here to overhear my conversation with Gerald. Not unless I count the new batch of listening devices which I borrowed from Pop's lair.

I've been tinkering with them to see about making a mic that is small enough to swallow and can filter out body sounds to pick up what the host hears. It's a fun side project for when I get bored practicing my newly honed superpower based lock picking skills. Turns out that what my sparks lack in power, I can make up for with finesse.

Both my folks are working. Which means Ger's parents are also working, since they all work together. Not that they talk about their jobs much at home. No, at home Balantin and Foxy aren't superpowered household names, they're just my ordinary run-of-the-mill parents. The world calls them heroes. I call them Moddy and Pop.

Gerald huffs into my ear. "I'm not lying, Iggy. It's not *really* lying to let them draw their own conclusions."

"It is when those conclusions are a lie," I say, rolling my eyes, even though he can't see it. Ger spends too much time with my Pop and his two dads if he's going to debate the definition of a lie when the intent here is clear. We're deceiving people. I whirl and pace back the other way.

"Look, don't you want to be in the same classes? If we come clean, they'll stick you on the sidekick track. You aren't my sidekick, Ig. Never have been, never will be. We are equal partners to the end," my best friend promises.

Ugh, my heart can't take that kind of sweetness from him. That right there is why I'm going along with this. Ger might not love me the way I want, but that doesn't really matter. He *does* love me. I flop onto my bed and curl up under my weighted blanket, wishing the pressure on my chest was him holding me tight. "The end of what, Ger? Do you really think you can pull both our weight forever?"

"Why do you think I can't?" he challenges me, with all the infuriating cocksure attitude of every neurotypical teenage boy I know.

"What if something happens to you because I'm not..." I gulp, unable to finish the sentence. I've had nightmares about something happening to him because of our ruse. Static fills the phone line when I get stressed. The little crackles of my power manifesting create interference until I can rein in my control. I press my thumb and forefinger against my closed eyes and focus on the patterns of light that bloom from the pressure to block out my nerves. It helps; the static fades.

The thing is, I grew up with heroes. I've sat by Moddy's hospital bed after they get hurt stopping the villains. Not Pop. He's more of a free agent than a true villain and he isn't one to go charging into danger. His work is quieter. But the fact remains, being a superhero isn't all about the glitz and glamor and saving the day.

Gerald should realize that it's actually dangerous work. He was the one holding my hand when I fell apart after visiting Moddy in the hospital. They made a full recovery from Vespula's neurotoxins, but it was still terrifying to see them helpless and small in a hospital bed. I couldn't bear it if Gerald got hurt because I'm too scared to tell the truth about my powers. Or my lack of them.

"You're not what?" Gerald demands. "You are perfect the way you are, Ig. Besides, you know the stupid tests aren't everything. I don't want to live in some hierarchy where one of us has to outrank the other. You help me with my crappy school grades, even though I know you have an easier time studying without me around. Why shouldn't I help you when I can?"

The tests he's referring to were all but a formality for me because our excursion with the potato cannon made headlines. Not just the *Supe Report* conspiracy blog either. No, we made the *Toronto Star*. So yeah, the entire city thinks I'm H class. H for hero as opposed to S for sidekick or B for those below even that cutoff.

At my actual ranking test, Gerald tagged along and easily manipulated the results. In most cases, it's easier to fix the results if you want to test as weaker than you are, but there are always workarounds. And confirmation bias was on our side. The kid of two supes who everyone saw call down a storm in a viral video clip would not test as anything but hero class.

"Your mom and my moddy don't stand on protocol," I point out. "We can be equals in every way that matters, even if I am classified as a sidekick."

"Sure. When it's just them, I know that's how it is. I know Mom and your moddy are friends outside of work. But when the cameras are rolling, all anyone cares about is Balantin. No one gives a rip if something happens to a sidekick, so long as the hero is victorious."

"That's not true!" I protest. But he's not wrong. If I was his sidekick, when we're trained, then he'd be the one making headlines and I'd get relegated to a footnote. A distraction or bait for his nemesis to kidnap. Not even the conspiracy bloggers are all that bothered over what happens to a mere sidekick or henchperson.

I think I've seen Gerald's parents mentioned by name in roughly one headline on the *Supe Report* blog. Even though most people write it off as full of conspiracies, I read it sometimes. It's one of the few supe chaser blogs run by an actual supe, the mysterious Bloggler. So that's probably why they mentioned Gerald's folks. A disaffected supe with weak powers is one of the few people who gets the full picture of what it's like to *be* a supe.

"It *is* true. Besides, I want to be in the same classes at university; we won't be if we're on separate tracks. We can keep making this work, Ig. Have a little faith in me."

I sigh and roll onto my back and reach for my headphones. My music helps to block out the rest of the world. I can picture Gerald's hopeful expression as he pleads for me to go along with his plan. "Okay. I won't say anything." I give in to his wiles. We say our goodnights and I curl up tighter with my music, hoping this isn't something I'll have reason to regret.

CHAPTER 2

Gerald

"**S**mile, Iggy." Mom gestures for my best buddy to lean closer to me for a photo in front of our new dorm. I glance over at Iggy, cute as hell, in their favorite pink narwhal hoodie. Their pale skin has a scattering of freckles I've fantasized about kissing. Their overgrown dark curls stand up in messy disarray, like usual when they go too long between haircuts.

By contrast, I got in the habit of keeping my light brown wavy hair trimmed short to avoid misgendering years ago. Even though both my dads have brown skin courtesy of their Mexican-Canadian heritage, I take after Mom's fair complexion. Even with a summer tan, I'm the palest of my siblings. That can get weird when ignorant strangers and gossip tabloids assume things about my family. At least today the cameras are here to capture a family memory, not splash my picture on a newsstand.

Ig's Pop has his camera aimed right at us. The shutter clicks away as he documents our first day at Super U. All five of our respective parents are alumni here, so they're allowed all over the secretive campus, unlike the non-powered parents and family.

Another freshman nearly levitates their suitcase right into Mom when they notice Ig's moddy. Balantin is one of the city's most famous defenders, so everyone here knows who they are. Several first gen students even cluster around to ask for autographs, or get selfies. I guess it hasn't sunk in that they are part of Balantin's world now.

That's why first-generation students have more restrictions on what their guests and visitors can see and do. It's about protecting our identities. The idea is some sort of mutually assured destruction where if we share another hero's identity, then we're all but asking to be outed ourselves. Plus, outing anyone is a dick move whether you're talking about another person's sexuality, gender identity or their mundane alter ego. At least, that's what I always say. Gerald's Rule numero uno: don't be a dick.

My second rule is that no one messes with my Iggy. That one I keep to myself. Ig's a bit of a runt. They can't help it. Or the way they think about the world in ways that always seemed to make them a magnet for bullies throughout grade school. Bullies they don't even realize are picking on them half the time. It makes me want to punch people when they make Ig think they're being friendly when they're really mocking them.

"Tell us more about dragon reproduction, Ignatius." Those little jerks will say, getting Ig all excited that someone shares their interests. And then they laugh about Ig's earnestness. Even though it would totally make sense for dragons to have hemipenes. If they weren't fictional.

I'm feeling murdery just thinking about the jerks we left behind after graduation. I hold Iggy a little closer and force a smile for the camera. Iggy glances at me, dark eyes open wide, like they don't get why I'm suddenly hugging the stuffing out of them, but they don't complain. I remind myself we never have to see our old classmates again. It's a big enough city to lose yourself in, and none of them had what we have. Powers.

The reason we're at Super U. Everyone calls all the globally accredited Super Hero Universities that, but technically, this particular school is Bertram R Arthur University. After one of the first geneticists to study us and figure out how the SUPE allele works. People in that field are still trying to figure out why kids like me, with three low-powered parents, come out as hero class and a kid like Ignatius, with two of the most powerful supes in the city as their genetic forebears, can barely work up enough of a charge to power a lightbulb. I mean, not Ig specifically, because as far as the world knows, they're an H class like me. I've worked hard to maintain that illusion. It's no mean feat, even for someone as powerful as me.

"Earth to Gerald," Mom says. I force a saccharine sweet smile for her, still holding Iggy close. I'm not a huge fan of her documenting my life, but I can't hate an excuse to hold Iggy. We don't touch as much these days. That's mostly my fault. I pushed them away when I started my transition because boys aren't supposed to be cuddly and affectionate with their friends. I grew out of thinking I had to live by everything boys are *supposed* to do, but by then things were different. Like, now touching Ig turns me on sometimes. And maybe no one's noticed, but I'm not taking any chances with our friendship.

I've watched enough teen dramas to know that first loves don't last forever and telling your best friend you love them is a terrible way to actually stay best friends. They've been by my side practically since we were in utero, so I'm not about to mess with that kind of history.

Our folks finish documenting the moment we move into our dorm, and I give Iggy a hearty slap on the back. "You ready for this?"

"Of course," Iggy says, tugging on their shirt hem like the fabric is bothering them. "Let's go see our room."

Our room. Damn, I did not think through just how tempting that thought is. And since we have the same class schedule, I'm going to be hard pressed to find any privacy to wank my attraction to them out of my system. This is going to be an interesting year.

We gather up our bags and narrowly dodge a couple of elemental kids having a water fight on the edge of the fountain in the middle of the quad. They continue to throw water around until one of the resident assistants, wearing a helpful nametag, intervenes. The RA reminds them powers are not to be used against another person outside of abilities and combat classes.

Until now, my abilities made me unique. Here, they're part of what makes me fit in. From the barely there fizzle of Ig's electrical manipulation to the kid lumbering past us using superstrength to carry a pushcart holding all their possessions into the dorm with a single trip, abilities are part of the fabric of life on campus.

For the next four years, we're going to be living

in a bubble where having abilities is the norm. Our lives are going to revolve around learning how to best use our superpowers once we finish our training and return to the mundane world. And when we graduate, we'll be heroes together, partners, just like it was always meant to be.

CHAPTER 3

Iggy

ollege is overwhelming. Orientation is
bright and loud and crowded. The other
students are all showing off their abilities,
so walking around campus is a blur of motion
and colored lights. The sounds merge into a
cacophony that echoes like it's trying to burst my
eardrums. Even the soft music playing through
my noise-canceling headphones can't entirely
block it all out. There's just so much noise.

I can't focus on anything the people on the big
stage are saying over all the static and the bright
lights. It doesn't help that even as oblivious as I
can be about people; I know that if I showed off
the pathetic sparks that are all I can manifest
with my superpowers, they'd laugh at me.
Especially since so many of them saw Moddy and
Pop and wanted their autographs, though the
Foxy fans were more discreet about approaching

us. Foxy, Pop's supe persona, isn't a bad guy, but he's barely on the allowable side of unsanctioned exercise of his superpowers.

After our parents leave us in our dorm to finish unpacking and settling in, I retreat to the little lair Gerald helped me set up first thing under his lofted bed. It's not much, a big round chair his mom calls a papasan that hugs my body with my familiar weighted blanket draped over it to mute the light and noise.

I've gotten good at not stimming in obvious ways in front of people; being socially ostracized will teach you to hide who you are real quick when your anxiety goes through the roof whenever people look at you too long. I can feel their eyes burning through me like they're made of lasers. Now that we're alone, I can curl my knees up to my chest, rub my hands over my face, and rock until everything else recedes, and it's just me in my safe little cocoon with no one to put on an act for.

I don't even realize that I'm crying until Gerald's big warm hand rubs my back through the heavily weighted dragon blanket. "You okay in there, Ig?" he asks. I know I take too long to parse what he said; it's hard to focus when I get overloaded.

"Mm." I force out a response. Words come slowly, hard to find because I just want to turn off the people-ing part of my brain and hide until we have to go to class tomorrow. There's too much going on and too many new scripts to learn. Tomorrow is looming like a giant void of things I don't know how to do and situations I have no experience with navigating and the only lifeline I've got is that Gerald has the same schedule, so I can follow his lead like I always do. I cling to that thought.

"You don't have to talk. If you want me to stay, make another noise, otherwise I'll leave you alone," Gerald offers. Part of me wants him to stay more than anything. But I really can't cope with any more stimulation right now. It's all I can do to stop my sparks from going haywire and messing with my headphones. Electric powers, even weak ones, are hell on electronics, and my soothing music is vital right now.

Even Gerald's usually comforting hand rubbing circles on my back feels like it's burning into me. It's all too much and everything is changing and I'm so afraid that I won't be able to live up to what everyone expects from me. I press my lips shut tight and stay silent. Gerald gives my back a final pat, then I hear him walk away, pick up something from his desk and leave. The door lock clicks behind him. I release a long shuddery breath and let go of having to act a certain way. Here I can curl up in my safe little nest and stop pretending I'm not panicking about how different my entire life is going to be, starting now.

CHAPTER 4

Gerald

I figured Ig would need some space after orientation. They were tapping their toes throughout the long speeches, welcoming us to campus and reminding us we're supposed to be some sort of superpowered community. That's always a sure sign there is too much going on and they can't focus. Their fingers twitched the way they do when they are forcing themself not to stim more obviously.

Some community, when they pack us all into an auditorium that echoes with all the new students' excited chatter while they shine too-bright lights on our faces. I wish I could make everyone turn down the volume for Iggy at events like that. I hope our big lectures aren't that bad. The lecture halls I've seen have better acoustics, at least. And the rules about not using our abilities in class should help, too.

I know from experience that Iggy will need some time alone to calm down, so I won't be going home any time soon. Might as well explore the campus. That way I can find all our classes tomorrow without stressing over it. One of us knowing where we're going should help Iggy cope. They hate not knowing what to do or drawing attention to themself.

Hate isn't the right word, exactly. It's more like they have to use every spoon they have running through every possible scenario and how they might react to it and whether that reaction is the right one and the potential consequences if it's the wrong one because they know neurotypicals don't always respond well to the actions that seem most reasonable to them, but that doesn't make it any easier to figure out which responses NTs want from them. And just listening to Ig try to explain it is exhausting, let alone trying to figure it all out on the fly.

So yeah, if I can tell them I know where we're going and what to do, it will make tomorrow easier. And then I won't feel as bad about asking them to help me with my homework and exasperating the crap out of them when I slack off with my constant distractions while we study.

I take a little over an hour to scout out all the classrooms on our schedule. That's partly from getting lost along the way a couple of times and trying to figure out the numbering for the classrooms in the Nutter building. It has the power usage classes, so the architecture is weird to accommodate various adaptations. That way we don't accidentally blow something up, punch through a support beam, or set the building on fire with a stray lightning bolt, or whatever else uncontrolled powers might do.

There's an open practice room where some upperclassmen are sparring when I wander past the viewing window. I check out their moves. I don't recognize the students, not surprising since I've only been here a day, but watching them has me itching for the day when Iggy and I can join the likes of Balantin protecting the city as part of Toronto's Hero Brigade. Nothing against Foxy, but I want to be a hero. With action figures and news coverage and the keys to the city.

Not that I'd tell anyone I want the accolades. A lifetime of watching the adults in my life in front of a camera spouting lines about being happy to serve the city and protect non-powered citizens from those who would abuse their powers has taught me what you can and can't say in front of a camera. No need for the Public Relations 101 class I've got this term to tell me the obvious. Then again, with my upbringing, I doubt most of the classes will have much to teach me. This program is more about getting the qualifications I need to be a hero.

A flash of fire inside the practice room draws my attention back to the sparring students. There's a tall Black person wearing a tight, presumably flame-resistant, super suit arcing flame between their hands facing off with a shorter Asian supe in a similar protective super suit. The second supe flashes around the room with what is either the most pronounced super-speed I've ever seen in action or else some form of line-of-sight teleportation. Hard to say with only the naked eye.

Speedy dodges fireballs, using the room's various obstacles to work their way closer to the fire wielder perched on a tower near the room's center. At first glance, it looks like Speedy is completely over-matched. Until the moment they zip in, just as a fire blast leaves their opponent's hands.

The fire must have some sort of refractory period, because Speedy has Fire pinned on the ground with power disrupter cuffs fastened around their wrists before they can light up another blast. The disrupter has to be touching skin to work, but the next attempted fireball fizzles and Speedy pumps a fist in the air in triumph while Fire stops trying to squirm free, admitting defeat.

They exchange words I can't hear through the viewing glass. Speedy releases Fire and helps them to their feet. The two shake hands and leave the practice room with the sort of playful casual touches that indicate they're close. The doors to the practice room shut automatically behind them and a reset sequence rearranges the various obstacles while fans vent out the lingering smoke from the fireballs. There's a flag at the top of the tower in the room's center now.

When the room is ready, another group of upperclassmen enter and take up positions around the perimeter. The tallest is white and blond, the person to their left is dark-haired and ochre skinned with muscles for days and the third has white skin, dyed-blue hair, and long elegant fingers. I watch in fascination as a timer counts down, and then all three of the new supes burst into motion. The tall one blasts a pathway over the first obstacle with ice. They skate along the ice as they materialize more of it in front of them. The muscular one plows through anything in their path, charging implacably, but slowly, in a straight line toward the tower. The third, with the blue hair, casually strolls forward. Frosty is laughing as they skate their way toward the center, taking the time to spin and direct a second blast of ice toward the big one. I gape at the display of Frosty skating backward as they use one hand to keep channeling an icy pathway to skate on and the other to trip up their opponents.

I'm too focused on the showy display to notice that I've got company.

"South's such a showoff," Speedy says, sounding exasperated, and I'm not sure if they popped into being at my side or if I didn't notice their more mundane approach. "Sorry to startle you." Speedy grins at me, then goes back to watching the spectacle. They sound more amused to have made me jump than apologetic.

"It's fine." I shrug it off. "I'm Gerald, he/him."

That gets me a side-eye from Speedy. "You a first gen, Gerald? Most of us don't go around using our legal names here."

"Yeah, well, I had to jump through all kinds of stupid hoops to get to pick Gerald, so hell if I'm not going to use my name." I bristle. Probably more than I should—Speedy didn't mean anything by it.

Speedy's expression softens and they stick out a hand to shake. "Ah, sorry, didn't mean any harm, Gerald. I go by Streak. She/her. And my future sidekick here is Cinder, also she/her."

Cinder is the person Streak was sparring with a minute ago and she joins us, pulling long magenta box braids into a ponytail.

"Is Streak telling you stories?" she asks me, then she leans in and gives Streak a kiss on the cheek. Streak turns so that it lands on her mouth and they seem to be lost in each other for a minute before they pull apart, smiling into each other's eyes. Something in me relaxes at the display of affection. Like these are my people. Or at least, I hope they can be.

"Nothing but the truth," Streak insists, still smiling at Cinder like she's the sun. "This is Gerald. He's a new freshman, right?"

"Yep." I wave to Cinder.

"Nice to meet you, Gerald. Are you a legacy or a first gen?" Cinder asks.

"Sort of a legacy. My folks sidekick for Balantin and Foxy," I say. The other two exchange a look, but they earn points from me for not fangirling or saying anything about my word choice, since technically my dads both hench for Foxy, it's a subtle difference. Heroes and sidekicks work for the common good or for companies that need superpowers to deliver goods and services. Villains and henchpeople freelance for their own purposes, usually nefarious. Not that there aren't freelance supes on all sides, but Foxy skirts the law, operating in the murky gray side of affairs.

"Cool. My mom's a minor supe attached to a tiny little town in the boonies," Streak says. "Did you watch our practice?"

"Yeah." I nod. "You're fast."

"Nah, I'm not super speedy, I sort of blur time? It's functionally teleportation, but I have to actually move from point A to point B. Except I can kind of smudge the difference between the two so it happens instantaneously. They consider it hero class because time manipulation is no joke, even if it's just a smidge of it and I can only use it on myself and my immediate vicinity. I can rewind a larger area for inanimate objects, but that's next to useless since it only works on a 3 second loop. Basically, I run fast, and it's hard for me to break dishes." She winks.

"Don't be modest, Streak, you're a badass chronomancer." Cinder nudges her with an elbow.

"Looked pretty badass to me." I gesture toward Cinder. "She's joking about you being a sidekick, though, right? I mean, you shoot fireballs."

"Fire*ball*," Cinder corrects me, emphasizing the singular with one raised finger. "Most fire manipulators have more juice than me. I can only maintain about the amount you saw me use in there. It's not quite enough to pass the qualifications for H class." Cinder shrugs it off. "No big deal. I don't need to be at the top billing for us to work together. It means we can look for work in smaller towns as a package deal without them having to budget for two superheroes."

"Oh, look! South wiped out!" Streak whoops and bangs on the glass, which apparently South can hear because they glance at us with a murderous scowl and flip her off. She returns the gesture.

"South's mom is my mom's nemesis. I mean, we aren't supposed to talk about that, but yeah," Streak says. "Anyway, the other two in there with him are Pugilist, AKA Pugsly, and Gill."

"Pugsly is basically a one-dude wrecking crew. He can plow through anything once he gets going, like a kinetic multiplier? Can put his hand through concrete so long as he keeps up momentum. Don't ask me how it works, but you can see it does." Cinder gestures to where Pugsly is pushing through what looks like a solid barrier. "And Gill can breathe underwater. Not the most useful skill for this course. He's got a smidge of water manipulation, too. Enough to gather up and use South's drips once he gets going, so—yep, there he goes!"

Sure enough, the third guy is making his move now; the melted ice that trails in South's wake from the start of the course coalesces in two big watery orbs that rise to surround Pugsly and South's heads, forcing them to focus on getting out from under water while Gill rushes the tower and pounds his way up the stairs toward the flag. Pugsly gets free of the water first, the orb splashing uselessly to the ground as he rips his hands through it. He takes a minute to get moving again, though, stuck in the obstacle he was walking through like it was nothing a moment ago. South freezes his orb and then shatters it, the shards tinkling to the ground at his feet and then he's off, speed skating along a spiral of ice around the tower to the top.

As Gill reaches for the flag, South shoots ice at him, freezing his hand in place with an icy tether inches from the goal. Gill yanks at his frozen hand uselessly. When South reaches for the flag himself, the tower shakes as Pugsly slams into it at ground level. The flag jolts. South slips and scrambles to regain his footing on the ice.

The tower shudders as Pugsly punches a support beam. The flag leans. South lunges. Another punch shatters Gill's icy manacle and sends both the flag and South tumbling. South blasts an icy ramp under his feet and slides down to safety. Gill follows him down by the same route, swimming in the melting ice South leaves behind him. They're both too late as the flag tumbles into Pugsly's waiting hand and he waves it in triumph. South stomps and looks like he's considering throwing more ice despite the game being over.

"Good." Streak grins. "I love watching South lose." South is scowling while Gill congratulates Pugsly. The three young men get into a shoving match as they leave the practice room, looking much less friendly than Cinder and Streak did when it was their turn.

"Boys." Streak rolls her eyes in exasperation at their behavior. She turns her back on the viewing window and crosses her arms as she looks me over. "Anyway, did you get lost or something? I figured most of the new baby frosh were busy unpacking and shit."

"No, my roommate needed the room," I reply, not wanting to get into the details.

"Sexiled on your first night? Your roomie moves fast." Streak winks.

I flush at the thought of Iggy needing the room for that. Nope. Not thinking about Ig and sex at all.

"Um. No. Ig's just, um, homesick." That's one way of putting it. Homesick and overwhelmed. Who wouldn't be? I'm feeling out of my depth here, too. And I don't have the added layer of everything being too loud and being told my coping mechanisms are inappropriate.

"Aw, does he need anything? Ice cream maybe?" Streak suggests heading toward the exit. Cinder and I follow, although I'm not sure why I'm going with them. They seem to assume I will, so I go along with it.

"They. And um, no, ice cream wouldn't help. They just need space to breathe for a while."

"My bad. Well, if they don't want ice cream, I know someone who does. Come on, we'll show you the market. You can use dining credit or cash to buy snacks."

"We don't have a freezer," I hedge, but I appreciate that Streak corrected herself on Ig's pronouns without making a big fuss about it. That makes me more comfortable with her.

"So? Guess you'll have to eat the whole pint then," Streak teases.

"Or you can stash your leftovers in ours—the freezer is miniscule, but it fits a couple pints of ice cream." Cinder offers.

"And the vodka," Streak adds. Cinder rolls her eyes.

"And the vodka that we shouldn't be sharing with our brand new baby freshman because he's probably still a minor."

"Nope, turned nineteen last week," I say with a grin. Perks of being among the oldest in our grade with our fall birthdays. Iggy is still eighteen for another month. We agreed not to drink until we're both old enough. So that won't be happening tonight.

No harm in getting ice cream with my new friends, though. This way I'll have people to ask when Ig inevitably has a million questions about how to use our dining credit or whether you are supposed to go to the practice hall already in your super suit or change there, and how the changing rooms work as far as which one to use, and whether people really just strip right there in front of everyone else. And, okay, I'm a little nervous about that part too, because as much as I'd prefer to go with the other guys, I don't really want to be flashing my bits in a men's locker room. I am thrilled with the results of my metoidioplasty, but old habits die hard and I don't want to be naked with a bunch of cis guys. Are there stalls? If so, will I end up getting harassed if I try to change in said stalls? Damn. Now I'm making myself nervous about tomorrow too. Time to turn off the overthinking and have some fun.

"Look at you, all grown up." Streak gives me a shoulder bump. "Cin, we're keeping this one. Wee baby frosh, consider yourself claimed. Which dorm are you in?"

"Steadman."

Cinder nods. "Cool, so, you and the roomie are elementals, then? That's where I'm at, too. Streak is technically supposed to be across campus with the other celestials, whose powers they can't adequately explain." She winks like she just said some sort of joke I don't get. "But they agreed to let her room with me in the elemental dorms. Perks of being an upperclassman. Steadman's the nicest dorm, since we've got the suite-style housing with the semi-private washrooms."

The two of them ask me questions about which profs I have for which classes and give me advice about which to avoid and tidbits about the campus as we walk to the market and I try to take in all the information so I'll know what to do in the coming weeks. They're like the uncensored and unsanctioned version of the campus tour we had to take earlier. That was when Iggy started to get overwhelmed, so I was more focused on squeezing their hand and trying to offer what comfort I could than actually paying attention. This impromptu tour is better, even if there are still a bunch of other students showing off their abilities despite the rules about when and where and how we can use powers on and off campus.

"I thought we were supposed to tone down the power displays?" I ask as we walk across a broad swath of grass and have to dodge a group of students playing frisbee with telekinesis. What's even the point?

"This is about typical," Cinder says, looking

around the quad. "I mean, they ask us to be more discreet around NPs, so when the parents of the first gens are around for orientation and stuff, or on game nights when there are NP super ball fans around the stadium. But otherwise, it's part of us. People are going to use their powers. The rules are all about making sure everyone does so safely."

"Yep," Streak agrees. "Games are all in fun, watch this." Then she blurs off, reappearing in midair to snatch the frisbee. In the next blink, she is standing with Cinder and I again, flipping the frisbee between her hands until one of the angry telekinetics gestures toward us and the frisbee bounces off Streak's face and zooms back to the game.

"Get your own team, Streak. This one is telepaths only."

"Sure thing, losers," Streak grumbles, rubbing at her forehead.

"You okay?" Cinder asks.

Streak waves away the concern. "Always. So, you've seen ours, Ger-bear, give us a quick show."

"Um, yeah, okay. I guess I can. What do you want me to do?" I glance around for inspiration.

"What *can* you do?" Streak asks, a challenge in her tone that has me eager to show off for my new friends.

"Wind control, mostly." I repeat the standard lie. It's a huge part of my power, the only part I've told anyone other than Iggy about. Most people don't have multiple powers. Those that do are generally weaker in one area than the other, or they tie together. Like Gill's water manipulation paired with water breathing. For me, I'm a storm caller, but there aren't many of those and the strongest and most famous of them was the Human Hurricane, a supervillain. There's this common misconception that stronger powers are more easily corrupted to villainy. Storm callers are considered dangerous and out of control.

Wind elementals, on the other hand, are common. Easy to train and unremarkable. Nothing to worry about. So I use my wind manipulation when people want to see or evaluate my powers. And I leave calling lightning for the times when Ig needs to put on a show of having more than the barest trace of being an electrical elemental.

Part of me wonders what it would be like to let loose with all of my power, like in the practice room where I watched Cinder and Streak, but the rooms are monitored and recorded and I have to be careful. Careful to stay off the League's radar if I don't want to be actively recruited as their next storm-calling super villain. Careful not to unmask our deception about Iggy's strength if I want to keep them close instead of having to watch them get treated like they are less because of crap they can't control all over again. Different shit, same outcome.

Ig is worth more than the strength of their abilities or how well they can navigate a world that refuses to adapt for them. I can't change the entire world on my own, but I can sure as shit make sure they get treated the same as me and the other H class students.

Streak is watching me with her arms crossed and an expectant look. Well, I won't pass up a chance to show off to my new friends. I sigh, and let the wind swell out of my lungs to blow the frisbee into a tree. The air flows out of me in a loud rush and Streak can't miss what I'm doing. I consider using enough force to embed the plastic in the trunk, but that hardly seems fair to the poor tree, so I flick my fingers and release the wind instead.

The telekinetic who told Streak to get her own team is still trying to pull on it with telekinesis. So when I release the frisbee, it flies directly into their stomach, doubling them over around it. I assume that's the same person who bounced it off my friend's forehead; poetic justice. Streak laughs heartily and ruffles my hair like I'm her kid brother or something. As the youngest of four by nearly a decade, heaven knows my parents already blessed me with enough overbearing older sisters, but I can overlook Streak acting like my big sisters because I like the approval in her smile.

CHAPTER 5

Iggy

My phone alarm wakes me on the first morning of classes. The familiar song and bedding make it even more jarring when I sit up and realize I'm not in my room at home. My heart races as the realization sinks in that this is home now.

I'm living in the dorms and I've got classes in an hour. That settles something inside me. Classes have been part of my routine for as long as I can remember. I know what's expected of me in a school setting. Heck, I'm the one Gerald depends on to make sure we get all our assignments done on time. I'm better than him at academics. At least, with subjects I'm interested in learning. Mostly the math and science Pop uses in his lab. And sometimes history, if it's the interesting bits that remind me of my favorite fantasy book plots. I can do this. University can't be that different from high school.

Then my entire world tilts as Gerald climbs out of his lofted bed in nothing but his boxers. Oh, fuck, how did I not realize that being roommates would mean seeing him first thing after he wakes up every day? And he'll see me.

It's not like I've never seen him shirtless. I've admired his muscled pecs from the time he started doing lifting for his gym credits at our high school after he started on T. But there's a difference between being shirtless together on a hot day in the summer, and being crotch to eyeballs with him in his undies.

"Hey, Ig, you okay?" Gerald asks, all concerned as I continue to stare at the front of his boxers. I can't quite seem to get the message through to my muscles to turn away, or get up, or anything to stop perving on him. Maybe because I don't fully want to. This is silly. We've had sleepovers before. Admittedly, not as many recently, because I've wanted to avoid this exact scenario ever since I opted to stop taking puberty blockers two years ago and started noticing that Gerald is hot. 'I want to lick him like a popsicle' levels of hot.

"Ig?" Gerald steps closer and rests a hand on my shoulder, snapping me out of my dazed thoughts about things I shouldn't want to do with my best friend. Gerald's hand pressing on me is anchoring, and I lean into the touch. Sometimes, like last night, when I've got too much going on and I'm already on my last nerve trying to process what's going on around me, being touched makes me feel like my nerves are on fire and I can't handle it. Most of the time, though, I like when Gerald touches me. I grab his wrist to keep him there and snuggle my cheek against his skin, sighing contentedly because Ger is safe to be myself around. If I want to touch his skin, he won't give me weird looks for acting on that impulse. Or rush me to answer with words when he asks a question.

I nod.

"You want to come with me to grab a shower before classes?" he asks.

I don't. I *really* don't. But I also don't want to draw attention to myself by being the weird kid who needs a shower. So I nod again.

Gerald gathers up both of our shower things and hands me the plastic tote Moddy packed for me with all my shower stuff. Then he drapes one of my purple and blue dragon print towels over the top. The smiling creatures make me grin— nothing too bad can be associated with cartoon dragons, right? Right.

Gerald slips on plastic flip-flops. I've got

similar shoes. I don't want to wear them. The hard plastic band irritates my skin, not as bad as the thong style ones that go between my toes and chafe like they are trying to saw my big toe off with every shift of my weight, but still not comfortable. And when they get wet, they squelch. Like they are trying to suck the skin off my feet. I shudder at the thought. But I also don't want to stand barefoot on slimy tiles where countless other students have done unspeakable naked things.

And now I'm fixated on the fact that I'm supposed to be naked in a public bathroom in, like, the next five minutes and I can't. Does not compute. I freeze up in the doorway, shaking my head.

"What's wrong?" Gerald asks.

I choke on any sort of response. Just no. Nope. University sucks, dorms suck. My life sucks right now.

"Hey, Ig, it's fine, you don't have to take a shower this morning if that's what's freaking you out."

It's like he can read my mind sometimes. Or he pays attention. But nope, he's wrong. I might avoid it today, but eventually I have to take a shower. I can't go indefinitely getting funkier and funkier until everyone is pointing and laughing at me.

"No." I shake my head again, forcing out the single word.

"Want to at least see the bathroom?"

"No."

Gerald sighs. "Ig," he says gently, "we'll be late for class if you stand here all morning."

"No."

"Yeah, we will." The words are a gentle correction, but they still sting. My powers fizzle over my forearms in crackling, tiny electric discharges, stress convincing my pathetic inner spark it needs to protect me. I rock onto my heels and rub at the sparks. Gerald massages his temples and knowing that he's frustrated enough not to try hiding it from me only makes it harder to handle the idea of leaving the safety of our room. "Okay. Come with me." He holds out his hand in an offer of solidarity.

"No." I bat him away. If he leaves me alone, I'll eventually be able to drag myself out of our room to assess the situation. I *can* do this on my own. It's just harder without help from someone who gets why I'm so upset about something that might seem minor to them.

"Ig, you can trust me, I won't let anything happen to you."

I know he's telling the truth. I can always trust Gerald. But I still can't seem to stop panicking. My heart is racing, my thoughts are a blank of fear and terrible what ifs. Electricity fizzes over most of my body now, too weak to worry about it for now. No matter how much I want to, I can't unfreeze my muscles or make my vocal cords shape any other words besides "no". No amount of willing myself to cooperate can override the way my adrenaline is pumping as if there's a two-ton mega tiger about to pounce on me instead of my best friend calmly suggesting we check out the communal showers.

I should have scouted them out last night, but all the orientation activities left me too exhausted to do more than drag myself from my chair to nestle under my covers and sleep. Not knowing what to expect is almost worse than the parade of potential horrors I'm imagining. Something out of the sports movies I've seen, maybe. An open tiled room with spigots, water pouring all around me and naked bodies writhing. I'm pretty sure that the showers aren't some sort of open orgy where everyone who isn't me is welcome, or I'd have heard about it, but that's all I can fixate on right now.

Gerald wraps his arms around me and squeezes. Can he feel my electricity, or does it get absorbed into his all-encompassing storm?

Sometimes it seems like my abilities are the palest reflection of him. Like he's so much a part of me that I got a tiny scrap of his powers. It's a foolish fantasy, but it makes me happy to think we fit together so well. It's not just our powers, either. We make a good team. Gerald is always coming up with our next adventure, and I'm usually the one who makes sure we survive his idea of the day unscathed. He's good at the big picture stuff and I handle the details, making sure we have the right materials so that a potato cannon doesn't explode in our faces, for instance.

Right now, his arms squeezing me tight calm my frantically beating heart. His familiar scent overrides the misfiring circuits in my brain telling me I'm in mortal danger and replaces them with a pervading sense of safety. Gerald is safety and comfort and home. I miss home so much right now. It's not just the shower, it's everything piled on top of that terrifying unknown stressing me out beyond my capacity to cope.

"Hush, Ig, I've got you," he murmurs near my ear and I slump in his embrace, letting him hold me up and make it all okay.

"It's a unisex washroom, Iggy. One that we share with one other dorm room. Remember? Steadman is all suites." Gerald hugs me tighter, the pressure of his embrace grounding me. "With a single shower stall, ok? The doors lock, so it will only be us. You and me, I won't let anyone bother you. Can you nod if that's alright?"

I take a deep, shuddery breath. His sleepy morning scent fills my senses, settling my agitated powers. It's enough to stop their erratic misfiring before I fry our electronics. It wouldn't be the first time, but I've gotten better about directing my sparks to frequencies that don't damage our tech. I draw in another deep inhale, and nod. Gerald holds me a minute longer, then pulls away. I make an undignified sound of protest, and grab for his hand. He lets me take it and leads me toward the semi-private washroom.

Sure enough, there is only one shower stall. The mirror is steamy, and the floor is damp. Guess our suitemates already used it this morning, whoever they are. The room sort of smells like mildew. I can handle the odor and dampness if it means being alone when I'm vulnerable, though. At least it's an honest stink. Not like the cloud of competing artificial fragrances that always drifted out of the showers after gym at my high school, despite rules against perfume. Or the ones Ger's older sisters all seem to douse themselves with. At least our high school had a fragrance free policy in class.

It's amazing how many fewer headaches I got after that policy took effect.

Gerald lets me shower first and I take my time getting clean, knowing he's standing outside, making sure no one hassles me. The warm water washes away my clammy fear sweat. I still feel like I've already run a marathon, the flood of adrenaline and endorphins taking their toll. And it's not even breakfast yet.

At least Gerald is here. I can be strong and brave for him. Like back in the warehouse, when I was the one he could rely on to rescue the kidnapped doctor. We've always had each other's backs. I can show him I'm more than the mess I acted like in our doorway. Some part of me knows he realizes I'm not at my best with everything in our lives changing this week, but it's hard to focus on that when I'm a giant ball of stress and anxiety.

This will get better. Once we settle into a new routine, it will be Ger relying on me to make sure we both get our assignments done on time and pass our academic classes, just like always. We make a good team. Gerald helps me step out of my comfort zone and I keep his impulsive plans from spiraling out of control.

I can get through this. I'll show everyone I'm good enough to follow in Moddy and Pop's footsteps. It's not like there was ever any other choice. No, from the moment I was born, Super U was my future. Only being an NP could have changed that fate, so I'm stuck here for the next four years. Well, I refuse to be a disappointment. I'm going to make the most of university. No matter the cost, I'm going to be the hero they all expect.

CHAPTER 6

Gerald

Iggy tries to pretend everything is fine as we make our way to the dining hall for breakfast. At least their pop left several cartons of the dinosaur oatmeal they prefer for breakfast in their closet and the cafeteria has hot water available.

So they make a bowl for themself while I take advantage of the waffle bar and add a couple of scoops of ice cream and chocolate syrup to the top. Sure, it's decadent, but I'm stressed about classes, too. And I can't show it without making everything worse.

Iggy bops along to the music in their headphones, ignoring the chaos around us as they devour their food. Once they finish their oatmeal, they sip their coffee while they watch me eat my breakfast sundae.

"Your waffle is getting all soggy," Iggy says in disgust.

I roll my eyes. Anyone else would be angling for a bite of my ice cream, but not Ig. They really are just concerned about my waffle. "I like it soggy."

"Why?"

"Because it's infused with sweet sugary goodness, Ig."

"Huh. I guess." They kick their feet under the table, tap their fingers on the bench and otherwise fidget while I take a few more bites. "Are we going to be in time for class?" They glance at their watch worriedly. "How far away is the building we need to go to?"

"Relax, we've got plenty of time. I checked how far everything is last night."

"How far is it, then?" Iggy sips their coffee.

"A five-minute walk." I take a bite of ice cream. I might have overestimated how hungry I was.

"That is not a distance."

"Fine. It is as far as I can walk in five minutes. You do the math," I grumble. They frown at me, like they're doing the math. I sigh. "Nevermind, Ig, let's just go." I don't really like soggy waffles anyway, and I've had my fill of ice cream for breakfast. We chug our coffee on the way to the tray-return with our dirty dishes.

The walk takes closer to ten minutes from the dining hall when the walkways are all crowded with students rolling out to their first classes of the day. My bad. We're still on time and Iggy chooses our seats without comment. In the front row, so there are no students sitting in front of us to distract them.

Most of the day goes better than I'd feared. Classes are a longstanding familiar part of our routine. Ig knows what's expected of them as a student in a classroom. Pay attention to the teacher, take notes, block out any extraneous crap that is going on. They still seem stressed out, but it's manageable.

I'm overwhelmed at the long lists of assignments in the syllabi we get handed in each class. But this is something Cinder warned me to expect. The long list is spread out over the course of the semester. Cut into weekly or daily tasks. It won't seem so daunting. I hope.

Monday, Wednesday, and Friday we have all lecture based classes, so it's not too different from high school, except everything is bigger. Iggy is good about the fiddly details of things, so I've always been able to count on them to help me stay on track with my studies. They have a calendar app that they update with all our assignments, tests, quizzes and projects. The syllabi should make it even easier to keep their calendar up to date.

Tomorrow will be different, though. We've got practical classes to learn about our abilities and see how everyone else's abilities work. Which means I'll have to get creative to keep our secret about Ig's power levels. That's a problem for tomorrow, though. Today, we get through all our classes and I find Cinder and Streak at dinner to introduce them to Iggy.

CHAPTER 7

Iggy

Meeting Gerald's new friends is weird. It's always been the two of us. We have been best friends since we were in diapers. I have a picture of us saved on my phone where we're wearing matching infant onesies that say BFFs on them. His is glittery and pink and mine is a shimmery blue, and we've joked that we ought to have traded countless times.

Hell, when we got old enough to swap outfits, we did that a lot. Until Moddy got wise that I wanted to wear the soft jersey glittery dresses sometimes and bought me some. And Ger's parents stopped foisting all the pink and purple unicorn attire they'd saved from his three older sisters onto him and let him pick his own clothing. I got some sweet comfy old hoodies out of the deal, since I didn't care if the graphics and colors were girly.

I've never had to meet Gerald's other friends because there has never been a time when he went off to meet people without me. We always make friends together.

I don't like how this new development knocks me off kilter. I always see us as a unit and this is concrete evidence Ger exists outside of 'us' and he could meet someone he wants to be a different type of 'us' with, and that upsets me. It upsets me a lot. Enough that I can tell I don't make the best first impression on Cinder and Streak because I'm having an internal freakout. No. Ger is mine. The idea of him with someone else is awful. Nope. Not happening.

"So, Ig, right? What is that short for?" Streak asks, leaning close enough that I can see her tonsils moving when she talks.

"Iggy," I correct her. "Only Gerald calls me Ig. And it's short for Ignatius."

"Iggy then, and is that your hero name?"

"No. Moddy and Pop figured I'd follow in the family footsteps with elemental manipulation."

"Your power is fire?" Streak asks.

"Nope." I check whether Ger is paying attention. He gives me a slight nod, so I point my finger at the cookie on Streak's plate and let a little spark arc toward it. Gerald takes what I started and zots it into a much more impressive jolt that incinerates the cookie and leaves the plate undamaged. He's a show off like that. And he did it for me. I give Streak a smug smile. More because of the tangible proof that Gerald is still mine than the display of my supposed powers. "Electric elemental powers."

"Hey, I was going to eat that!" Streak pouts. Gerald blows out a heavy breath, directing the wind to get her another cookie from the dessert bar not ten feet away from our seats. He blows around a few napkins and gets a glower from another student for messing up their hair with a bit of stray breeze, but Gerald doesn't seem to notice. Streak smiles appreciatively and ruffles his hair.

"Looks like we picked a bright one to be our new frosh," she says.

"And it looks like we got a twofer. Very nice, Iggy." Cinder nods my way in appreciation. "As for us, I work with fire."

"And I can alter time in a limited fashion," Streak says, sounding bored. "You two have got to stop with telling everyone your real names, though. Or at least come up with your alters before someone else does and something you don't like sticks."

"That's what happened to Streak." Cinder nods

her agreement.

"Yeah." Streak grimaces. "Still better than being called Speed. I am *not* a street drug. So, we've got wind and electricity to work with, huh?" Streak cracks her knuckles.

"Yep," Gerald agrees.

"And you are quite enamored of your legal name, huh?" Streak nudges Gerald with her elbow and I bristle at the familiarity of her touching him. "So, how about we honor the initial and go with Gust?"

Gerald nods. "Yeah, that works for me. I'm still probably going to go by Ger, though," he adds with a cheeky grin.

"And for you, hmm." Streak turns to eye me up and down. Like I'm some puzzle she needs to solve. I hate that look. I'm not a puzzle, I'm a person. Arms crossed, I sulk, tuning them out as Cinder and Streak toss out potential hero names for me. Each one is worse than the last. Volt, Static, Shock, and Electro. They sound like a cut rate list of video game moves. I shrink in my seat, hating it all, but unsure how to make it stop short of storming off in a huff.

"Zap," Gerald interjects.

I like that better. It feels nice in my mouth, the buzz of the z and the snap of the p at the end.

Short and to the point, like Iggy. I can live with going by Zap. And it helps that Gerald suggested it.

"Yes," I say, too enthusiastically, if the reactions from the others are anything to go by. "Zap, call me that one."

So they do. Throughout dessert, and a walk back to Streak and Cinder's dorm room, where we play some video game I've never heard of before. *Day Dreamer*—it's some sort of action RPG that they swear has an outstanding plot, but it has a team PVP mode where Ger and I can play against Cinder and Streak. The pair sit cuddled together, but I think little of it until they win the first match. Then Streak tips Cinder's chin up for a kiss. Oh. Girlfriends.

No wonder Gerald seems so at ease with them right away. They're queer, like us. It makes me slightly less possessive of him, knowing that these new friends of his are together. The evening is more fun after that. I don't have to make small talk, just play the game and throw around occasional trash talk about winning. That's an easy social script to follow.

It's fun, even. We play until their neighbor pounds on the wall for us to tone it down. We turn off the console. Gerald and I say our goodbyes and we leave with promises to hang out again soon. I'm okay with that. Mostly. New friends are exhausting, but I enjoyed our evening together once I got past my jealousy.

Later, when it's Gerald and me alone in our dorm, watching a video together in my bed before we go to sleep, Ger complains that Zap and Gust sound like sidekick names. Since I barely have enough juice to be a sidekick without him boosting me, I shrug it off.

Zap is fine for me. But he's right about Gust. He should have said something to Streak when she suggested it. Nicknames have a way of sticking, whether or not you like them. Lucky for me, I've never minded being exactly who I am.

CHAPTER 8

Gerald

Our second day of classes is more stressful than the first. Mostly because we have Powers 101 classes. For most of the day, we are learning about how other people's abilities work. It's boring, and stuff I mostly learned as a child growing up in a super-powered family.

Two of my older sisters are S class supes with elemental control who work for the hydro company. The third refused to be ranked, but I think her telepathy is almost as strong as my storm powers. She does security consultations with protection against supervillain plots as her area of focus.

I understand the typical uses and limitations of most power classes. Between Ig's folks and mine, I've listened to an encyclopedia's worth of theory and strategizing about powers and their real world uses. And it's boring. Boring theories. Boring to watch our first gen classmates stumble through the basics and the legacies flaunt their powers as if the exercises are any real challenge worth showing off with.

There is one guy among the telepathic powers who catches my attention; he's only an S class, but he's got flair. At first, it was the unusual hero moniker that caught my ear. Weevil. Not exactly something most people would pick for themselves. When I get a better look, I recognize him as the freshman who was carrying South's tray for him last night. He uses his telepathy to control bugs.

Mind control that only works on insects. No wonder that got him a sidekick classification. Not the glamor most people imagine when they picture the daring defender of their city. Or any of the other things supes do. That's the sort of power that the League might want to exploit, though. Perhaps I should consider befriending him; image problems aside, bug control could be hella useful. Weevil's interesting display of getting a bunch of ants to complete our assigned task of pushing a button from across the practice room is cool, but then it's over and I'm back to languishing in my boredom. I didn't bother with a notebook, so I distract myself by fiddling with my keycard to while away the long hours of class.

By the time we get to elemental powers, I'm tuned out completely. I lost track of my keycard at some point when a big fat spider startled me into dropping it under the seat in front of me. I need to remember to retrieve it before class ends, but I don't want to cause a ruckus by reaching under the seat of the girl in front of me.

Ig looks like they are barely hanging on to their focus. They keep their nose buried in their notebook, scribbling notes I know damn well they don't need to take because they know this crap forward and backward, better than me. But it helps them to focus on the profs and tune out all the background noise of people showing off their powers, so I don't bother trying to distract them. But not being able to bug them only adds to the tedium.

When it's finally my turn to demonstrate my powers for the class, I half-ass a little breeze to set off a buzzer at the far end of the room.

"Gust, he/him, elemental control of wind." I state my alter ego, pronoun, and power before rattling off my student ID so the prof can mark me down on their attendance sheet without giving the entire class my real name. Not that they couldn't find it easily enough after the fuss the *Supe Report* made over Ig and me last spring.

I'm tempted to 'accidentally' blow the

lecturer's notes all over the room, but that would only buy me trouble I don't need during my first week. I'm turning over a new leaf with university and being a serious student, like I promised Ig and my folks.

I get a bored approval from the professor and then it's Ig's turn since we're going down each row. I have to elbow them to get their attention and they give me a blank look, like they aren't sure what they are supposed to do. I gesture to the target.

"Oh, um, electric elemental control," Ig says. Then they recite their student ID number as they let sparks sizzle along their fingers.

I nudge the electric charge they started into something powerful enough to trip the circuit and make the buzzer sound. It results in a bright flash of light that makes Ig squint and wrinkle their nose in distaste. We're sitting close enough and I've gotten good enough at not having to physically direct the charge so that no one would notice I was providing the juice that Ig is pretending to control. No one will know unless they are already looking for the lie. It might get tricky to maintain when we start using the big practice rooms where they can measure power signatures, but if we never give them a reason to suspect anything, then I doubt anyone will go looking for such an absurd deception.

"Very good. Do you have your alter ego figured out yet?" our prof asks.

"Zap, they/them," Iggy says, staring fixedly at their notes. The lecturer writes something on the attendance sheet before moving on to the next elemental student so they can prove their hero ranking in the most boring way possible. Just like everyone else. It makes for a long day. I'm more than ready to head home by the end, and so is Iggy.

We're almost back to our dorm when I check my pockets. "Shit, I just realized I dropped my ID card during class," I say, stopping to confirm it's missing.

"You lost it?" Ig demands. They look frazzled after our second day of classes and the stress of performing with their powers in front of the entire first year class. Not to mention the several faculty and older students who dropped by the lecture hall to assess the new students' talent.

"Yeah." I shrug. "No big deal, I'll go back and grab it."

"I can come with you," Iggy offers with a weary sigh.

"Nah, don't worry about it. We're almost back to the dorm. Go on ahead and I'll catch up when I've got my card." I gesture toward our dorm.

We're in sight of Steadman, no sense in both of us traipsing back across campus after a long and draining day.

"You should hurry. The class buildings are card access only after five," Iggy points out. There should be plenty of time if I don't get sidetracked. "Right, I'll call you to let me into the dorm if I don't find it, okay?"

"Okay." Ig agrees. "Don't make us late for dinner. The tables in the dining hall got crowded last night." They take out their phone and fiddle with the settings, presumably to take it off of silent mode now that we are done with classes for the day. They dig through their bag for their headphones, too. Probably to block out the other students for the rest of the walk home.

"Crap, batteries are dead." They scowl and stuff the headphones back into their bag. That sucks. I've noticed Iggy using the noise-canceling features more often than usual between classes. They even had to add a modified battery pack to make it safer for them to use their powers to boost the charge level without blowing a circuit, but at least it helps them to get through the day with all the distractions on campus.

"I can walk you the rest of the way first," I offer, though I might need to borrow their student ID to get into the building after hours if I do that.

"No, it's fine. I can walk home without you holding my hand, Ger," Iggy snaps. "I'm not some little kid."

"No, you're right. I know you can." I squeeze their shoulder in a silent apology. Iggy shrugs me off. Okay, they sound more tired than I thought. They ought to get home to where they can decompress from our day as soon as possible. So much for asking them to come with me in case I'm too late. They've been getting good at opening locks with their powers. It's not a huge deal though. If the doors lock before I get there, I can always ask someone else to key me into the building, no big deal.

"Hurry or you'll be too late," Iggy says. Then they turn and stride toward our dorm and I jog off in the opposite direction to retrieve my keycard before the building gets locked up for the night.

CHAPTER 9

Iggy

"**H**ey, fresh meat!" someone I don't recognize calls to me as I'm approaching my dorm without Gerald. I startle, letting sparks dance over my hands at the implicit threat of being addressed out of the blue like that by a stranger.

I'm pretty sure that isn't a friendly thing to call someone. That's the sort of thing someone says when they want to razz me. Not one hundred percent on that, though, since Cinder and Streak called Gerald and I their wee baby frosh and Ger says that's meant to be affectionate. Fresh meat could be a similar friendly sort of slur? I don't like it. Looking at the imposing guy who said it, I'm not convinced that I'm supposed to.

"Hello?" I ask, trying to rein in my sparks. They're a nuisance and a reminder of everything

I'm not. My actual powers are a disappointment.

Moddy and Pop were so excited the day my superpowers came in. And then they kept checking in, and looking more and more concerned the longer I went without getting much more than a fizzle. They tried to hide it, and they kept up a good facade of believing I'd get stronger with time and practice. My ability to manipulate the charges I make got better, but they never got stronger. I can mess with fine tuning the wattage and amplitude, but I can't make a lightning strike.

Then Ger and I fucked everything up with the warehouse fire, and they were so proud it hurt. I couldn't correct them, and Gerald said that I should continue to pretend and that he'd help me. He's always kept the electrical component of his abilities a secret and only uses it now to make me look like I can do more than I can. That feels like my fault. Even if he hid that part of himself for reasons that had nothing to do with me at first. He didn't want to be seen as too powerful or a threat. I know our ruse is holding him back or putting him at risk of being called a liar and a cheat. But I can't make myself put a stop to it.

If I was as strong as Gerald and I pretend, I could use a jolt of electricity to warn this stranger off, but I can't and something tells me I can't risk letting them realize that I'm weaker than I seem.

"I've seen you with Cinderella and Streaker, right?"

I take longer than I maybe should to realize they mean Ger's new friends. This person, with their nasty nicknames, rubs me the wrong way. I nod, unwilling to spare the effort to reply with words. They aren't worth it. I turn back toward the dorm, but they wave their hand and ice blooms at their feet, letting them glide effortlessly in front of me. The move forces me to stop or slip.

"I'm talking to you," they say. I'm not sure what that's supposed to mean. They can talk all they want, it doesn't obligate me to listen. I move to step around the ice patch and they gesture again, making it spread further and once again gliding into my way. "That means look at me. They call you Zap, right?" They give my sparking hands a sneering glance. "From the looks of it, Bug Zapper is more accurate. How did *you* test at hero class?"

I make brief eye contact to assess the threat. Silly, since I can't tell if they want to talk at me or threaten me or what, and their face isn't giving me any answers. All I accomplish is the usual crawly sensation in my guts that I get when I have to look into someone's eyes. The racing thoughts about whether it's enough or too much and am I doing it right?

They might have a message for Cinder and Streak since they brought up my connection to them? The stranger's eyes make me uncomfortable. It's like they're stabbing right into mine and I can't make myself hold eye contact without my sparks sizzling all over my body. The scent of singed hair and clothing fills my nostrils. And burnt circuitry. Awesome, there goes my custom watch again, along with all the biometric data it was tracking for me. Most of the time, I have enough control not to burn myself, but that is fraying right now. Another way my powers fall short. I shift my stare to their forehead in hopes they won't notice that I'm not quite focused on them. The trick eases enough of my discomfort that I can rein in the sparks.

"They assessed me as an H class during my classification exams, same as anyone else," I answer their question, though I've learned that neurotypicals rarely ask the questions they really want answered. I can't read their mind to figure out what they meant, though, so if they want more from me they'll have to actually ask me. Sure enough, they let out an irritated huff.

"Oh, think you're a wise guy, Bug Zapper?"

"No." For one, I'm not really a guy and for another, I don't think I'm particularly wise, neither of which is what they probably meant.

But I'm not wasting effort on a more nuanced answer for the likes of this bully. "Did you want something, or can I go back to my dorm now?"

"I was going to ask why a dynamic duo like you and Gusty were slumming it with the losers, but I guess I can see why, if you can't even get it up to defend yourself. I expected more after what Weevil said about your demo in your elemental powers practice earlier. Weevil made it sound like you could blast away my ice without a thought, but it looks like he was wrong." They arch a brow at me as if they expect me to do something. I run their words through my head and try to parse the stupid NT garble that apparently means something other than what they said. Weevil was one of the other first years. I don't remember his power, but I think he was an S class. A future sidekick. Did this bully claim him the way Cinder and Streak took Ger and me under their wing?

Oh. Do they want me to blast their ice with my lightning? Yeah, that isn't happening without Ger. I'd only embarrass myself if I tried. But if I don't, will that raise their suspicions more? This is some real BS. If I focus the sparks on the soles of my shoes, that might be enough to grip the ice and walk away?

It takes more juice than usual to light up the rubber soles of my shoes. The electric impulses

I control fizzle faster, the further they get from my skin. With the rubber in the way, that effect happens faster, but if I focus, I manage to step onto this asshole's ice as though I'm walking on a clear sidewalk. The ice crunches unpleasantly underfoot and I almost lose my concentration at the visceral crackling sound of it echoing in my head. But this is the fastest route away from the jerk, so I keep my head down, focus on the little electric spikes giving me traction and forge ahead to get away from them.

For a second, it seems like they're going to let me walk away. The ice in front of me pulls back, and then it flows up my legs, encasing my feet up to the ankle in a searing cold that burns my skin. My sparks flare up my legs, fleeing the icy burn and leaping up to spring uselessly from my fingers and fizzle out.

The bully gets right up in my face now, too close for me to look away. I glare at their forehead, wishing for the billionth time in my life that I was powerful enough to make them regret targeting me. That follows fast with shame at wanting to hurt someone. Moddy and Pop would be truly disappointed in me if I used my powers to harm someone just because I felt threatened. Even a bully doesn't deserve to be electrocuted. Foxy gets a bad rap, but Pop isn't the sort of villain who goes around hurting people.

"Huh, guess you really are a dud. Shall I leave you here for everyone to see you can't even unfreeze a little ice? I'm sure someone stronger will come along before you get frostbite." The bully pats my cheek. It's not a friendly touch. More like they want to show me they could do much worse to me and we both know I'm powerless to stop them. That doesn't stop me from letting electricity arc between my skin and their fingers; they pull back, shaking out their hand with an irritated scowl pronounced enough for me to clearly read their emotions, even as ice coats their hand.

They retaliate by using the ice-coated digits to grab my jaw and force me to look at them. I focus on their forehead again, letting my fear and hate and discomfort pour into my glare. I hate this person, and I don't even know their name. "Word to the wise, sidekick, I don't know what game you two think you're playing, but Gusty has genuine talent. If you care about him, you won't hold him back when the time comes for him to show his true power, understand?"

"No," I reply, hatred like I've only experienced once before is vibrating along my every nerve and I just want to get away from them. Never see them again, though that's impossible since they've got elemental powers like Gerald and me, so they live in Steadman Hall with us.

"Well, for both your sakes, I hope you figure it out by the time he makes his choice. In the meantime, don't be such a cling-on—you'll ruin his chances at making the sort of alliances he needs to succeed in the real world, if he's constantly babysitting you."

The bully stares at me a moment longer, then they release me with a final rough pat on the cheek that makes me want to scrub away the lingering memory of their touch. They turn on their heel to skate away on a moving patch of ice that unfurls ahead of them. The frozen shackles around my feet flow after them, releasing me once they get far enough away. I glare after them, still frozen despite my lack of restraints. My feet are all pins and needles of shooting pain from the lingering cold and my soggy shoes drag on my feet like they are made of gooey lead, too heavy to lift. Any motion sets off a cascade of agonizing pin pricks when I shift my weight.

I hate being held powerless at another supe's mercy and this encounter reminds me too much of that other time. With Teller. I shake my head to drive away the intrusive memories and keep shaking it. A few people walk past and give me weird looks. I don't engage with them. I want nothing to do with them or anyone I don't know and trust.

I'm still shaking my head, otherwise keeping

as still as possible when Gerald jogs back along the path. It takes everything I've got not to succumb to the miserable lingering effects of being literally frozen in place while my mind goes to the static place of being threatened and overwhelmed.

"Ig? What happened?" Gerald asks, his voice too soft.

I shake my head harder; the rush of fight or flight has passed and I don't have the energy to put the confrontation into words. And even if I could, what would I say? It was somehow connected to him and our lies. I don't want to worry him over stuff I don't really understand, so I just keep shaking my head. The movement feels good, draining away some of the jangling fear and inability to move, so I do it again, even though I know if I keep it up, I'll draw unwanted attention. Ger puts his arm around my shoulders and guides me toward the dorm. I let him; my feet don't hurt as much now. With Gerald to lead the way, I don't have to think, only follow him to our room where I'm safe from prying eyes and threats from unknown bullies.

CHAPTER 10

Iggy

The first week of classes goes as well as I dared to hope. I'm falling into the new routine without a hitch. The schoolwork is more intense, but it's all subjects I enjoy. Settling in is easy once I learn what to expect and we can establish a schedule that works for us.

Which is good, because Gerald's constant mother henning is starting to grate on my nerves. I hate feeling like he sees me as someone he needs to protect. As he's told me countless times, we're a team. I don't want him to treat me like I'm fragile just because I sometimes need extra help.

Campus life suits me once I adjust to everything. By the end of our second week, I've established my daily routine and I'm getting more at home in our cozy dorm room. Gerald and I luck out in that our suitemates seem to prefer evening showers, so there isn't much conflict over our morning ablutions. It means I don't have as much stress over that as I'd worried I would. Watching him change at bedtime is still uncomfortably arousing. He's caught me watching more than once, but he doesn't make a big deal about it. Which I appreciate because I'd doubtless freeze up if confronted on the matter.

There is no socially acceptable script for explaining why you're checking out your best friend. Not without making everything awkward. None that I've found, anyway. And I've looked online for the right thing to say. There's nothing foolproof, so I am keeping my mouth shut and trying not to let my eyes wander too much.

Instead, I try to focus on other things. Like how Gerald was right that no one will look too closely at my alleged power levels if we don't give them a reason to. Not counting that one asshole who froze my feet. That guy doesn't count at all. For anything. So far, we've carried off the ruse that I'm powerful enough to be an H class and Gerald doesn't have any powers behind manipulating the wind.

Everyone in our classes calls him Gust, which I kind of hate. He's more of a Gale than a Gust. He says that sounds like a girl's name, though. That's silly, but I don't really get the need to gender all the things. Names are just names. Same with toys and clothing and colors. People have gender, stuff doesn't. Unless it's sentient stuff. That could be cool. Regardless, I don't see how inanimate objects can have an internal sense of self or adhere to some rigid social structure, but my grasp on that is fuzzy at best.

Ger should go by something like Storm Surge. Something more impressive than a mere breeze. I'm happy enough to have everyone except Ger call me Zap. To him, I'm still Ig, and that also suits me fine. I don't care if people know my real name; with my parents being who they are, it's not like it's a real secret. Everyone knows I'm Foxy and Balantin's kid.

The one who, according to the really hardcore supe watchers, shouldn't exist because heroes don't consort with people who may or may not be villains, depending on how loose or strict of a definition you use. It was a scandal when I was born and their relationship came to light. Whenever Moddy does something heroic, or Pop pulls a particularly ballsy stunt, our entire family inevitably gets pulled into the spotlight, headlining in everything from the *Toronto Star* to the *Supe Report*.

Sometimes it sucks to have a parent who is the face of my city's Hero Brigade. No wonder most of our classmates hide who they really are from everyone, but for me and Ger, the cat's been out of the bag from the start.

Moddy, Pop, and Ger's folks weren't happy about it. Gerald's family didn't have it quite as bad, except we were so inseparable as kids that he always got pulled into my limelight. As we got older, Gerald got the idea that he had to protect me from it. That got pretty nasty when we both turned out trans.

Superheroes are a favorite cash cow for entertainment magazines and shows. So they were happy to make a story out of Ger and me, even on the flimsiest of pretexts. Let alone Moddy 'raising me to be just like them' and refusing to settle into society's arbitrary gender boxes. The sheer stupidity of that makes me mad. As if Moddy and I *choose* to be different. So that we can be endlessly mocked and harassed. Sure.

And thoughts of bullies bring me back to the asshole who froze my feet to the ground on our second day of classes. I know who he is now. He's only cornered me once, after the first time. It was the next morning, while I was making my oatmeal. Streak was getting her coffee at the same time as me. She ran him off with veiled threats that I'm not entirely sure I understood. She told me his name is South and not to let him bother me. After that, he mostly shoots me strange looks or watches me too intensely from across the dining hall or the quad. It's like he's waiting for me to confirm my weakness with evidence he can exploit.

By the middle of the second week without him approaching me directly again, I've managed to stop worrying about South. Mostly. It's not really his threats that are keeping me up late, staring at the ceiling. Even if they triggered the nightmares I've been having about Teller giving me commands. The nightmares are vague, and it's mostly the sense of powerlessness that sticks with me late at night when I can't fall back asleep.

That's when I hear something in the darkness. I can't seem to tear my brain away from fixating on the soft repetitive noises.

Then, when I realize what I'm listening to, I pretend not to hear the furtive sounds of Gerald touching himself late at night. It's not like we have any real privacy for him to find another time or place to do it. Except maybe the shower, but it's late. If not for the unfamiliar room making sleep so elusive, I'd be out like a light at this hour. He has no reason to expect I'd be awake.

I know he gets horny pretty regularly. That was one side effect he mentioned when he started T, so this is something I should have expected when we moved in together. I figured it would happen. Still, thinking of him aroused does things to my own libido.

I want to watch the way pleasure washes over him. Study how he touches himself. Run my fingers over his body in loving caresses. Just thinking about it makes me ache for my release. It's not like I can tell Gerald I'm crushing on him. He's my best friend.

And I'm totally perving on him right now. Listening to the symphony of his pleasure in our dark dorm room. The rhythmic rustling of his bedding, the soft catch in his breath, his bitten-back moans. The slick wet squelch of lubricated flesh as he jerks off to some fantasy I'd give anything to be a part of.

My hand slips under my waistband, as if it has a mind of its own, fingers curling around my hardening length. I buck into my tight fist. My shaft feels hot to the touch, getting harder by the moment and filling me with longing. I grip myself tighter, squeezing as if I can force away the desire building in my balls.

I can't hold it back, though, and trying only makes me ache for more. The slick sounds of Gerald fucking his own hand or a toy have me exploring every inch of my dick and imagining what it would be like if it was his hand on me. His erection thrusting into my fist. I want that. Him panting with desire, his face inches from mine in the dark, his body curled against mine, warm and solid as we both climb toward our peak.

A little moan slips past my lips as I jerk myself harder. The dry friction aches almost as much as it sends shivers of pleasure cascading along my spine. The soft sounds from the other bunk pause.

"Ig?" Gerald calls my name. Oh, fuck. A single syllable has never held so much power over me. "You awake?" His voice, husky with lust, is enough to drive me wild.

"Mmph." I have no idea what the right answer to that is. This is uncharted territory and my usual social scripts do not apply. All I know is listening to him jerk off is hotter than any porn. Maybe I should stop, but I can't seem to tear my hand away from my dick. Enough moisture leaks from my tip to make it easier to stroke myself without lube. My hand flies along my shaft and I'm close, so close to the edge. He can hear me, too. He has to realize I'm getting off with him.

"Is this okay, Ig?" Gerald asks, and the sounds of him getting off resume, slow and tentative.

"Yeah," I pant back. "Ger. Gerald. Don't stop. I..." Words fail me as I arch into the pleasure. I'm lost in imagining his hand on my shaft, his voice whispering my name in the dark. "Mm. More."

"Oh, fuck, Ig." His voice is strained, but the wet squelching sounds pick up in tempo as he continues to fuck whatever unseen toy he has up there. "Sorry," he pants, "I didn't realize you were awake."

"Ngh." I grunt and pump myself harder. "I'm not sorry. Say my name again." I whisper that last request, unsure if he can hear me or if I want him to realize how much he turns me on.

Masturbating together in the dark, separated by the distance between our bunks, is one thing. Doing it with his name on my lips might cross lines. I can't seem to help myself. Can't care enough to stop. He's so perfect. I want his powerful arms wrapped around me. His solid chest pressed against my back like when we snuggle. I want to watch my sparks arc between us, feel the tingle dancing from my fingers to his junk, and vice versa as we touch each other all over.

Gerald isn't like anyone else. He listens to what I need and does his best to give it to me. Even when it doesn't come naturally to him. I crave him in ways I can't always articulate. Least of all now, with lust soaking my every thought. Gerald's touch is like being wrapped in my blanket, safe from all the overwhelming sensations that bombard me all day long. "Ger."

"Oh, fuck, Iggy!" His voice ticks up an octave as his movements become frantic, and then the sounds of fucking fade to a low primal moan as he comes. And his voice, dripping with pleasure, calling for me while he orgasms, tips me over the edge, too. My release rolls over me like an avalanche, lighting up every nerve ending with cascades of little blueish sparks of light in the darkness. Sticky cum pumps out to coat my fingers and make a mess of my pajamas. Ugh. I lay panting and spent in my bunk until my breathing steadies.

"You still awake?" Gerald's question is tentative.

"Yeah."

"That, uh, doesn't change anything, right?"

"Right." My voice is flat at the unexpected sting of his rejection. It's far easier to fall back on stupid trivia to keep myself from blurting that it meant the world to me. That it changes everything, if he wants me like I want him. "Sexual release is a basic biological drive. Like thirst or hunger."

"Right, Ig." Gerald chuckles. "The two of us getting off together is no different from sharing a midnight snack."

"Right." I rub at my sternum to ease the

strange ache there, disappointment pooling low in my gut. "I need to go wash up." I get out of bed, grab a change of clothing, and flee to the single occupancy washroom. Once I've locked myself in, I set to scrubbing away the evidence of what just happened. Funny how fast it went from the best orgasm of my life to something I regret doing. I wanted it to mean more, even though I know better. Gerald could have anyone he wants, so it's foolish to think he'd want me.

There's a knock on the door, and I freeze up. I don't want to deal with people-ing right now. It's too much.

"Ig?" Gerald calls through the door. My name still sounds damn good coming from him. He must not be upset if he followed me, right? We can carry on the same as always. Nothing has to change just because he made me come my brains out with nothing more than my own hand and his voice in the darkness.

"Ngh." I grunt a non-reply to acknowledge that I'm listening.

"I'm sorry that I upset you. Like you said, nothing has to change. We both have basic biological needs. There's no harm in meeting them together. Come back to bed?"

"Mhm." I hum.

"At least tell me if you're okay?" Gerald presses

the issue. I push my fingers against my eyelids and watch the sparks dance in the darkness until I can string together a response.

"Just not tired." Which is true, all the sleepy lassitude from coming has drained away and now I'm jittery and on edge.

"If you're not sleepy, we can watch cartoons in bed and snuggle."

"Same as always?" My voice doesn't even quaver, go me. Guess that's what happens when you spend most of your life masking; you get good at hiding your true feelings.

"Yep. You and me forever, Ig. Nothing's ever going to change that," Gerald promises.

"Best friends forever," I agree. No matter how much I wish he'd see me as more. I finish up with the water, pull on the fresh lounge pants I grabbed on my way out of our room, and open the door to join Gerald. He falls into step beside me and we go back to our room.

Gerald grabs my phone from my desk. The brightness setting on his always bothers my eyes. He unplugs my device, then hands it over so I can unlock it and pull up a streaming app. I hold open my blankets for him to join me. This is something we've done countless times at sleepovers when our folks were out doing their supe thing. We huddle close to share the tiny screen on the dimmer setting that I prefer. I know this script and it's easy, so easy, to let him climb into my bed with me and pretend we didn't cross any lines. Problems don't exist if you don't acknowledge them, right?

His arms around me in my bed are as comforting as they've always been. Gerald knows me. The things to avoid, like bright lights, featherlight caresses that tickle and squirm, or the weird sounds mouths sometimes make that feel like they can burrow right into my brain with all the finesse of a rusty spoon. How I prefer to be touched, with deep pressure instead of light brushes. He's always been good about giving me what I need from him. But there's a hollow ache of longing for something more now that I can't seem to shake. I sigh and snuggle closer to him, zoning out to the familiar cartoon on the screen and his steady breathing.

CHAPTER 11

Gerald

Iggy's morning wood poking me in the thigh isn't a new thing. Normally, I just roll away and pretend not to notice. We've slept together in the platonic sense countless times. There were kids at school who thought that was weird around the time puberty started going through our ranks. Some of my friends weren't allowed to invite me to slumber parties after I started to transition. That was a mindfuck.

On the one hand, totally unfair social ostracization from my peers. On the other hand, it meant I was getting treated like any other boy. But Ig and my respective parents were always good about trusting us to make good choices and not treating either of us any differently because of our genitals.

My sisters had sleepovers with their friends,

regardless of gender, throughout school, so we already had a precedent in my household for sleepovers with friends and significant others. My folks figured teenagers are going to do what they're going to do, and they'd rather it happen in as safe an environment as possible. They basically only cared that everyone was on board with anything that happened and that if someone with a dick was involved, condoms were available in the washroom. That, and if you made a mess, you washed your own bedding.

By the time I was old enough for the fact Ig and I don't have the same genitals to be a concern to anyone, I was in no way ready for any type of sexual relationship. We kept having sleepovers. And if I occasionally snuck off to the washroom after they fell asleep to rub one out when the constant horniness of puberty and my hypersensitive t-dick kicked in, well, that was no one's business but my own.

Now, though, now I know what Iggy sounds like when they come. How they say my name in the throes of passion. And I know they don't want it to change things. So I won't let it alter our usual routines, no matter how much I'd love to rut my own arousal against Ig's hard cock this morning.

I tear myself away and blink blearily at the clock on Ig's desk. My pulse kicks up as I realize we must have slept through their alarm. We're late for class. Not good. This is going to throw off our entire day even more than last night's interrupted sleep.

"Ig, wake up." I give their shoulder a firm squeeze.

"Five more minutes," Iggy grumbles and rolls into a ball, blankets clutched tight around them.

"No time, we're already late for class."

That has them bolting upright. "What? But my alarm... shit, we never plugged my phone in last night."

"Yep. Alarm died." I stride across the room to pull out fresh clothing and apply an extra layer of deodorant in lieu of a shower. "Come on, if we hurry we can get to class while the prof is still collecting today's homework." I finish dressing, grab my bag and tear open a Pop-Tart from the stash I keep for mornings like this.

Iggy paws through their laundry for a clean shirt, sniffs their pits and grimaces. "No time for a shower?" they ask pleadingly. It's not about the shower. I get that. It's about breaking from the certainty of our routine. And possibly a little about not being completely clear on acceptable standards of daily hygiene. It's a university campus, they are hardly going to stand out for going one morning without a shower. Heck, they'd barely stand out if they showed up to class sleep-tousled and wearing pajamas. But telling them that won't make this morning any smoother. It will just make them fixate on the illogic of social mores.

"You had one last night, remember?" I say, hoping that will defuse the situation.

Iggy sighs. "No oatmeal either."

"I've got Pop-Tarts, so we can eat breakfast on the way to class. Put on your shirt, Ig."

"Pop-Tarts don't have dinosaurs," Iggy complains. But they don't comment further as they finish changing and follow my lead with the deodorant and a quick comb of their hair. I try not to act too impatient as they double check their school bag has everything they need, plug in their phone to charge while we're in class, and spend an age untying their shoes, putting them on and re-tying them when they could just shove their feet in like anyone else would. That's not how Iggy does it and that's okay.

I grab an extra Pop-Tart for them and we leave. They nibble at the food all the way to class. And we make it to our seats just in time to get a quiz I forgot about entirely. One that I am *so* not ready for. Not only do I hate having to work under a time crunch because it stresses me out, but I've also been slacking on my studies. Between knowing just enough to get cocky and all my newfound freedom, I haven't been keeping up with the reading for class.

I dart an anxious glance from the quiz's five short-answer questions toward Iggy. The first question has me stumped. I don't even have a pencil with me, since note-taking seemed like a waste of time. Iggy is already bent over their paper, filling in answers, just like all the other students around us. They're good at masking and fitting into a school routine, even if it takes a ton of energy for them. I'm the only one quietly panicking.

I fidget. When my chair scrapes, Iggy wordlessly hands me a spare pencil along with miming a deep breath and an encouraging smile. Right, breathe. Iggy knows quizzes like this are not my thing. At least I can guess at the answers now. I might have been a tad overconfident about my academics. I scribble in answers for the three questions I know, BS my way through the other two, and hope I can pull up a failing grade if I study more before the next quiz. After class, Iggy lets me vent about how unfair quizzes are as a concept, and how the one we just took was particularly cruel and unusual.

"I just don't think five questions are enough to get a fair assessment. And who cares if I can recall the dates when they isolated specific gene sequences, let alone what those genes are, right? I know the basic history of when the SUPE allele first appeared and gave Orian and her nemesis their powers. And how she paved the way for the superheroes of today."

"You ran out of time and wrote some BS about it, huh?" Iggy interrupts my rant.

"Yeah." I sigh. "It's just silly that a handful of random questions on a time crunch might deprive the city of my heroic protection."

"Relax, Ger." Iggy snorts at my dramatics and hubris. "No one can stop you from doing anything you put your mind to. You are going to be an epic superhero once we graduate." They squeeze my hand in solidarity. "Besides, the second page of the syllabus says the prof drops the lowest quiz grade for the term, so you won't flunk out over one bad quiz. I'll remind you to study for the next one."

"Thanks, Ig. You're the best. We are going to be the best heroes this city has ever seen." I push through the lingering awkwardness from last night to give them a quick hug.

That helps pull me out of my funk. Iggy is great at keeping me from losing track of what I need to do for school. For all that they have been leaning on me more than usual to get through the transition to university, I lean on them too.

I meant what I said about always being there for each other. Ig's not the only one who needs help sometimes. I've been the one crying in their arms and needing their support on plenty of occasions. When my dysphoria gets to be too much, or I dive into something without thinking it through, they're the one who is always there for me. The one I can lean on without judgment or intrusive questions. Sure, that happens less often recently, but it's still a part of my life and Ig gets it. We complement each other like no one else.

The rest of the day goes better, falling back into our usual routine. We have dinner with Streak and Cinder, like we've made a habit of doing every night. Ig seems to be warming up to them more. We study for a while after we eat. And when we get into our separate beds at the end of the night, I try not to feel guilty or weird about quietly getting off to the sounds of Iggy jerking themself.

CHAPTER 12

Iggy

W hile we were growing up, our parents did the best they could to shield us from their fame, but it is what it is. The flashbulbs and screamed questions always made me freeze up. Adrenaline makes my brain crash when I get cornered by people looking to get a scoop on my family for their latest hero story.

It's not like I fall apart or throw a tantrum. I just can't seem to make myself move when my body is convinced I'm about to be attacked. With how aggressive some of the entertainment reporters get, my endocrine system might have the right idea.

It certainly felt like an attack when they were lying in wait to ambush me outside of my school as a young teen. Gerald was always there to make sure we got home safe, though, and tell the assholes with cameras that we had no comment. I rely on him too much. He almost never complains, and he rarely asks for much in return.

Tonight, he wants me to come to the big super ball game with him. It's the first home game of the season. I've never been much of a sports fan, but he likes super ball. At first, I thought it was one of those things where he thought he had to geek out over sports because 'boys like sports', blah blah blah, manly man bullshit. But it turns out he was actually into playing. And then, with his powers coming in, the only organized sport he can play is super ball. His powers might give him an unfair edge at regular sports. Our school didn't have enough supes for a team. The city has a junior league, but Gerald never went to tryouts and he changed the subject whenever I suggested it, so I learned to leave it alone.

He still enjoys watching. I don't. It's loud and chaotic, and there is too much going on for me to concentrate. I dislike being lost in a crowd. The way the noise from the cheering crowd resonates in my chest like it might vibrate me apart, the way the bleachers shake under me like they might collapse. The bright glare of stadium lights burning my eyes. No, thank you.

But Gerald gave me the puppy dog eyes, so I gave in and agreed to watch the first home game of the season with him. He might not admit it, but I don't think he wants to be alone in the sizeable crowd, either. So this is something I can do for him after all the help he's given me with getting used to campus life. Cinder and Streak are on the team, so we have to go to support our friends, apparently. I want to say they aren't *my* friends; they're his friends. But they've been nice to me. And I don't like the idea of him having friends we don't share.

So I put on the oversized school hoodie Gerald bought for me, and we tromp out into the cool evening to the stadium to line up for the student seating. The cozy hoodie blunts some of my discomfort. I like how the hood conceals the fact I'm wearing my headphones, my music blunting extraneous sounds to a dull roar. When I pull the hood tight around my face, it blocks out flashes of light and motion in my periphery. Like blinders on an easily spooked horse. Not that I have much experience with horses. I had a slight obsession with them for a while as a kid, but that turned into devouring books with horses in them. Which meant teen dramas about horse-loving girls and fantasy novels, mostly. The fantasy novels were long enough to last me more than a few hours, so those became my favorites. From there, my interest in horses got subsumed in all things draconic.

Dragons have elemental powers, just like

Gerald. The most common trope is fire breathers like Moddy. But there are ice dragons and storm dragons and space dragons and basically anything else you can imagine.

I know they aren't supposed to be real, but before Orian and Capricorn, superheroes weren't real either. So it could happen. We could get our own dragons. How cool would that be? Cooler than waiting in line with my student ID card pressing a line into my palm because I'm gripping it too tight to block out the antics taking place all around me. Someone starts some sort of stomping, chanting cheer for our team and the entire line seems to know it. Everyone but me.

I try not to let it bother me. I'm used to being on the outside of this sort of thing. But usually Ger is on the outside with me and when I look over at him, he's stomping along with the rest of them. It makes me feel even more alone. An outsider observing them.

I huddle into my new hoodie and wish I could just go home, but I've got to sit through the game first. The chant seems to last an eternity. When it finally dies away, they let us into the designated student section, checking our IDs instead of tickets since students can attend the games for free.

There are more chants and cheers and songs once we get into the stadium. The student seating is near our team's bench, and Ger leads the way to seats near the front. Fewer distractions. Good. I sit to wait for the game to begin, but most of the other students are standing and buzzing with energy. The fizz of electric impulses on my skin when I get too overwhelmed isn't out of place among my excited peers. I wish I had the concentration to snuff it out, but I don't. So I let the sparks dance around my hands and focus on the pretty patterns they make without my control. It's a pleasant distraction until our team takes the field for warm-ups.

Cinder is easy to spot, despite her uniform; her brightly colored hair is like a beacon. Streak is harder to pick out until she blurs across the field to grab the ball out of the air, South skating hot on her heels. The two of them hate each other off the field, but when they are playing together, they seem to get along just fine. Weird. Sports are weird.

But watching the upperclassmen flaunt their skills isn't terrible. If only that was all there was to it. At least our team doesn't have all kinds of loud flashy powers on display. At the moment, Cinder's little puffs of flame are the most distracting thing on the field, and growing up with Balantin, I'm used to fire manipulation.

Tonight's game is against a team from the

US. All the accredited North American Super U teams play in the same league since there aren't enough of us in any one country to have meaningful competition. I rarely follow sports, but Gerald has been reading up ever since Cinder and Streak suggested he should try for the team next year.

Freshmen almost never get to play, but next year he could have a shot. He's good enough with his powers to have a solid chance, but I hope he decides not to play. I don't want him to spend all his time with his team instead of me. Ugh. Nope, I'm supposed to be working on that. I know I get clingy with him, especially when I'm already insecure about other stuff in my life. Ger says he doesn't mind, but he seems relieved when I tell him I'm sitting out tonight's after-game party. We could probably both use some time to do our own things. And he should join the team next year, if he wants to. It might even be good for both of us to have time apart with how overprotective he's been since the semester started.

The announcer interrupts my thoughts to describe the teams. I listen long enough to determine that we're playing against a super university out in the middle of nowhere in the midwestern US. I sort of wonder what it would be like to live in a vast empty countryside, but it's hard to imagine as a lifelong city dweller.

The movies make it seem like those sorts of places are all cows and cornfields as far as the eye can see. Pretty sure that's not accurate, but I'm not all that invested in finding out more. Not unless those fields of cows turn out to be an all you can eat buffet for the aforementioned dragons that I'm still holding out hope for humanity to discover. I increase the volume of my music to block out the too-loud pep rally songs blaring over the speakers as the game commences.

I don't follow super ball, so I'm not really sure who is winning or what's going on. Ger seems excited, though. And Cinder and Streak are on the field a lot, scoring points or whatever. Some of the other team's players are impressive too, if I'm honest. Doesn't erase the fact I'd rather be anywhere else. I get through the evening unscathed. By the end, I mostly pick up on when to cheer along with the rest of the student section, even if I have no interest in learning their chants.

I'm exhausted by the end of the match. Gerald drags me off to meet up with Cinder and Streak to celebrate on the field, so between that and the cheering fans all around us, I figure we won. Go team?

CHAPTER 13

Gerald

Iggy bails on coming out to celebrate after the game. I hate that it comes as a relief to only have to worry about myself for a few hours. It feels selfish not to want my best friend there, but we could both use time to ourselves. I walk them home while Streak and the team get showered and changed. Iggy is still buzzing from all the energy at the game and I know to expect a crash before long, so I want to be sure they get home safe.

As soon as we enter our room, Iggy retreats into their chair to curl up under their dragon blanket and come down from all the action. Their project of choice tonight appears to be some bit of tech that would be right at home in Foxy's lab. I don't get the impression they enjoyed the game tonight.

"Thanks for coming with me," I say, hating that we aren't in sync. In high school, there were plenty of parties I attended without them because they weren't into it and I wanted to try the stereotypical teenage experience. This seems different, though. Bigger. Because I'm going out with friends, instead of solo. I'm looking forward to socializing and meeting the rest of the super ball team. The party would be a special type of hell for Iggy, but it's the sort of thing I enjoy occasionally.

"Mm," Ig grunts, not looking up from tinkering with their gadget.

"You're cool with me going out, right?"

"Mhm," Ig agrees, rocking in their chair and prying open the casing on the small plastic object.

"Okay, so, like, I'll be back late. Don't wait up or anything, I'll try not to wake you when I get home."

"Mhm."

"Bye, Ig."

Iggy wiggles their fingers at me in a halfhearted sort of wave, but doesn't stop poking at the circuits inside the device or otherwise acknowledge me. I'm used to that, too. They spent the entire night pushing their limits to join me in doing something I know they didn't enjoy, and they've spaced out now because they did that for me. So I should be used to them needing to decompress. I am used to it. I'm just also a touch insecure about our friendship with everything changing so much. Their quick dismissal stings. That isn't Iggy's problem to fix, though; it's mine. I double check I have my wallet, phone, and student ID before I shut the door behind me, letting it slam with more force than needed.

No more thinking about Iggy tonight. Streak sent me a text with where to meet her and I jog across campus to catch a ride to the bar. To my surprise, South, Pugsly, and Gill are loitering in the parking lot with Streak and Cinder. The rest of the team and their friends are around too, so maybe it shouldn't shock me. Whatever their personal feelings about each other, they put that aside during the game. I guess that extends to celebratory drinks afterward as well.

"Hey." I wave as I approach the group.

"There's Gust," South says. My hero name sounds mocking coming from him. I ignore him and join Cinder.

"There you are!" Cin hugs me. And I congratulate her on a great game.

"No Zap tonight?" Streak glances past me,

like she expects them to materialize out of the shadows. Not impossible, there's a villain out in BC known for shadow manipulation, but that isn't Ig's power.

"Not tonight, they had a headache after the game." I fudge the truth. It's more complicated than a headache, but I won't get into that. People understand and sympathize with headaches after a noisy event. I don't want them to look down on Ig for who they are by trying to explain how hard it is for them to attend sporting events and deal with crowds.

"Aw, hope they get better soon," Cinder sympathizes. "They totally have to come along next time!"

"For sure." I don't know how likely that is, but I nod anyway.

"Pile in, we're rolling out." Streak gestures to her car and I slide into the back seat. Cinder sits up front. To my surprise, South, Pugsly, and Gill all squeeze in with me. Pugsly and Gill double up their seat belt by the window, which leaves me pressed against South. He flashes me a cocky grin and pats my thigh, just above the knee. "Guess we're getting cozy, huh?"

"Guess so," I agree, resisting the urge to make myself shrink in to take up as little space as possible. That impulse makes me feel small and pathetic and it's something I've worked hard to overcome. I refuse to let South, or anyone else, intimidate me.

The others rehash their game all the way to the bar where we're meeting the rest of the team for the after party. I decline Streak's offer to buy the first round. Iggy and I still have our deal about waiting to drink until their birthday, even if I agreed to visit the bar without them. I'm not going back on my promise. At least, that was my plan. But at some point around the time South and his crew bring a round of refills for our table, the ginger ale I've been sipping starts to taste different without me registering the change right away. It just tastes flatter, less sweet, like when the syrup in a fountain drink machine runs low.

Around the time the room starts to spin, I realize the weird taste might mean something is wrong. Cinder and Streak aren't sitting with us anymore. They got up to dance a while ago, and I don't know anyone else here well enough to ask for help. I stand to excuse myself to the washroom, hoping I can walk off the lightheaded sensation. My grip on my powers seems to slip more with every lazy rotation the bar makes. I've never experienced this untethered sensation before and I don't care for it at all.

I stumble while trying to push away from the

table. My blundering knocks over my chair and I almost plow into someone with a tray of drinks. I heave a gust of air to stabilize the tray, which sloshes fizzy liquid from a few of the cups and earns me a pointed scowl from the server. South smirks at me and raises his glass from across the table, like he's saying cheers.

I stammer an apology, and weave my way to the washroom in the back of the bar, ignoring the people at our table calling after me. They sound surprised and concerned, but with my head spinning and my thoughts in a foggy haze, I'm not in any state for dealing with people.

I trusted Cinder and Streak when they said I didn't have to drink to go out with them. But there was definitely something more than soda in my drink. I'm certain of that now. Guess I shouldn't have trusted the rest of the team to live up to that promise. The betrayal hurts.

I stumble into the door, trying to pull it open until I lean against it and it swings inward. That almost lands me on my ass on the dirty floor tiles. I use a gust of wind to steady myself, and slam the door between me and the bar. A twist of my wrist sends a tendril of wind to set the bolt, locking the door. Loosening my control enough to use the wind has the storm coiled close to the surface tonight. I don't think I like the way alcohol affects me.

It's unnerving how lowering my inhibitions makes it harder to reign in the electricity crackling along my nerves, until I'm convinced if I can't discharge it, I'll burn from the inside out. I never use this part of myself without Ig around; it's too dangerous if we want to keep up our illusions. But I'm alone in the locked bathroom. My head is spinning. I'm not sure if I can keep a handle on my powers long enough to get back to campus if I don't let off some steam. So I let the power arc between my hands in a white-blue flash of light.

Someone claps. Not the thunderclap of sound that sometimes accompanies my more impressive electric blasts. The ones I have perfected attributing to Iggy. Actual clapping, coming from what I thought was an unoccupied stall. It sends ice down my spine, because someone saw. Someone who might unravel everything.

"Hm, I thought there was something fishy about you and Zap. Are you a storm caller, Gusty?" Gill steps out of the stall, spinning a ball of what I can only assume is toilet water on one finger. When I don't reply, he flings the ball at me. "Think fast."

I throw up a hand and blow out a breath of wind to scatter the droplets like rain. Despite my power over the storm, my control of water is nonexistent. I can only push it around or send a charge through it, not control it directly. The wind is enough to shield me.

A lock scrape in the door behind me and all the water droplets freeze, tinkling to the ground like shards of glass as South joins us. "Well, well, well, is our little Gust more of a Gale?" he drawls.

"Shut up!" I ball my hands into fists as the fear and adrenaline burn away most of the fuzzy-headedness that drove me to seek the refuge of the washroom in the first place. I'm still tipsy, but for the moment, I'm also focused on the threat.

"What else can you do, Gusty?" South steps into my personal space and eyes me up and down, like he can see my powers through my skin or something. Maybe he's drunk, too, if he thinks that.

I shiver at the intensity of his attention. It's not just that he's standing too close and threatening to expose my secrets. It's also years of fear about being confronted in a washroom and told I don't belong. Over the past year, I've gotten more comfortable with my body and how well I fit in gendered spaces, but how in the hells did I think this was a safe place to retreat? It's not safe and I don't feel safe with South and Gill surrounding me.

"Nothing. I don't know what you thought you saw, but it's nothing." I'm not about to show a pair of bullies just how scared they've made me.

"Hmm, no, that won't work, try again." South holds up his phone and plays a video that Gill must have sent him. It shows me with lightning arcing between my hands.

"Photoshop." I try to make myself sound casual, as if this is no big deal.

"Maybe, but if this leaks, there will always be doubt. Always questions. Rumors you and your precious Bug Zapper won't be able to put to bed, because they'll be the truth, won't they?" South gets right in my face and smirks at me as he reveals just how much he knows. Or suspects. He can't know. We've been so careful.

The *if* isn't lost on me, even in the midst of my spinning head and the urge to lash out and protect myself from the threat. If they only wanted to ruin me and Ig, then they would have already shared the video. I'm a little long on the uptake under the circumstances, but now I realize that this is blackmail, pure and simple. "What do you want?"

"You. No more of this Gusty garbage. Stop slumming it with Bug Zapper, Cinderella, and Streaker and join us at the big boys' table. You can be Whirlwind. Be a real somebody instead of a two-bit nobody so you can keep your loser friends afloat."

"I think it's a bit late for a new alias." I cross my arms, taking strength in the slight gesture of defiance.

"You still don't get it, huh?" South sounds faux-regretful as he slings an arm around my shoulder and makes a sweeping gesture with his other hand, like he wants to show me some fantastic vista. The only thing I see is the wet washroom and Gill's leering face. "Let me spell it out for you, Gusty. On campus, you're Gust. In class, Gust. With your family and friends, Gust, or Gerald, though, you might want to think twice about being so loose with your legal name, all things considered. Then you come to us for extracurricular training and you become Whirlwind. You'll receive instructions and a package in your campus mailbox first thing tomorrow. A new super suit that should hide your identity as Whirlwind. Starting tomorrow, you train with us. When we call, you come to us. You work for us. And you will cooperate with us, or you'll regret it. I don't think you're eager to see how your Bug Zapper does as a sub-sidekick B class... where they belong. And that is the least of what my people can do, capisce?" South grips the back of my neck and gives me a little shake before stepping back to look at me. His expression remains bored. Like my reply doesn't matter to him in the least.

"Yeah. Okay." I nod stiffly. "I understand."

"Good." South throws his heavy arm back around my shoulders, and guides me toward our table. "Next round is on you. Might as well enjoy your first time getting wasted, kiddo, starting tomorrow you're on the same strict training regimen as the rest of us. The League doesn't take subpar supes."

Gill follows right behind us, in case I make a move to get away. I won't, though, not if it means Ig gets outed as having weaker powers and the world finding out my secrets.

CHAPTER 14

Iggy

I t takes ages to calm down after the game. I spend several hours poking at the health tracker watch I fried with an ill-timed spark when South cornered me. The familiar task lets my brain zone out while I relax into my hobby. It's a shame my interest in electronics makes a crappy combination with my sometimes volatile superpowers. I'm going to need more solder from Pop's lair to finish the job. My watch remains bricked when I crawl into bed hours later.

I pretend to be asleep when Gerald stumbles in after his night out to celebrate with the team. He reeks of alcohol and I can't help how much it stings that he went out drinking without me. We agreed to do that together.

This is the sort of thing I don't think he gets. How deep it cuts that he broke his word to me.

Did he? Why else would he stumble to his bed, though? Or not even whisper my name to see if I'm still awake. Usually, he'd at least do that much. Tonight he doesn't.

I curl tighter under my covers and try to let the hurt roll off my back. This is a stupid thing to cry about. I knuckle my eyelids to stem the flow of tears and fix in on the pretty patterns floating in the darkness behind my closed eyelids to distract myself. So what if he went out without me? Maybe him drifting away from me is for the best. I don't want to hold him back.

I muffle a disgruntled sound in my pillow, even thinking that makes something in me recoil in horrified fear. Gerald isn't like that. He would be the first to tell me that line of reasoning is ableist bullshit. He's told me I can't hold him back by being myself because he wouldn't want to move ahead with anyone who would look down on me for who I am. No, Gerald won't leave me behind, even if he broke his promise. I'm sure he'll have a valid explanation in the morning.

I fall asleep to the sound of Ger's even breathing. The adrenaline crash from being at the game with the roaring crowd and bright lights finally beats out the keyed-up jitters from being overstimulated. The distant imagined echoes of screaming fans and the spectacle of both teams' powers on display haunt my fitful sleep.

The next morning Gerald has a headache, and I'm as hungover from lack of sleep and emotional burnout as he looks. Neither of us brings up last night. We eat our breakfast in our room instead of venturing to the dining hall. Technically, we're not supposed to have a coffee maker or the hot plate I use to make my oatmeal in our room. So I make Gerald bring them to our hall's shared kitchenette to plug them in there, despite his grumbled complaints that no one actually follows those rules.

I'd rather not consider the rest of our neighbors being reckless with the building we all have to live in, but Gerald has a point. Everyone in our dorm has elemental powers, so a fire is pretty unlikely to engulf the building without someone being able to put it out. I mean, unless it's one of the residents powering the flames.

Good thing South controls ice, or I'd be worried about that asshole setting the building on fire just to watch it burn. After our encounter on the walkway, I don't trust him at all.

Gerald and I spend the day lounging in our room and playing *Conker's Bad Fur Day*, which never fails to cheer me up. The multiplayer mode is infinitely quotable and silly and has the allure of the illicit, since the mature rating meant I wasn't allowed to play it as a kid.

Most of the time, I'm a rules follower. Rules make it easier to fit in and do what's expected. But Gerald smuggled his eldest sister's copy to my place when I was sick once in the sixth grade. Ever since then, this game is Ger and my thing and I love playing it with him as we quote the familiar dialog to each other.

It's the first time since we've been on campus that I've really enjoyed myself without reservations. With just the two of us, I don't have to edit my behavior or my words. I can repeat the silly voices and rock in my seat or let my fingers wiggle and hands flap when we win a game, without mockery.

When Gerald notices me stimming, he doesn't get weird about it. He just smiles at me and offers to play again. All day long, until we miss dinner at the dining hall and order a pizza instead. Even then, we don't stop playing. We follow the same pattern of every lazy Saturday since we were kids. Only better, since we don't have to beg our parents for permission to have a sleepover. Gerald just snuggles into my bed next to me when he gets tired. We keep playing until I fall asleep with my controller still in my hands and my best friend snoring on my pillow a few inches away. It's a perfect day, perfect enough to pretend last night never happened and nothing will ever change between Gerald and me. That we can truly be best friends forever.

CHAPTER 15

Gerald

Watching Iggy flap their hands around when they win our game makes my heart ache with the realization that it's been months since I've seen them happy enough to do that. And the fact I didn't notice until now makes me a crappy friend. That, on top of breaking our promise last night, however unintentionally, has guilt gnawing at me. I never want to be the reason Iggy is sad, but I saw their tear-streaked cheeks and red-rimmed eyes when we woke up this morning.

Ig might not be the best at reading social cues, but they are observant when it comes to the things they care about. And I know I'm among the things they care about most in the world. When they first told me I was one of their special interests, it was overwhelming. But I think for Ig, that was just another way of saying they love me. And yeah, it can get intense, but so can my crush on them. Just different types of love, or something.

All I know for sure is that seeing them happy and uninhibited about expressing it makes my heart swell with pride. With me, they are secure enough to be themself. And just like that, my world is back on its proper axis after South's vague threats and the last few weeks of struggling to adjust to all the freedom being out from under my parents' roof and at university has to offer.

Sure, I *can* stay out all night with my friends and get wasted at a bar. I *can* blow off my studies to goof around in the practice rooms with Cin and Streak playing with my powers. Upperclassmen are allowed to book the practice rooms whenever they want to hone their skills. I *can* be whoever I want at school. Gust, the guy who follows after the upperclassmen who took a shine to me like a pliant puppy. Or Whirlwind, the villain in training who blows off his friends to get ahead. Or Storm Surge, the hero I'm pretty sure Ig and our families expect me to be. That's the hero alias Ig uses for me, when it's just us.

Being here, at Super U, is like a clean slate. But what I really want to be is Gerald; the boy who loves his best friend. I didn't have to go to university to know that. And I don't think I enjoy being pulled in so many directions. I don't like feeling that if I go out with Cinder and Streak, I'm betraying Ig. Or that staying in with Ig is letting my new friends down. Or that if I don't go along with South's demands, something terrible will happen and it will be my fault. I'm not sure what to do about that, exactly. But for the space of a lazy weekend, I can just stay in my cozy bubble with Iggy. It can just be us again, like it's always been since we were babies.

The bubble can't last, though. Not long after Iggy falls asleep, curled against my chest, their phone chirps with the sound they use for getting alerts about their folks. Mine buzzes, too, so, probably Balantin is making more headlines. I grab both phones and mute them before the noise wakes Iggy.

Then I check mine. Sure enough, there is a breaking news story about Iggy's moddy and my mom rescuing motorists from a collapsing overpass. The video clip with the article shows Balantin in their super suit holding flames at bay while my mom uses her super strength to carry a carload of people to safety on a precariously teetering bridge. Once the bystanders are safe, Balantin lets go of the rogue flames that are consuming an overturned transport trailer. They turn their attention to fusing the broken steel girders so that the overpass doesn't crumble onto the traffic below. From there, they turn their focus to the flames, only to reveal that there is someone in the midst of the crowd below. They are wearing a familiar super suit with the League's twin fangs logo stamped onto their facemask.

I watch in horror as the flames lick Balantin's face, then go out, like the other fire wielder is toying with them. The villain sends a slow lick of flame toward a child at the edge of the crowd, then turns and flees. Balantin doesn't even hesitate in leaping to the child's defense despite their smoldering super suit and the damage to their person.

Whoever is recording catches Mom in the corner of the frame. She isn't in a position where she can see the villain, just that Ig's moddy is hurt and fighting to rescue a kid. My mom runs to her hero's side, as any good sidekick would. The kid is safe. The villain escapes. The video clip ends.

More alerts pop up, from every supe news source in the city. The *Supe Report* blog seems weirdly focused on the contents of the overturned truck. I skim the article in horrified fascination. Bloggler recognized the logo on the boxes inside the burning trailer was from some sort of electronic chip manufacturer.

The story from the blog details how this attack is an even bigger blow since shortages in the raw materials used to make them are causing massive back-orders for all kinds of gadgets you wouldn't think require a chip. That all seems like pointless information when clearly the League threatening everyday citizens and hurting Balantin when the hero leapt into the fray is the important part of the story. Who cares about a bunch of back-ordered cars and ovens? What good will smart chips do for the League?

I have a text on my phone from an unknown number. The first message is a link to the video I just watched. Another comes in a moment later.

Unknown: Do not think of ignoring your promises. Check your mailbox, Whirlwind. Next time we have to remind you of your duties, you won't like the consequences.

I want to send back an expletive-filled rant with all my rage. The implication that they hit a target they knew Balantin and my mother would have to respond to as leverage to get to me is staggering. I want to destroy them, the way they destroyed the bridge.

They could have killed people. And for what? To send a stupid message? Ig's moddy got hurt for nothing. Well, not nothing. They were helping people. But those people shouldn't have needed saving from the League. Might not have if I'd just done what South told me to do. What I had agreed to, even if it was under duress.

This is why I've always hidden the extent of my powers, even before it mattered to cover for Iggy. Why it never seemed like much of a hardship to all but give over control of half of my abilities to Iggy. If there was a way to actually transfer my control of electricity to them, I'd sign up for that in a heartbeat. But that's not how anything works. And burying my head in the sand about South's threats will not make them go away.

I disentangle myself from Iggy. They mumble a sleepy protest and I want nothing more than to fall asleep beside them, hold them all night long, even if it's just platonic snuggling. I'd give almost anything to be close to them in whatever way they want me. But keeping them and our families safe is more important than what I want. I slip out of their bed and slink out our door to check my campus mailbox in the downstairs lobby.

When I unlock it, a plain envelope that I can only assume is from South sits there, along with a few flyers for campus events and the key to the parcel delivery box. I retrieve the plain brown package from the parcel box and leave the key. I don't open the note or the parcel in the dorm lobby. Instead, I take them to our suite's washroom and lock myself in, not caring if our suitemates need the facilities. I just need a moment of privacy to think.

The envelope from the League has nothing on the outside to show where it came from. Just my mailbox number. When I open it and pull out the folded note, the paper feels thick and expensive in my hands. The embossed twin fangs League logo stands out at the top of the page. The note is a simple script font, a single printed line. No handwriting that might connect it to South. I know it's from him, anyway. Or whoever else the League has tasked with recruiting new supes on campus.

Welcome to the team, Whirlwind.

That's it. Nothing more, no matter how I tilt the page seeking a trace of hidden ink. I crumple it, and then think better of throwing it away where someone might find it and link it to me. Instead, I set it aside and tear open the parcel. The brown paper packaging parts to reveal a gray-blue super suit, like a storm cloud.

I shake out the folds to see the whole thing. With the full hood to obscure my features, the suit will cover every inch of me, save the lower half of my face. The accents are in the cerulean blue of a clear sky and the overall design looks like a storm devouring a sunny day. Or at least that's what it seems to imply to my jaded eye. The part that makes me go numb is the sigil over the chest and forehead.

I've seen something similar before. This one is an update on an older design, but it's clearly a modern take on the vintage villain's emblem. The Human Hurricane.

So, they mean to advertise me as the famous villain's second coming or something to that effect. He's one reason I've always hidden the extent of my powers. But the League knows now. They know, and they know who I am and where to strike to hurt me. If there is a way out of accepting the gift of this suit, and the demands that come along with it, I can't think of it.

Instead of fighting the inevitable, I fold the super suit up into a tight little square. I've long since learned how to fold the resilient material that can dampen other supes' powers and natural forces alike to protect the wearer. As I'm folding, I find the second note pinned near the neck of the suit.

Enjoy your new suit, but do not allow it to be traced to your legal identity or your hero name.

You'll be told when to wear it. Keep it secret, keep it safe.

For now, report to your contact daily for instruction. DO NOT record any names on your phone. We will contact you. We expect you to train with S in the practice rooms each day after classes.

No more gallivanting with jumped up sidekicks. You are one of the elite now; act like it! Do not squander your talents or the opportunities we can offer you. Live up to your full potential.

This note doesn't bear the League insignia. Clearly, they figured the source of my instructions was clear enough not to require further explanation. I crumple the second note along with the first, and ball both up with the packaging they used to wrap Whirlwind's suit. After a moment spent composing myself, I stride out of the bathroom with my head held high. I'll figure this all out. First order of business, take the ball of wadded up paper around the corner to our hall's trash room where I bury it in the stinkiest bag of waste I can find. Somewhere no one is likely to find it.

Then I return to the washroom to wash my hands, though that does nothing for the filthy way just handling the villain suit that was commissioned for me feels. I don't want this. But I don't see a way to stop it, either. Not without giving up everything and putting everyone I love in greater danger. So I slip back into my room to hide the new super suit at the back of my closet, where Iggy is unlikely to find it. It's not like we go through each other's clothing.

When it's done, I stand and look uncertainly between my cold, lonely bed, lofted up near the ceiling, and the cozy spot beside Iggy that I had to abandon earlier.

I long to crawl back into their bed as though I'd never left. But that isn't fair. Not with what I'm hiding now. Not when even our friendship is enough to paint a target on Ig's back. I can't always be around to protect them. South already showed me that on the second day of classes when he cornered Iggy on their way back to the dorm.

I climb into my lonely bed and ignore the way Iggy mumbles my name in their sleep. Their hand stretches across the empty blankets where I lay when they fell asleep. It looks as though they are unconsciously searching for me. I turn my back and try to sleep. I fail at that too.

CHAPTER 16

Iggy

Sunday when I wake up, the first thing I notice is the lingering scent of Ger's manly man shampoo on my pillows. He's such a sucker for any branding that affirms his masculinity. It's kind of cute. And my pillow smells nice, if a little strong. My smile fades as I realize the man who left the traces of his scent in my bed isn't lying next to me.

I sit up, frowning, to look for him. Gerald isn't in his bed either. Or our room. When I check my phone, I have a ton of notifications. Either I slept through a hell of a lot of buzzing and chirping from my phone last night, or Gerald silenced it to let me sleep. That's the sort of overprotective thing he'd do. I quash the flare of irritation at him treating me like a kid or something. And then I see the headline alert and irritation turns to anger.

Moddy got hurt while I was lying in bed dreaming about my crush. And he kept that from me. Kept me from knowing and from reaching out to make sure it's nothing serious. What if it was? What if Moddy died while I slept away half the day? This is not okay.

I ignore my unread texts from Gerald and hit the button to call Moddy back, since they and Pop have both tried to call several times. The fact Moddy's number is on my missed call log could be a good sign that they're okay. Or at least okay enough to call me. Or it could be subterfuge, meant to downplay the injuries if the worst happened.

"There you are." Moddy's gentle smile is obvious in their voice when they pick up on the second ring. "Is everything alright? We've been trying to get a hold of you, Ignatius."

"Moddy?" I grip the phone tight, unable to get out my questions. My throat feels rigid, my words locked away by fear for them.

"So, you heard about the League's latest antics." Their steady voice reassures me that everything will be alright. "I'm fine, darling. And so is Eloise. No one was seriously injured."

Relief floods through me in a riptide. Moddy and Gerald's mom are both safe. The sudden jolt from anxiety and fear to hearing everything is alright reminds me of being tossed by the waves when we went to a water park as kids. I got pulled out too far and nearly drowned and my body seems to think this is the same as that, tossing me under a flood of feelings I can't control and I can't seem to get my head above the waves.

"Breathe, Ignatius, I'm here. I'm okay. And you're okay too." Moddy lets the reassurances pour from their mouth like rain and eventually it gets through to me. I stop shaking from the adrenaline and undirected anger, hurt, and fear. It's a miracle I didn't fry my phone with how upset I was. A miracle and extra-strength EM shielding that Pop helped me cook up in the lair.

"Sorry," I mumble into the phone.

"Nothing to forgive. We handled the incident. Everyone is fine. Why don't you and Gerald come home for a visit? I can have your pop make us a nice roast. Gerald's family is joining us. You two should, too. You can bring home your laundry to save some quarters. And see for yourself that I'm all in one piece."

"What does laundry have to do with quarters?" I ask, secure in knowing Moddy will understand that I'm genuinely confused and not being a smartass.

"Oh." Moddy doesn't sound irritated at being corrected. They usually don't, not like some people. "Did they upgrade the machines? We used to have to put in coins to wash a load of laundry."

"Oh. No, we have laundry cards. I guess you can use coins to load them. Or a bank card. I use my bank card."

"Then you can save some of your money by doing laundry at home, Iggy," Moddy cajoles.

"I should study tonight. And we have class tomorrow," I state.

"You can study here, or before I pick you up. And I'll have you back on campus in plenty of time to get a good night's sleep for your classes, Iggy," Moddy offers.

I want to see them. Hug them. So even though it's going to screw up my plans for the day to make sure I stay ahead on my assignments, I agree to dinner at home. The stress of that might make it hard for me to focus on my textbooks, but I'm stressed about the video of Moddy getting hurt already. What's a little more stress? I stand and pace off some of my nervous energy. The movement helps.

"Okay. I don't know if Gerald has plans. But yes. I want to come home."

"I'll be there to pick you up outside your dorm around four then. Text when you speak to Ger about joining us."

"Okay. Thanks, Moddy."

"I love you, Ignatius. Pop and I both. We're so very proud of you. You remember that, yeah?"

"I love you too, Moddy. And Pop. See you tonight." I hang up and stare at my phone screen. I'm not sure I want to read the messages from Gerald. But I can't seem to help myself.

I dive in, unsure what to expect. His terse messages dash my hopes for an explanation of why he's gone. Or an apology for turning off my phone and his other recent weird behavior. He just says that he left to practice using his powers so he can try out for the super ball team next year. He's meeting up with some upperclassmen for extra training sessions. Something about that seems off, but I get sidetracked by reading all the alerts about last night's League attack. Considering that Moddy was there, learning what happened seems like a more pressing concern. So I set aside my worries and irritation until Gerald gets home to talk about it in person.

CHAPTER 17

Gerald

"Gusty, so glad you could join us. You're late." South smirks at me from across the practice room. "We'll have to reset the scenario, Gill, see to it." Gill turns to obey with alacrity. Upon his inputting a command at a console designed for that purpose, the training room's various obstacles reset for a new scenario designed for four. South and his cronies move to take up their starting positions.

Not long after stowing my Whirlwind super suit in the back of my closet where Ig is least likely to stumble across it, I'd received another message from the same unknown number that has to be South summoning me to a morning practice session in the training rooms. So after a long night of tossing and turning, here I am.

"Sorry, I didn't get your message right away," I reply, hurrying to take up my position at the last remaining open starting point.

"This scenario is two-on-two combat. You and Pugsly versus me and Gill. Whichever team is subdued first loses. Show us what you've got, no holding back except for not actually killing anyone, clear?" South ignores my excuses.

"Crystal." I nod my understanding as the countdown timer to the start of the scenario begins in big red numerals.

The hardest part of this whole thing might be hiding my true abilities. South and Gill might know, or suspect, but if I slip up here, the computer that records everything happening in the training room will soon make it so that everyone knows I can control more than the wind. I brace myself for the start signal, then launch myself toward Gill. He's the least powerful of my enemies; if I can knock him out of the action fast, then Pugsly and I will both be free to focus on South.

It's a shame we didn't have time to share tactics before we began. I'm sure if I voice my concerns, South will turn it back onto me for not arriving on time. There's no point in complaining to teammates who are coercing my cooperation. I dodge past obstacles, borrowing the strength of the wind to hasten my dodging movements as padded pistons thrust at me to slow my passage.

Gill and South are both ignoring Pugsly as they angle toward me. South skates along an icy pathway through the air, going over much of the course, though there are swinging pendulums and the occasional gout of flame or motion-triggered bolts thrown toward him near the top of the room that forces him to dodge around. Gill darts and leaps through the obstacles at ground level. Pugsly, impervious to obstacles so long as he maintains enough momentum, simply stalks implacably toward where we are all converging.

I throw a blast of air to send South off course at the critical moment when he tries to dodge and a swinging ram knocks him sideways off his icy pathway. He recovers fast, creating a platform that breaks his fall and continuing toward me with a rictus grin.

"Such feeble efforts. Next time press your advantage, Gust," he calls to me with a patronizing shake of his head.

While I'm distracted by delaying South, I lose sight of Gill, eeling his way between moving obstacles. Until he pops up atop a nearby tower and douses me in water. I almost laugh at the harmless attack, which causes me to hesitate a blink before blowing the clinging moisture away from myself, directing the wind to blast the water away from my face first.

It's a mere nuisance, no great rush to dispel it. A bit of water will hardly even slow me down, and the student issue super suit I'm wearing repels most of the moisture, anyway. But before I can so much as scoff at the foolish waste of Gill's power and clear my face, South flicks his wrist in my direction and I'm encased in ice from the neck down, unable to move and frigid within the solid coating. The super suit might protect my skin from the searing cold or the risk of frostbite, but it's not a pleasant sensation to be trapped in ice.

"Blow as hard as you want, little squall. You won't catch us, nor gain your freedom from South. You'll only chill the ice more and keep it harder longer," Gill sneers at me.

I can read the deeper meaning that South's got me trapped in more ways than one and the sooner I accept it, the easier it will be. That might even be true, for him at least, but I don't give up without a fight. Gill turns his back on me, cracking his knuckles before going after my nominal teammate. I try to blow the water wielder off his tower perch, but he just lets the force of my wind propel his jump that much further to land in a clear spot and cut off Pugsly's approach toward South with a large pole that my partner for this exercise picked up from the many removable parts of the training room to use as an improvised weapon.

South doesn't waste time gloating over incapacitating me. He falls on Pugsly from the other side, trapping the other supe between two targets. It crosses my mind that if I let them beat me this handily every time we practice, perhaps they will reassess my usefulness. Whirlwind is a name to make the city's defenders quake before us. If I fail to live up to the promise of that name, will they lose interest in me? And what will that mean for Gust? Should I let these bullies force me away from my dreams of defending the city alongside Balantin and my mom? Because if I lower myself for them, by making Ig and myself seem weak and unthreatening, then how are we supposed to convince anyone we're up to taking up our parents' mantles here?

No. That's a coward's way out of this. Say what they might about me—I'll never be a coward. So, I won't allow South and Gill to defeat me this easily. Now to figure out a way to get loose.

Lightning might shatter the ice encasing me. Or it might just reveal my true strength to no good purpose. No. Only the wind is at my disposal in the training rooms. That's something I can't afford to compromise.

Across the room, Pugsly has planted his feet

at the center of the clearing and started twirling the large heavy pole about him in wide arcing swings. He's holding our opponents back with the weapon, batting away all the water and ice they lob at him. Neither South nor Gill can slip past his guard and it appears as if the pole is weaving an impenetrable defense around his body, as unstoppable as he is once he is in motion.

Well, I can make use of the room just as easily as my teammate. It's easy to stir up a breeze with my mouth free to blow. I can control the wind even without that much impetus to direct it, but it never hurts to give the impression of a weakness that I don't truly have to better obscure my true weaknesses. That's a trick my fathers taught me after years working alongside Foxy.

Ig's Pop is a wily supe, and his sidekicks are no less sly than him. They have to be to keep up with his plans. My folks are more than mere sidekicks to Ig's parents. I understand that. But there's still a deference between them I never want to experience between Ig and me, no matter which side of the hierarchy I fall on.

Iggy just naturally ignores that sort of social nuance. When we work together, I want it to be a fully egalitarian arrangement. I refuse to settle for anything less. So our power imbalance can never come to light, and if that means dancing to

South's tune until I can best him and the League at their own game, then so be it.

My wind flows around me at my behest until I find one of the spent motion activated bolts that South triggered earlier. I can force it aloft and sling it at my ice prison. The first strike chips off a chunk near my shoulder. My second attempt hits more firmly and sends a crack spidering through the ice at my back. The third wind-powered blow combined with me squirming against my bindings with all my might sends chunks of ice flying. Without letting it falter, I direct my wind to sweep that same ice toward my opponents. I let the wind carry me toward them, too. I follow the flying ice shards to Pugsly's defense. In unison, we press an attack now that we are both free to strike.

South easily freezes the slushy ice chunks I send toward him, flinging an arm out to catch it and reform it into an icy spear, arrowing toward me. I dodge, shearing off the point of the ice shaft with a concentrated gust of air, honed razor fine to cut.

Pugsly takes advantage of the distraction to dart his stick at South and knock him sprawling. I focus a blast of wind at him, pinning him to the ground even as Gill makes the ice melt rise from around South to surround my head. That seems to be Gill's favorite trick, and I'm ready for it, using my control of the wind to pull air into my lungs, even through the sphere of water. With South pinned down, there's little danger of it freezing around me.

Most elemental powers rely on physical gestures and the ability to see what we seek to influence, at least to some extent. Not that the strongest and most skilled can't move beyond those crutches. Balantin can call a flame unerringly without seeing it or lifting a finger. South is neither extraordinarily skilled nor terribly strong, in my estimation. Sure, he's got a cocky swagger, like many with H class powers. When he wants to put on a show, he's capable of flair, but he's no Balantin.

With one hand pointed at South, I keep up the windy onslaught pinning him to the ground, and with the other I send a breeze to help my ally disperse the water bubble around his head. The water splatters around him, only to reform around his ankles with Gill grim-faced and determined to pin him in place. If we're each focused on pinioning the other's partner, would the match end in a draw? No matter, I intend to end this confrontation with an unambiguous win.

I ignore the water restraining Pugsly and send my wind looping around the room to pick up speed and strength. By the time it loops back to us, it is a powerful fist of air that plucks up Pugsly's dropped staff and slams it into Gill's midriff. The projectile passes easily through the wall of water that he hastily throws up to shield himself. I push, letting the wind flow until Gill fetches up against a wall and the pole pins him in place. I hold a hand toward each of my opponents and let the wind buffet them mercilessly. If we were outside, it could pick up grit to scour their skin and force them to admit defeat.

"Yield?" Pugsly asks, going to stand over South. He presses a meaty palm on his vanquished foe's head, applying only a fraction of the crushing pressure his power makes him easily capable of.

"I yield," South spits, irritated. I don't immediately drop my wind. Not until Gill also yields, making our victory official.

Gill struggles feebly against the force restraining him, only slumping in defeat once South gives up too. "I yield," he echoes the words.

I'm still caught up in the idea of using a sandstorm to scour away any claim they think they have on me. It would not be a pleasant lesson for them to learn. Their super suits would protect them from serious harm, even then, but I like the idea of scraping my mark into their exposed skin, showing them I'm not someone to trifle with. Stricken at the vicious turn of my thoughts, my grip on the wind falters.

No. This isn't who I am. Even the vindictive thought has me flushing hot with shame. Iggy would never be okay with me attacking someone with that kind of cruelty. It's the sort of thing the nebulous concept of Whirlwind would do. The act of a supervillain.

Abruptly, I pull the wind away from my helpless victims and stumble backward, as though I can distance myself from my own thoughts. I fetch up against a low metal barrier that can move into different configurations along a track. For now, the scenario settings have it locked in place, forming a solid barrier against my retreat. A bulwark to lean against as I reel from the bloodthirsty images in my head.

I'm startled by a movement in the shadows near the doorway. I can't make out who is there. Their super suit blends with the shadows.

"He'll do."

The supe who steps forth into the room is someone I recognize. Or at least, their suit is. Not Umbra, as I'd at first feared. No, this is a lesser villain than the one I've heard rumors of terrorizing the populace out west. The spider silk touch of a telepath playing in my head reveals this villain's identity to me. Teller. If I can trust the latest rumors from the *Supe Report*, he's taken over complete leadership for the League here in our city.

Teller turns his back on us and steps back into the shadows. The door to the practice room slides open to allow him to exit, but he pauses, silhouetted against the fluorescent light of the hallway.

A voice nudges at my mind, the discomforting tingle of a telepath forcing his thoughts into my awareness sinks chilling claws into my spine.

'You'll do quite nicely, Whirlwind. It won't take much for us to nurture that cruel streak of yours, will it?'

I brace against the wall, breathing heavily at the horror of what I could be with these people. What I could let them shape me into. I grasp desperately at the idea that it wasn't truly my idea, that this villain planted the suggestion in my brain. I'd never actually use the wind to strip the flesh from anyone. Not even South and Gill. Not even for threatening me.

I don't expect a reply, but I get one nonetheless. The impression of humorless laughter and the mental image of Iggy. *'Wouldn't you? Not even for your precious sidekick?'* The laughter fades. *'I do not need to plant thoughts, hero-ling. I only seek to nurture that which has already taken root. You hunger for power and fame.*

We're just offering you an easier path to take it for yourself. Imagine what you could be with us at your back. Think of all the riches you could lie at your love's feet if you only give in to your own desires.'

I don't want to give in. Power isn't all I want. And though I've dreamed of glory and a gleaming city's adoration, that isn't what I truly want either. But thinking of that here and now feels like a trap. In class, we've been told that the best defense against telepathy is to fill your mind with something else. Leave no room for the telepath to sink roots into your psyche.

So I focus on Iggy. The brilliant smile they aimed at me during our game yesterday. Our shared sleepy snuggles, soft and warm before I got the alert that brought it all crashing down to reality. Their delighted flapping, that they only share with people they trust not to look down on them for it or correct it as aberrant behavior. Those people who don't try to understand aren't worth a lick if they can't see how wonderful Ig is. I see Iggy's happy stims as the unbridled joy they are. Carefree Iggy at their most relaxed and happy. That was all mine only yesterday. I might be as greedy and selfish as the League thinks, because I want all of that to myself. There isn't much I wouldn't do to make sure that Iggy remains all mine.

'*Good. Very good.*' The thought is a faint echo.

Teller is no longer standing in the open doorway. He's gone. The sharp prickle of another invading my mind has faded to less than a dull ache and I'm uncertain whether I imagine that last comment or if he truly is pleased with me.

I don't care. I've done what they wanted. The rest of the day is for me and Ig. Let them try to stop me. I walk out of the practice room without a backward glance. South calls something after me, but I just raise a finger to flip him off. He isn't in control here. His boss seemed satisfied with my efforts; I'm leaving.

The door closes behind me. I don't see any sign of the telepath who observed our session and spoke to me lingering in the hallway. I rush through changing out of my generic practice super suit, and sprint back to the dorms, letting the wind lend my feet a bit of swiftness so I don't have to see the others if they decide to follow me home. Once I've put some distance between us, I slow my steps so I can text Iggy that I'm sorry and I'm on my way to our room.

CHAPTER 18

Iggy

By the time Gerald comes back to the dorm, there isn't time to confront him about sneaking out and silencing my phone. He already texted me half a dozen times, apologizing for it on his walk back to our dorm, anyway. I prefer not to dwell on things like that. Sometimes I just have to accept that neurotypical people do things that don't make sense to me. Even Gerald.

Just like I do things that confuse them. Case in point, I've spent most of the day huddled in my chair cave under the weighted blanket that sometimes helps when I can't cope. It's not helping as much as listening to the voicemails Moddy left last night reassuring me that they're fine on a loop. I'm an emotional mess today. The useless adrenaline rush of learning about danger well after it has passed is still jangling my nerves.

When Gerald gets back to our room, his eyes seek me out in my blanket lair right away. Before he can comment, I extend my parents' invitation to join us for dinner. To my surprise, he doesn't agree right away. Gerald always jumps at the chance to eat at my place. Always. I don't get why today is different.

"Pop is making a roast," I inform him. Sure that will jar him out of his uncharacteristic reticence.

"Sunday nights are for studying, right?" he asks. I hate when he throws our schedule in my face. Obviously, I'm aware that we spend Sunday nights studying. That's how we've done things for as many years as I can recall. But if I can adjust to studying on campus, then I can readjust to studying at the kitchen counter where we've done our Sunday studying since we were kids.

"We can study at home," I snap. I shouldn't be peeved at him. That was the same excuse I gave Moddy earlier.

Ger is watching me, his focus making me twitchy and uncomfortable.

"What?" He knows I don't always have the mental spoons to deal with last-minute schedule changes. They throw my entire day out of whack and I'm wrongfooted until I can get my activities back on track. And it's worse when I'm already on edge, like today.

"Nothing, Ig." He rubs at his temples. That's something I've learned he does when he's tired. Only took years of observation to figure it out. Ger is worth observing. He flashes me a wan smile that I know he doesn't mean. "If you want me with you to visit your folks, then I'll tag along. It's natural that you're worried about your moddy."

"Thank you. Pack your laundry and books." I wave toward the jumbled mess of discarded clothing and precariously stacked school books and notes on his side of our room. Ger isn't the tidiest. He's also right about me worrying. Reading the headlines and watching the video of the bridge attack has me too fixated on what could have happened last night to focus on my studies until I see for myself that my family is safe.

That was one benefit of living at home that I took for granted. Whenever Balantin or Foxy made headlines, they came straight home to me as soon as possible afterward. It made the gap between seeing their names as a breaking news headline and seeing them safe shorter.

I haven't been able to focus on anything all day. Between not knowing where I stand with Gerald after he took off on me this morning with only his cryptic texts about practicing his powers and worrying about Moddy, it's been a crappy day. At least Gerald sent me a text before heading home to apologize and tell me he was on his way. It gave me time to work up to forgiving him before I saw him.

"I'll pack up in a minute. Are we okay?"

"Why wouldn't we be?" I ask.

"Because I silenced your phone last night, and I wasn't here when you woke up and saw the headlines," Gerald says.

"You already explained you wanted to let me sleep, and you knew I wouldn't if I saw that. I forgave you. What else is there?" I ask. Ger knows I don't hold grudges. It's a silly question.

"I wanted to be here for you, when you woke up." Gerald says in his apologetic tone. Experience with him tells me he feels guilty, and that's why he won't drop the subject. He's bringing it up to assuage his guilty conscience. It's got nothing to do with me. So it's easy to just give him whatever absolution he thinks he needs, now that I realize that's what he wants.

"It's fine. We're not little kids anymore, Gerald. Sometimes supes have to keep secrets. Even from each other. I understand what it's like."

"I don't want it to be like that between us." Gerald protests.

I shrug pragmatically. It's like that between our parents. Foxy and Balantin aren't always on the same side. Rarely in direct opposition, but there are things my father does that my moddy wouldn't be able to ignore, if they knew in advance. And things that both of my folks keep from their sidekicks, or that Ger's parents have to keep from each other. Work is work, and home is home. That's how they always say they get past those secrets. I don't love it, but I understand the practicality of it all. Keeping things separate is a rule that makes it possible for my parents to be together, no matter what their jobs require of them.

It's a rule that I've accepted will probably have to be a part of my life if I want to keep both Gerald and Gust close. Ger and I aren't little kids anymore, to share all our secrets. Being supes might mean we have to keep things from each other. Even if we are a team, at home and at school. Just like we've kept my pathetically weak powers a secret from everyone else.

Gerald doesn't cheer up at all over the course of the evening. Pop mentions some new tracking tech he's working on in his lab. A swallowable locator chip that syncs with a smartphone app and can stream the user's vital signs. It's the sort of toy I'd normally pester him to see in action, but I'm distracted and worried.

Not even seeing his sisters at our big family dinner brings Gerald out of his shell. Not being able to figure out what he needs has me frustrated.

The actual dinner is nice. Good homey food and the familiar sort of chaos with my folks and their sidekicks gathering together. Gerald's family is a part of my family, too. It's good to see everyone. Especially visual confirmation that Moddy and Eloise are all in one piece, but we don't stay long after the meal. When Pop drops us back off at the dorms, I go straight to bed, not even bothering to listen in to see what Gerald is doing in his bunk.

CHAPTER 19

Gerald

After the first training session with South and his cohorts, I get a text from him daily telling me when and where to meet. We train on campus, in a reserved practice room. Most days, they book a time for later in the evening, after Iggy has settled into bed for the night. So it doesn't interfere with joining Cinder, Streak, and Iggy for their training sessions, too.

If that was all it was, I wouldn't mind South's attention. Extra training with my superpowers, without having to split my focus to keep up the ruse about Ig's powers, is no hardship. I enjoy letting loose with people I don't mind roughing up.

After the ways South and his friends have threatened the people I care about, I have no compunctions against flinging Gill into a wall hard enough to make him lose control of his powers. Or shoving South off the ice ramp he built to the top of the practice room. His super suit should absorb enough impact that he won't die from the fall. At worst, he might break a bone or two and free me from having to work with the League, at least for a short while during his convalescence.

Then again, the campus health center has supes with healing abilities, so even a bad break probably wouldn't hold him back for long. It might just make him more angry at me. He and his crew don't trust me, or care too much about fair play during our training sessions, either. They know my loyalty isn't to them.

Daily training isn't where the demands stop. I never thought it would be. Several weeks pass without incidents, though. Then we have a long weekend for homecoming and shit hits the fan. It starts out innocently enough.

Iggy comes with me to watch the alumni super ball match in the stadium. Our parents are on the field, playing against our friends on the university team. During halftime, I go to grab snacks. When I get back, Pugsly and Gill are sitting on either side of Iggy in their sweaty team uniforms. Pugsly has his arm around Iggy's shoulders. Gill is talking animatedly. Iggy slouches low in their seat to make the smallest target possible. I almost drop the nachos I'm carrying to go right over and tell them off. But then a familiar tingle goes up my spine and I recognize I'm being observed.

'Zap is fine where they are for now. Go with South if you would like that to remain true.' Teller's distinctive mental voice makes me want to scrub the inside of my head.

No. I don't want to go anywhere with South. Not when Ig is with people who I don't trust at all. Not even in a crowded stadium. In front of thousands of potential witnesses. Not even when Balantin and Foxy are sitting with my folks on the alumni team's bench less than ten yards from where Iggy is sitting.

Iggy is unaware of the danger flanking them. Or maybe not unaware. They are swaying nervously in their seat with their hands wedged under their thighs to keep from more obvious stimming.

Gill makes eye contact with me, a bubble of water forming casually over his hand, spinning on his finger. It's an aquatic parody of a basketball trick. It's a threat and I know it. I've experienced what Gill can do with a ball of water like that.

The mental image of Iggy gasping water into their lungs presses into my mind, as though plucked from my worst fears, and zoomed in until it's all I can see. It's not my own thought, or rather, it is, but weaponized against me. By Teller. He's still got his spidery mental fingers messing with my mind.

'*Go now.*' The telepathic command is impossible to disobey.

South waves up at me from the field with two fingers. I walk woodenly down the stadium steps, dumping my snacks in the trash along the way. South meets me at the barrier between the spectator seating and the field.

"There you are! Come on, we haven't got long; the halftime show only lasts half an hour. You brought the super suit?"

I'd received a text to bring my Whirlwind attire today, and I learned my lesson about ignoring these orders after the first time. So I've got my villain super suit wadded up in the pocket of my cargo shorts, an uncomfortable lump of cybernetic fabric. I nod.

"Good. Let's go." South nods and vaults over the railing to join me in the stands. He leads the way to the nearest exit. I take one last glance at Iggy before we leave the stadium, to remind myself why I'm going along with this. I was hoping to catch Iggy's eye, give them some sort of warning to watch their back with Gill and

Pugsly. Iggy is intent on staring at their lap. They don't see me. But to my relief, Cinder and Streak have joined the others near Iggy. Streak catches my eye and scowls at seeing me leaving with South. She and Cinder must have noticed Gill and Pugsly.

At least Iggy has backup I trust now. Good. Streak and Cinder won't let them get hurt. Although the fact they don't think Iggy is perfectly capable of defending themself might mean they have suspicions about Ig and my longstanding ruse.

That's a problem for later. All that matters right now is doing what I must to protect Iggy and keep the League from targeting the people we love. So I shrug at Streak's questioning look, and follow South away from the stadium.

We don't go far, just to the nearest academic building. There aren't any classes at this hour, so the doors are keycard access only. South lets us in, using an ID that isn't his.

"We can change in here." South shoves me toward the nearest washroom when I hesitate. He locks the door and we change into our super suits.

"When we're on League business, like today, I'm Arctic Blast, got it?" South demands as he dons his villain mask. So, that's his villain name. I'd wondered. Arctic Blast made his debut two years ago, when South would have been a freshman.

No matter how much I currently dislike him, I know better than to out him. It's against the supe code, even if he is a villain. And he could just as easily retaliate by telling the entire world that I'm Whirlwind, or revealing everything I want to keep hidden. It wouldn't fix anything. It shouldn't be a surprise that he isn't doing whatever he has planned as South.

When we're done changing, Whirlwind looks out at me from the mirror, standing beside Arctic Blast, for all the world like we are teammates. The thought of working for the League turns my stomach, but I don't have a choice. Teller might be reluctant to use compulsion on me, but there is no guarantee he won't if I force his hand. Better to go along with this until it crosses a line.

"Got it?" South, or Arctic Blast, prompts me since I still haven't replied.

"Sure." I can't tear my eyes off our reflection. In the mirror, Whirlwind and Arctic Blast stand shoulder to shoulder looking way more intimidating in actual villain suits than we would if we were wearing the simpler generic super suit designs of the student gear we use for practice. Arctic Blast looks different in his suit, more formidable. We both do.

For half a heartbeat, I wonder what it might be like if I chose this path for myself instead of being coerced. I want to be part of a tight-knit team of supes. Something like the League or the Brigade. But not if it means turning villain. It's not as if Arctic and I are gearing up to rescue kittens and orphans. I don't want to be a big name supe if it means hurting people.

"Stop wasting time, Whirlwind, we've got work to do." South jolts me out of my thoughts.

"What work?" I ask, more to stall him than because I want an answer. The less I'm involved in the League's plans, the happier I'll be.

Arctic Blast makes the final adjustments to his suit, snugging his gloves more firmly onto his fingers. Then he leads me back out of the lecture building. He explains our role in the plan as we go, and reminds me that Iggy is the league's hostage against my good behavior.

I don't dare risk my best friend's safety to defy him. Besides, he's not asking me to do much, just add a few special effects to the halftime show, really. From what Arctic Blast is saying, this is essentially theatrics to announce the league's newest recruit. Me.

CHAPTER 20

Iggy

Something is definitely wrong. I suspected as much when Ger didn't come right back with our snacks. Sure, the concession stand lines are long during intermission, or halftime, or whatever the sportsball term is for the long bit between people trying to score points. But this is ridiculous.

Nerves over why Gerald is taking so long build on top of the general overstimulation from attending a game and I can't help rocking in my seat and rubbing at my eyes to relieve the strain as much as possible.

Then South's cronies join me and my stomach twists with growing dread. Just what I need on top of the general unease from just sitting in the crowded, noisy stands. Why now? When I'm already riding the edge of control?

Everything in the stadium is too loud and too bright and as much as I want to support my family and friends, I might ask Gerald to take me home before the big halftime show starts. It's all too much and every new sound reverberates like a jackhammer pounding at my skull. Every bright flash is like an explosion going off far too close for comfort.

The ball of water Gill is spinning on his finger nauseates me. Too much. It's all too much. Every touch of Pugsly's arm around me, every whiff of his sweat from being on the field has me cringing and wishing I could be anywhere else. I fix my eyes down on my lap and try to hold as still as possible. I feel like I might puke if I move.

Then Streak is there, challenging them. Cinder joins us, too. Still no sign of Gerald. Where is he? Did they do something to him before coming for me? Why isn't South with them? He's cornered me before. More than once. Enough that I dread seeing him.

"Zap?" That's Cinder's voice, not the first time she's called me, but I wasn't hearing the supe alias as my name.

"Yeah?" I say, focusing on a spot just behind her head. Eye contact is beyond me right now, with the noisy crowd pressing in on me and scraping against my raw nerves. It's only because

I'm looking past her that I glimpse the plume of distant smoke before the big sodium lights over the field clang on in tandem with the loud crackle of the speakers declaring the Hero Brigade is taking center field for a demo.

This isn't super ball. It's a blatant effort to recruit young supes to work for the civil service. Working for the city to stop the League of Villains and pitch in for public works projects that need a bit of superpowered flair. The major perk to joining the Brigade is fame. Any hero class supe can become a household name as one of the GTA's defenders. Private sector work pays the big bucks for powerful supes, but they prefer their employees to keep a lower profile unless you have a power that works well for the company's image and branding. At least, that's what Moddy says when they're complaining about their co-workers at the Brigade having egos the size of Niagara Falls.

"You okay?" Cinder asks, bringing my attention back to the tableau around me. I grimace at Gill's too close presence.

"Bug Zapper is fine. Aren't you?" Gill sends his globe of water to dance in front of my face, shedding droplets that flick irritatingly against my over-sensitized skin. I squirm and force myself to nod even though I'm itching to get away from here and look up what's going on downtown. The glare of the stadium lights makes it impossible to keep track of the smoke. It could be nothing, a trick of the light. I don't think so, though.

"Fine." I agree. I'm not sure why, maybe a part of me hopes if I go along, they'll leave me alone. As if that's ever worked.

"Uh huh, we're supposed to be with the team in the lockers during halftime. Where's your boss?" Streak demands, hands on her hips.

"Busy," Gill replies with a shrug. He doesn't question her calling South his boss. "Don't worry about it. We're just keeping Bug Zapper company until their date gets back, right, Zap?"

Pugsly's arm around me tightens and I grunt in pain. It's all too much. The nausea crawls in my belly at his touch and smell invading my senses.

And then the show on the field really gets going. Supes showing off for the crowd. Balantin is among them, shooting fire from their hands. Their fire leaps to twine with the illusion of a dragon being cast by their teammate, Lustra. They both do their part of the choreography. Lustra is a supe Moddy dislikes working with in the field, because Lustra is all flash and photo ops.

From watching them together, you'd never

guess how much they butt heads behind the scenes. For a moment, watching Moddy put on a show is enough to distract me from the confrontation with South's flunkies. Then the lights go out and the announcer's voice is no longer broadcasting the Hero Brigade's stats over the loudspeaker. His recitation is cut short and replaced by words that echo in my mind instead of my ears.

'We interrupt this blatant display of anti-free-supe propaganda to bring you the League's newest up-and-coming star. We present: Whirlwind, performing today with the League's very own Arctic Blast. Feast your eyes on the newest generation of supes who aren't afraid to be super.'

And then the lights flash back on to illuminate a pair of supes in blue-hued super suits rising over the stands on a column of ice, the wind billowing ostentatious capes out behind them.

My heart drops. South and Ger are both not where they should be, and these two have ice and wind powers, so I have a pretty good idea who is wearing the fancy super suits.

There is a long moment of silence as they pose, and then the Brigade goes on the offensive, trying to reclaim control of the situation.

The lights flicker again, and Balantin's fire rushes upward to illuminate the stadium from above, where the heat shouldn't bother anyone. Lustra casts another of her illusions, two enormous serpents who chase Arctic Blast along his moving ice paths; the creatures cavorting in his wake overshadow his display and make it seem silly. Balantin doesn't hesitate to put aside all differences to work with their teammate.

It only takes a well-placed flame to melt Arctic Blasts' ice path and knock him out of the sky when he swoops low over the field where he won't land on any fans should he fall. The Brigade would have captured him for sure, if Whirlwind hadn't been there to catch him, and to use the storm to carry them both away from the stadium on a coil of wind stronger than anything that Gerald usually tries to command. And if I know anything from following supe news, they'd end up charged with everything from public endangerment to interfering with a Brigade-sanctioned event if they were caught at the scene. We're talking about a criminal record and major fines, at a minimum.

As it is, the two villains beat a hasty retreat over the stadium wall, back the way they came. Balantin and Lustra don't pursue, since neither of them is a flyer and calming the panicky crowd is a bigger priority. Lustra uses her illusion powers to project her voice and try to calm the masses.

"Remain where you are. The situation is under control," she bellows. I can see Pop working his way to the technical room, where the announcer's voice remains silenced.

The crowd isn't listening to Lustra. I wonder if part of that panic is Teller's lingering touch, inciting the spectators. Outright coercion on a crowd this size isn't possible. Not without the power-augmenting ray gun that Gerald and I destroyed his plans for building. He couldn't possibly have built it. Not when the Brigade has the doctor who designed the ray in protective custody. They gave Dr. Lewis a brand new identity to keep him out of enemy hands.

So, no, mass coercion is impossible. But magnifying the natural tendency of a mob toward panic wouldn't take much effort from Teller. My gut is still roiling with nausea and watching Gerald face off with Moddy as part of the League of Villains is a scenario plucked from my nightmares. Gerald wouldn't join them willingly. Not the Ger I love. That isn't him.

But neither is breaking promises and disappearing on me at all hours like he has been for weeks now. Instead of listening to him get off in the dark of night lately, I've only heard him sneaking off to do I don't know what with I don't know who. His League contacts, I suppose, considering this display. It doesn't add up.

Gerald isn't a villain. Nothing makes any sense anymore.

What did they even hope to accomplish here? The Brigade members are moving through the stands now, trying to keep everyone calm as they evacuate the stadium. The announcer comes back over the loudspeaker. I glimpse Pop standing with him, using his technical skills to restore the lights and sound system to their proper function.

Foxy working against the League to help the Brigade restore order. Pop'll hate the optics of that. He has more fellow feeling with the League's philosophy than the Hero Brigade. Even though in practice he aligns more with the Brigade's actions. It's not enough to get him to join either group. Pop isn't a joiner. He's like me in that sense.

"The rest of the game is canceled. Please follow the stadium staff's instructions for an orderly and safe evacuation. Remain in your seats until your row is asked to leave, then file out calmly. Your safety is our primary concern..." blah blah blah. The milling crowd shoves toward the exits. It's loud, and everyone is pushing and jockeying for position. Somewhere in the chaos, Gill and Pugsly slipped away. Now I'm flanked by Cinder and Streak. Both of them look grim.

"Did you know about this?" Streak asks me.

For once, I understand exactly what the vague question means, since I have essentially the same question on a loop in my head. How could Gerald have gone rogue like this? How could he hide something so major from me? "There has to be a mistake. He wouldn't do this."

They both shoot pitying looks at me. At least, I'm pretty sure that's what those sad looking half-smiles mean. It's okay that they don't believe me. Cinder and Streak don't know Gerald like I do. My phone is buzzing with alerts, but the crush of spectators carries us toward the exit, so I can't really check it right now. It's all I can do to hold it together in the howling press of the crowd.

"Come on, they're calling our row." Cinder grabs my elbow to steer me out of the stadium, following along with the rest of the anxious crowd. Her hands on me feel wrong. Like crawling ants. I don't like it, but I fear that without her support I'll fall flat on my face, so I allow Cinder to steer me out of the stands and back toward our residence hall. Campus is buzzing with talk of what just happened and what it might mean.

I ignore the knots of people gossiping. Instead, I stride straight to the haven of my room where I can check my messages and let my folks know I'm okay. Not that they'll get my messages until the current situation is under control. They're always in the thick of any crisis.

Except, as my notifications load, I realize the halftime show disruption was nothing more than a distraction from the League's actual plan. The headline alerts about Moddy and Pop are all about the attack on the alumni game. There aren't any injuries being reported, at least. But I have another notification set for League activity. And sure enough, that one's triggered too. The *Supe Report* has a new article posted.

The local supe blog never fails to irritate me with more vague conjecture than actual information, but in this case, they're reporting several coordinated attacks around downtown. The same area where I saw the smoke right before the League interrupted the halftime show. Almost like showing off Gerald in his villain guise was nothing more than a distraction to pin down Moddy and the rest of the Brigade's heavy hitters far from the real action instead of responding to any other disruptions.

Sure enough, the blog lists multiple villain sightings around the city. But that's not the part that scares me. No. It's the fact that the pattern of locations is bone-chillingly familiar from something that I thought was no longer a threat. And now Gerald is somehow tied up in the middle of it.

CHAPTER 21

Gerald

I t's a darn good thing that I've been doing double the usual training lately. My sessions with Iggy, Cinder, and Streak have me in good enough condition for my classes. But the additional sessions with South and his minions are probably the difference between the two of us crashing into the astroturf and getting away over the stadium wall on a gust of wind when Balantin melted his ice.

My control isn't quite strong enough for sustained flight. Not yet. But it's enough to grant us a clean getaway. Not that we'd done more than disrupt the Brigade's showing off. I rarely agree with Teller, but really, all we did was counter their propaganda with some of our own. That doesn't seem so bad.

When we touch down outside the stadium,

South jerks out of my arms. "Set me down here; I don't need your help." He brushes at his super suit, like my touch left him smeared in filth.

I roll my eyes at that. "Next time I could let you fall."

"I'd have corrected. It takes more than a bit of fire to ground me," South insists.

"Sure." I glance around the full parking lot. There aren't many people out here at the moment, but it's only a matter of time before they evacuate the stands. We're conspicuous here in our recognizable super suits. "We should go change." I start toward the disused restroom where we left our clothing. South falls into step at my side, grumbling about Balantin and the Brigade. I'm not in the mood for his shit. And none of this makes sense.

Did they just want to expose me to the people I care about as a traitor? What purpose does that serve? Better to keep my betrayal a surprise, right? Unless there was a greater purpose behind tonight's disruption of the game. Or they just wanted to cut me off from any hope of backing out of our arrangement. They don't know Iggy or my family if they think exposing me will be enough to cut me off from their support. At least, I don't think that will happen. All I want right now is to get home and try to explain myself to Iggy.

South lets us into the building and we hastily change, South back into his team uniform and me into my street clothes. South stuffs both super suits into a backpack and hands it to me. "Take care of these."

"What, now?" I ask, struck by the fact I have to face the people I care about after essentially coming out as a villain. I try to convince myself that most of the crowd probably won't be able to ID me. Wind elemental control isn't all that rare. No one has to know Gust and Whirlwind are one and the same. But Iggy and our folks will put the pieces together. It makes my stomach lurch. South and I leave the empty restroom and head toward the exit. "People might guess it was us out there."

South shrugs laconically, pausing in front of the doors that let out onto the green. "Probably. But the golden rule around here is that you don't expose another supe's real world identity. So no one will hassle you, Gusty. Even if they suspect." He ruffles my hair, the touch overfamiliar. Like he's some indulgent big brother.

Ugh, as if I don't have enough big siblings to patronize me when I make silly mistakes. Mistakes like going along with this. I should have asked the people I love for help to get out of this situation before I got in so deep over my head. My thoughts keep coming back to how I'm going to face everyone now.

"But they'll know."

South claps me on the back. "Yep. And they might not trust you the way they did before, but it hardly matters. You're one of us now, Whirlwind. Maybe showing everyone that truth will help you accept your place on the team. It's for the best, really. Now, get home and get some rest. We've got your first proper mission tomorrow." He pushes through the double doors and descends the steps into the crowd streaming away from the super ball field.

South saunters away, tipping me a mocking wave over his shoulder without so much as glancing back at me. I steel myself for whatever comes next and join the crowd, too. No one says anything to me, too caught up in the evening's drama to notice one more person joining the press.

By the time I reach my door, I've relaxed from the initial adrenaline high. The tense fear that I had some sort of target on my back had my skin prickling with nerves every step of the way. Some part of me is convinced that one of the other students or sports fans will leap out and accuse me of being part of the League. That doesn't happen. No one seems to notice me at all. To most of them, I'm just another anonymous freshman.

I pause with my hand on the doorknob. Iggy would have come straight home after what happened. The game would have been enough overstimulation to drive them into their chair lair to recuperate and relax on its own, let alone everything else that went down during the halftime show. This is it. I'm about to face Iggy's disappointment and I don't know if I can handle seeing hurt and betrayal on my best friend's face.

When I open the door, Iggy is a lump under their weighted blanket. They scramble out of the chair at the sound of the door opening.

"Gerald?" they sound so tentative, gaze darting over me like they expect to see something other than my familiar form in our doorway.

"Yeah, Ig, it's just me." I say, keeping my tone soft.

"Whirlwind." They state it, voice and face flat.

"That's me too." I admit.

"Why?"

"It doesn't matter, does it?"

"It does. It matters. Ger... I'm scared."

"It was just a show," I soothe, making no move to get closer and risk seeing fear of me on my friend's face along with the obvious doubt in their demeanor toward me.

I'm itching to go to them. Hold them. I want Ig to comfort me the way they have after countless childhood misdeeds, but I don't deserve that. And Iggy has already spent the better part of the day bombarded with too much input to handle me falling apart on them, too.

Iggy shakes their head emphatically, hand pressed hard against their sternum to self soothe. I recognize the signs that they are freaking out, and it's at least partially my fault. "It was a distraction." They shake their head again, like they can't quite make themself stop the repetitive movement. "Look." Iggy thrusts their phone out toward me, wincing when our fingers brush as I take the device and scroll through the blog post they've got pulled up on the screen.

"What's this?" I recognize the blog. It's all the same supe chaser who usually makes shit up to fill a weekly column. The author doesn't get how official superheroes actually operate. I might have a bit of a negative bias, though, because they covered the story last spring. When I burned down the warehouse and Iggy took the heat for my rash actions. It was worth it to destroy Teller's augmentation ray plans, though.

Teller is slimy enough without the sort of tech he was planning on using the captured Dr.

Lewis to develop. I shudder at the thought of Teller's greasy mental voice compelling me to act. Bad enough that he's got enough leverage to manipulate my compliance. How much worse would it be if he could command it at will with his powers? No. It's unthinkable.

The Brigade agreed about the dire threat Teller could pose. They put Dr. Lewis into protective custody and I destroyed the papers Blot tried to rescue from the fire.

"The *Supe Report*." Ig takes my question at face value, drawing me out of thoughts of the past. "Bloggler's writing about what happened tonight."

"I see." I focus on the article to see if it has anything to add to what little I already know about tonight's events.

"Look at the map." Iggy's voice remains flat. When they get like this, it's a sign they're overwhelmed. Letting any of their fear and worry out would open up the floodgates and they are trying their best to stave off the kind of meltdown that will see them hiding under the warm weight of their blankets for hours. That crash is inevitable at this point, and it's not anything Iggy can really control. I just hate that I had any part in causing their upset. And how helpless I am to make it better for them.

For now, the best I can do is listen to them. I open the link to the blogger's scribbled map overlay. And I go cold at the pattern that emerges. Every site that the blogger has circled corresponds to a potential source for a component that I saw listed on those blueprints last spring.

Teller wanted to build some sort of psychic amplifier. The sites on the map include the microchip transport truck from the bridge attack last month. A clinic that does medical imaging, a jewelry store, an electronics big box store, a lab at U of T, and most chilling of all, a building full of condos. A private residence listed alongside all the other places is not a good sign.

Each of the circled locations links to another page on the blog. Clicking through brings up a summary of the target's stats and links to what little reporting is available relating to the attacks. The circle around the condo pulls up an array of surveillance photos of what appear to be the building's residents. One of whom is a man bearing a striking resemblance to Dr. Lewis.

The low-resolution image has Nathan Steele listed as his name, but there is a question mark drawn next to it. Several of the other tenants have names next to them as well. But the blogger seems to have dug deep enough to realize that Steele isn't the doctor's real name.

It strikes me as reckless to publish that information, but then again, I'm privy to the details of the doctor's story and this blogger isn't. I understand why the League would have taken him. And I can guess what they are planning to build with his help. If we don't stop them before they can complete the device, it might not be possible to stop it, ever.

In light of this, South dragging me in front of a giant crowd, including members of the Brigade who were sure to recognize me, takes on a whole new meaning. He intended to discredit me. Burn my bridges. I was a cocky fool and now everyone will pay the price if I can't fix this. I have to either come forward with what I suspect and convince the Brigade I'm on their side rather than leading them into a trap for the League, or I have to stop Teller myself.

"He's going to build it." Iggy says what we're both thinking.

"No. Not if we can stop him." I hand back Iggy's phone.

They stuff it into their hoodie pocket, then slouch back to rocking in their chair. "Can we, though?" Their voice comes out small and defeated.

"Yeah, Iggy. You and I can do anything. Haven't I told you that enough times? Together, we're unstoppable."

Iggy shakes their head. "We aren't together, though. You're with *them*. Have been all semester." And now the overwhelm seems to take over. They wrap their blanket around themself tighter, rock faster, and try to weather the emotional storm.

I know better than to pursue an argument when they're this overwrought. It's been a long-ass day and Iggy needs to rest more than we need to hash this out right this minute. The League might have a jumble of components, but I saw the plans. It will take them time to assemble the device Teller intends to build.

South said he needs me to help him with something tomorrow. Probably getting more components for the ray. A coolant, perhaps? Something that uses the amount of power the ray design called for would need something to keep it from overheating. So we've got time to figure out a plan. We can afford to take tonight to recuperate. Not that we have a choice. I need Iggy and Iggy needs rest.

"Want to snuggle up in your bed and sleep?" I suggest softly. Iggy usually loves snuggling with me. But tonight they hesitate.

"Dunno," they eventually mumble.

"I messed up by keeping stuff from you, but I

swear to you, Ignatius, I'd never betray you of my free will," I promise.

"Threats?"

"Yeah. Can we talk in the morning?"

Iggy nods, getting their whole body in on the movement.

"Snuggles?" I offer, hopefully.

Iggy shakes their head. And I don't push them. I try to hide my disappointment as I get ready for bed. It hurts to go through the motions like everything is fine while Iggy hides. Most of the time, I'm not a part of the outside world that Iggy needs a break from. I'm used to being a part of their refuge. Tonight, I'm a huge part of why they are quietly melting down in their little blanket fort under my lofted bed. And there's nothing I can do to fix it.

I just hope like hell that I'm not as impotent to fix the massive screwup of believing Teller and the League would give up on these plans after the fire destroyed the originals. We mentioned what we saw, but not all the details. That seems like such an arrogant mistake now. Burning the blueprints was only ever going to be a setback.

I should have gone to Balantin with everything I knew while I had the chance. Insisted the Brigade follow up more. But it's too late for that now. Even if Iggy's moddy believes me, there's no way the Brigade will act on any intelligence I bring them after the show I put on today. Sleep is a long time coming.

CHAPTER 22

Iggy

When I wake up the morning after the League tried to turn everyone against Gerald, my head is fuzzy. My neck is sore from sleeping curled up in my chair. My eyes are gummy from crying and my throat is sore and dry. Emotional hangovers are pretty similar to what I understand about waking up with an alcohol-related hangover.

That thought sends a pang through my chest. Gerald and I were supposed to try drinking together. On my birthday. We meant for it to be a first we shared. He couldn't wait one more freaking month to keep that promise. And I never asked why.

He never explained himself either, though. That probably should be the least of my complaints this morning, but it's stuck in my head and I need to know what happened that night. The night before the bridge attack. Is it silly to think the League somehow made Gerald break our promise? Yeah. But I can't quite make myself believe he'd do that if he'd had a choice. I don't think he's changed that much in so short a time. It doesn't fit who I know my best friend to be, and I hate it when things don't fit.

"Gerald?" I ask. It doesn't quite occur to me that he might still be asleep until I get his muzzy response.

"Mhm?" He sounds more than half asleep. I should maybe apologize, but he's already awake at this point and I need answers.

"Why did you get drunk without me?"

"Huh?" His bed creaks above me as he shifts around up there.

"The night before Moddy got hurt on the bridge, you came home drunk."

"I was hoping you didn't notice that."

"Of course I noticed. You reeked of it. Why did you do it?"

Gerald sighs, like I'm bothering him and he doesn't want to snap at me. Even knowing he's annoyed will not deter me. He owes me answers.

"Well?" I reach up to prod at the bed.

"It's not what you think." Gerald swings his legs onto the ladder and climbs down to talk.

"You don't know what I think. Unless you've developed another power without telling me?" I cross my arms protectively over my chest.

"No, Ig, no new powers." Gerald slumps down onto the edge of my mattress to sit where I can see him. "South and Gill bought the second round for the table. My soda tasted off, but I didn't realize they spiked it until I'd already finished the glass. It was strong enough that I felt sick."

My stomach flips like I might be sick, too. I was mad at him, and someone had slipped something into his drink without his consent. My queasiness grows the more I consider it. The things that could have happened to him. What if they put more than alcohol in his glass? What if... a thousand terrible fates could have befallen him, and I blamed him for it. "No." I'm rocking in my seat, agitation growing.

"Yeah, Ig," Gerald rubs his hands over his face, "I realize it sounds far-fetched, but I think South got me something strong so he could get me alone. Because they threatened me. He and Gill. In the bathroom."

"No. No, no." I put my hands over my ears so I don't have to hear what South did to my Gerald.

South has scared me before, and that was in public places. I can't listen to this. "I don't... Ger, he didn't..." I can't finish the question.

"Hey, no. It's okay, Iggy." Gerald opens his arms to me, and I fall against his chest, letting him hold and comfort me, even though I should be the one comforting him. He was the one South drugged and... nope. I can't go there. "He didn't hurt me, Ig. I'm okay. But they threatened to out you as an S class, and make sure everyone knew what I really am."

"What you really are?" I repeat, looking up at him in search of some clue about what he means.

"That I've got storm powers. Just like the Human Hurricane. And I could have killed someone with that warehouse fire. I didn't have control, Iggy. Not the kind it takes to be a hero, anyway. A genuine hero."

"You do. You have to, because I think they're going to build the amplifier and we're the only ones who saw those plans."

"I should have taken them with us instead of burning them. Or at least told someone what we found in more detail."

"I suppose. But it's too late to change anything now. No point talking about should-haves." I shrug out of his arms and swipe at my eyes. They aren't still teary. I cried every tear I had last night, but the excuse to touch my face helps ground me. Soothes away more of the fear that I don't have time to indulge in until we handle Teller. "So. How do we stop them?"

"You're asking me?" Gerald hunches his shoulders.

"Yes." I nod. "Because you're the hero. I don't mind being your sidekick, I've never minded."

"You're not, though. You're my partner in, well, not crime."

"Partner in crime-stopping?" I suggest. He laughs like it's a joke. Neurotypicals have a weird idea of what's funny. But I delight in making Gerald smile. He looks more like the earnest boy I fell in love with when he's laughing. Less like the scared young man who came home with a super villain suit bulging in his backpack last night.

"Yeah. Partners." He holds out his hand to me. I wrap my fingers around his palm and squeeze.

"Partners. So, we need to get close if we're going to stop them. Think Whirlwind can get an invitation to the main event?"

"I doubt it, but I'll try. If nothing else, South invited me along to help with his next League assignment tonight. I might find out something that will help us. Top priority is to get Dr. Lewis away from them, though. He's an NP and he should have been better protected."

I shake my head. "No. Our priority has to be stopping Teller from completing the device. Getting the doctor away from him is part of that, but if he gets a working prototype completed, a lot more lives will be at risk. We can't let him control them, Gerald." I shudder, remembering the time Teller unleashed his compulsion on me.

I'd been ten, playing in the living room while Teller and Pop had a chat in the kitchen about something supe related. Moddy was out. I was being loud. Teller yelled at me. Pop told him off, demanded that he leave me alone or their business wasn't happening. Teller backed down at first. But I was in the middle of something, too focused on my game to care what the jerk of a visitor in the other room said. Pop wasn't mad at me, so I kept playing. Teller told me to shut up again. Pop got between us.

Then Teller unleashed his powers on us both. It escalated into a meltdown, and before I knew it, the telepath was standing over me. He forced me to meet his eyes with a single sharp command that rang inside my head until I thought I might explode if I didn't obey. It hurt. And the command to settle down and act my age hurt. Everything about that day hurt.

He barked at me, "Children should sit quietly while their elders talk." And he put the full force of his powers into the command. It punched into my head, an unshakable need to do as he said. So I sat, unable to defy his coercion.

I'd been trapped, powerless to control my own body, sitting motionless on the couch until he finished his conversation with my pop and left. It seemed like an eternity before the command snapped free and I could move. I'd spent that eternity aching to stim and rock and deal with all the terror he'd inspired by looming over me. Instead, I'd remained a captive to his will, still and silent.

Pop couldn't help me, caught in a coercion of his own. He refused to work with the League at all after that. They'd collaborated before. I think he may have even considered joining. But after that incident, his hatred for the League rivaled his disdain for the Hero Brigade.

One thing I've always known is that my parents adore me. That will never change. But I can't be sure if they will trust what Gerald and I know after last night. Moddy won't accept that the League hasn't compromised Ger. Pop, well, if it was anyone other than Teller, he might listen. But after what happened… I don't think he'd risk this being a trap.

That only leaves us. Gerald and me against the world. That's what he's always wanted, ever since he was old enough to understand that we could be superheroes. That the powers on the news were our birthright, encoded into our DNA. Setting us apart and making us special. He always said it had to mean something. Be for a purpose.

I've given up on explaining the genetics to Gerald. That it's just a matter of certain heritable traits aligning in a particular way. Some higher power didn't choose him, his alleles just aligned to give him a set of traits that most people don't have. The reasons aren't any more profound than why he has brown eyes and light brown hair. Sure, it's complex and fascinating if you're into genetics. But it isn't some deep and meaningful higher calling.

Ger doesn't see it that way, though. Moddy and the Brigade make it sound like being a hero is this almost spiritual thing, and Gerald believes it. With all his heart. It took me a long time to realize that. He sees being a hero as some sort of mystical claim on his life. Or something. I'm fuzzy on the details because it seems silly to me.

Our powers aren't some omen or mark of fate. It's all random probabilities that bring together the exact combinations of gene sequences that give rise to any power, strong or weak. Sure, there is some evidence that the SUPE allele influences sperm motility and egg quality and that certain combinations of SUPE allele configurations are more or less likely to result in viable embryos, but that isn't destiny. It's nature.

"Iggy?" Gerald sounds worried, like he's said my name more than once while I was zoning out to my memories of that day with Teller.

"We can't let him build that amplifier, Gerald. No one should ever experience what it's like to be stripped of free will. No one."

"We won't let that happen," Gerald promises. I wish it was a promise he could truly keep rather than more of his bravado. It still feels nice when he pats my back in the soothing circles I like and lets me cling to him until I'm less overwhelmed by what we have to do and the villain we have to face to do it. Alone.

"I'm scared." I admit. His arms around me make that safe to admit. Not for the first time, I wish I had the words to ask him for more. His lips on mine. I've wondered about it a lot, what being his lover would feel like. Wild fantasies about it flit through my dreams most nights, now that I've heard him call my name while we both jerked ourselves off before bed.

If I'm honest, I've wanted him to view me as a potential romantic partner ever since the first time I saw him kiss a boy on the playground and hold his hand when we were twelve. He's dated plenty of people since then, none of them stuck around. The idea I'd just be another in a long line of failed relationships made it impossible to redefine our friendship. It's still not something I know how to ask for, and now is not the time to broach the subject. So I keep my mouth shut. Stopping Teller comes first.

"Me too," Gerald admits, rocking me from side to side. "But we have to try."

CHAPTER 23

Gerald

Cinder opens the door a crack when I knock. She stands there, peering suspiciously through a narrow opening like she expects me to attack her or something. "Hello?" Her tone implies that she has nothing to say to me and she doubts I have anything to say that she wants to hear. She's probably right, but I'm hoping that if she hears me out, she'll still be willing to help us.

"Uh, yeah, hi. Can I talk to you both?"

Our first move is to gather a team. Going to the Brigade with what we suspect is out, but we need more allies. Streak and Cinder have been good friends to me all semester and they have skills we can use to infiltrate the League's base of operations. I hope.

"Now's not a great time." Cinder leans into the

door, pressing the small opening she made for me to talk through even smaller.

"What is there to talk about? We all recognized you last night, Gust," Streak snaps from behind her girlfriend.

So far, my request for help isn't going well.

"Please, just give me a chance to explain?" I glance over at Iggy for encouragement. They shrug, looking uncomfortable with being involved.

"What is there to explain? You joined the League." Streak's voice sounds as cold as South's ice.

"I didn't!" I protest. "It wasn't my choice."

Streak snorts derisively. "That's bull. You had a choice. No one forced you to put on that suit and drag South's ass out of there when he'd have gotten captured. That was all you, Whirlwind." Streak pushes past Cinder and out into the hallway to confront me. She shoves my chest hard and I stagger back a step, wondering if she put some of her power into the push.

I wince at the villain name being flung at me like a curse. "Gust. Please. I'm Gust."

Cinder's hard expression softens. "What happened?" she asks, relenting enough to come out and stand next to her fuming girlfriend.

Cinder puts a soothing hand on Streak's shoulder, trying to calm her.

I glance up and down the hall, but it's early on a Saturday and after last night's excitement, just about everyone seems to be asleep in their rooms. "South threatened Iggy if I didn't cooperate."

"So you went along and didn't think to ask your friends for help?" Streak crosses her arms, still not convinced of my sincerity.

"I was afraid to drag you into things. And Teller was there for some of it. I figured it would be easier to stand up to them when it really counted if I cooperated without Teller forcing me to."

"Well, you seem to be fine with dragging us in now." Streak glowers at me, arms crossed over her chest.

"What changed?" Cinder asks.

"We shouldn't talk about it here," Iggy interrupts. They tug at their earlobe and fidget from foot to foot, stimming to stem their anxiety.

"Where, then?" Cinder asks.

"My car." Streak uses her powers to blur back into the dorm room without waiting for a response from the rest of us. As far as I'm concerned, her car works as well as anywhere we might go to talk. She reappears in the hall, striding past us, keys held high. "Come on."

Cinder follows her girlfriend with a shrug. Iggy and I exchange a glance and fall into step with our friends. By the time we get to the parking lot behind our building, Streak has flashed ahead and is pulling up to the curb with the car. We all pile inside, Cinder in the front and Iggy and I in the back.

"Buckle up, we're going for a spin." Streak puts the car into gear without waiting for a reply. We do up our seatbelts as Streak pulls out of the lot. "Over the summer we outfitted my car with top of the line anti-surveillance tech my mom gets from the Hero's Guild back home." Streak explains once we're cruising along on the 401, headed further away from the city. Streak easily slides between lanes to pass any car going slower than us. Her driving makes me queasy. Or maybe it's the fear that she won't agree to help us.

"We can talk freely here," Cinder adds, peering over her shoulder at Iggy and me. She flashes us an encouraging smile.

"So, spill," Streak demands, swerving around another car. Iggy hunches over, hugging their knees. Whether from the G forces of Streak's angry driving or the tension between us, I'm not sure. Likely a mixture of both. I can't blame them. They look about as miserable with the situation as I feel. This is all my fault, So I've got to fix it for both of us. I offer Iggy my hand, but they don't uncurl enough to take it. Fair enough.

"I'll admit I screwed up. I should have told you all when the League first approached me. But I didn't take it seriously enough. And then when they showed me the consequences of defying them, I didn't want to get you involved. I still don't, but this is bigger than any one of us, and there is no one else I can turn to for help after last night. No one else will believe me."

"What makes you think we do?" Streak growls. The car engine whines as she pushes it faster. I don't dare glance at the speedometer to see just how fast she's going. Somewhere in the felony speeding range.

"Easy, babe, why don't we hear them out? Getting us into a wreck won't help anything." Cinder puts a soothing hand on her furious partner's thigh.

Streak huffs out an angry breath. "I control time; it's not like we actually *can* crash when I can rewind the car to the moment before impact and then fast forward us into a safe trajectory." But she slows the car and stops hopping between lanes. If nothing else, I'm sure her car's engine will thank her for showing restraint.

From the amount she downplays her ability to control time, I'd never have guessed it was strong enough to do what she just described. Maybe I should have realized it after seeing her on the super ball pitch. It's remarkable how few goals make it into our net when she is on the defensive. Almost like the ball slips around the hoop to avoid giving the opposition a point in the seconds after it appears they've scored.

"Start at the beginning and tell us everything, Gust." Cinder turns an encouraging smile on me. It has to be a good sign that she is back to using my hero name, right?

I nod and take a deep breath to gather myself. "To give you the complete picture, we should start last spring, with Iggy and my science fair project..." Iggy reaches over to take my hand, squeezing to show their support. That, more than anything, helps me spill out the entire sordid tale. Everything from our stumbling on the League's meeting to destroying the original plans for the augmentation ray and on through South recruiting me, last night's distraction, and the *Supe Report* blog's map of recent League activity.

"Wait. Did you say the *Supe Report*?" Streak glances back at me.

"Yeah, I get that most of the people on campus

consider them a conspiracy site, but the blog had all the missing pieces. Whoever is running it put together all the seemingly unrelated villain attacks and stitched it into a picture we can't ignore. Based on the map, Teller probably has access to all the components he needs to build the amplifier."

"And he took the scientist who designed it for him?" Cinder asks.

"We're pretty sure, yeah. Dr. Lewis was under the Brigade's protection. They're hardly going to tell Whirlwind about his current whereabouts. But one attack was at a residential property with ties to the Brigade. I'm pretty sure it's where they stashed him after we rescued him," I reply.

Cinder bites her lip. "So, what do you want us to do?"

"Stop the League before they build the device. Rescue Dr. Lewis. Destroy the plans and get Teller locked up so that he can't try this again. If he actually builds the device, he'd be practically unstoppable."

Iggy shudders. "He can't make it. He can't. No one should ever feel like that."

Cinder's frown softens with sympathy, and she turns toward Ig. "Has he used it on you?"

Iggy nods without a word, huddling closer

in on themself and jamming both hands under their thighs. I ache to hold them. Offer any comfort I can, but I'm pretty sure it would still be unwelcome. We aren't completely back to our usual ease with each other, and I only have myself to blame for that.

I should have told Iggy what was going on. Protecting them is no excuse for sneaking around and lying. If anything, it makes my actions worse, because it's as much as saying I don't trust Ig to protect themself, or help me with this. I do, though, more than anyone. I shattered something precious between my friends and me when I made the choice to go along with South and Teller's instructions. Now I can only hope it's not too broken to fix.

"Well, for what it's worth, I'm in. You still should have told us. But I get why you felt like you couldn't. Just don't do it again, got it?" Cinder tosses her long magenta locks over her shoulder.

"Thank you, I won't. Promise. Streak?" I turn to watch her reaction.

"What she said." Streak glances back at me. "I'm pissed, but I get it. I'd have done the same to protect Cin. Except I wouldn't have been an idiot and kept it all from her. Men," she snorts, "always thinking you have to do it all on your own."

"Hey! I resemble that remark," I complain, but I can't help a slight smile at her acceptance. It's not blanket forgiveness, but at least I haven't burned bridges with my closest friends.

"We need a plan to stop Teller and get the Brigade to put him in lockdown before he hurts anyone else," Iggy insists, not giving me time to bask in Streak's forgiveness.

"I've got an idea. Not sure how much you'll like it, but if the Brigade is out and most of our classmates saw Whirlwind's little performance last night, we can't be too picky about our allies. Not if we want to avoid fueling the rumors about Gust's involvement with the League." Cinder types something into the GPS app on her phone and pops it into the dashboard holder for Streak to follow.

Streak grimaces but nods. "I suppose it's better than nothing."

"Where are we going?" I ask.

"To visit an old friend." Cinder flashes me a cheeky grin. "You might recognize her alias."

"Bloggler." Streak growls the name like she finds it personally offensive.

"She runs the *Supe Report*." Iggy states the fact with no inflection. I recognize the alias, and the fact she is a low level supe; that doesn't explain

Streak's animosity.

"Cinder dated her for a hot second back in first year."

"And I chose you, babe. Once you got around to letting me know you were an option." Cinder leans in to kiss Streak's cheek. "Bloggler can help us, and we're still on friendly terms."

Streak sighs, sounding defeated. "I know. And even I'll admit that she knows her shit, even if she is only a B class."

"Her powers might give us an advantage with planning our next move," Cinder says.

"Pattern recognition is a parlor trick, not a superpower," Streak grumbles, but she pulls into the next exit lane to follow the GPS's chirpy instructions about making a U-turn and heading back into the city.

CHAPTER 24

Iggy

When we get to Bloggler's place, Streak doesn't bother with the metered parking on the street. Instead, she pulls into the laneway behind the strip of businesses and parks in a driveway marked private, boxing in an older sedan as though she has every right to park there.

"B lives in the second floor walkup above the beauty supply store." Streak juts her chin toward the building in front of us. "We should split up for this. Gust, you're with me. Zap, go around the front with Cinder. You two approach her while Gust and I set up back here in case she bolts."

"Um, why would we expect her to bolt? I thought you knew her?" Gerald protests as we all get out of the car.

"Let's just say there are reasons she runs

an anonymous, fringy, conspiracy-peddling, superpower-tracking blog? B isn't exactly the most trusting person. Come on, this will be fine." Cinder gestures for me to go with her, so I follow her around the building to the front.

Small businesses line the sidewalks along this stretch of Eglinton. The address we're looking for sits tucked between a laundromat and a Chinese restaurant. The delicious aroma of whatever they're cooking reminds me it's been ages since I last ate a proper meal. We should have had breakfast before getting Cinder and Streak, but time is of the essence.

Cinder marches right up to the unobtrusive door to her ex's private residence. She rings the doorbell, then knocks sharply in a pattern. We wait. I shuffle anxiously, unsure of what to expect. I think I can make out the sound of footsteps on the stairs inside. Cinder repeats the same pattern of knocks.

The lock clicks and someone opens the door a crack, the security chain prevents us from entering or getting a clear view of the person on the other side. "What are you doing here?" Bloggler demands.

"I came to ask about the blog," I answer truthfully.

The door starts to shut, but Cinder puts out a

hand to stop it before it slams. "Come on, B. Zap misspoke, we need your expertise on a matter you've covered on the blog. At least hear us out first? For old time's sake?"

"I don't need the details to tell you I'm not doing it. Whatever 'it' is. You made your loyalties crystal clear, Cinder. You have your hero to grovel after, leave me out of it." Bloggler pushes on the door again. Cinder doesn't budge.

"It's not like that. Streak is my partner, but I don't mindlessly follow her every whim. We're a partnership of equals."

"Sure." Bloggler snorts. "I'm sure she says that now. But who is the one getting the big bucks and celebrity status, product endorsements, the whole superhero treatment, and who is the one getting tossed in front of villains like cannon fodder?"

Cinder sighs. This argument sounds awfully familiar. *The same things that Gerald says when I press him on keeping up the ruse that I rank as an H class and keeping my true power level a secret. I wouldn't mind being a sidekick, the only downside would be disappointing my parents. Not that they've ever made me feel lesser from not living up to whatever abstract visions they had for my future when I was a baby, but they named me to be a hero and they were so thrilled with me testing at an H class that I worry there* might be a first time for everything. I don't want to find out by seeing them disappointed. I also don't want the limelight. But try telling that to Gerald, who grew up dreaming of it, always in someone's shadow with his three older siblings.

"Sometimes it's better not to be the center of attention," I grumble, interrupting Bloggler's rant without thinking it through.

"Who's this?" Bloggler's attention turns to me. She allows the door to inch open more, the chain pulled taut.

"Zap. And they're the one that wants to see your map," Cinder says.

"My map? It's all there on the site. Why did you come here to see what I've already made public?" Bloggler demands.

"I want to see what isn't public," I explain. "The raw data you're working from. So that we can pinpoint Teller's base of operation for this."

"This?" Bloggler asks.

"His augmentation ray. Or psychic amplifier, whatever you want to call it."

"You know what he's after?" Bloggler leans closer to me.

"Yes." I try to meet her eyes; neurotypicals are more inclined to listen when you look at their eyes, for unknowable reasons. It makes me feel all squirmy inside, but this is important.

"How?" Her eyes narrow in the tiny sliver of her face that is visible. I glance away, wishing she would just let us inside instead of talking through a door.

"I saw the plans. It's a long story, but the originals got destroyed in a warehouse fire last spring. But all the recent league activity on your map corresponds to components for the device."

"An augmentation device?" Bloggler asks. Something in her tone relaxes Cinder's guard.

"For his powers." I nod. "He's strong enough to compel control of his victims on his own for brief, simple actions. With the augmentation ray, who knows what he might do?" I shiver and hug myself at the thought. I hate the idea of Teller being unleashed on an unwary defenseless populace.

Bloggler shuts the door. Guess that's her answer then. We'll need to make a plan without her help. Cinder isn't moving to go back around to the car yet. I wait for her next move. Something scrapes on the other side of the door, and then it opens again, without the chain this time. The petite, lighter skinned Black woman on the other side of the door glances up and down the sidewalk, then gestures for us to follow her inside.

"Well? Don't just stand there, we've got lots of ground to cover if we're going to stop what the League has set in motion."

"Thank you, B. I owe you one." Cinder claps her shoulder on the way past her as we file inside and up the stairs to the second-floor apartment.

Bloggler harrumphs. "You already owe me more than one, Cin. Where's your hero?"

"Around the back." Cinder gestures.

"Better call her in. Does this one also have a hero to answer to?"

"Gust. He's with Streak. I'll let them both in the back door if you want to take Zap to look at the data," Cinder offers.

"Of course, make yourselves at home." Bloggler waves her hands as she talks. "Not like we broke up for a reason or anything."

"Thanks." Cinder heads off down the hallway. I follow Bloggler into a stuffy, cluttered kitchen with printouts of headlines, newspaper cutouts, and magazine clippings on every surface and a laptop with about a bazillion tabs open whirs angrily in the middle of the chaos. It's sitting on some sort of fan to keep it cool.

I survey the disarray, trying to decide where to begin.

"Excuse the mess," Bloggler says.

I shrug. My fingers are twitching to straighten up the piles, but I figure she's got some kind of organizational scheme going on amidst the chaos. I hope so. I'm still not entirely sure how she's supposed to help. Like she told Cinder, we saw the map. We have a map detailing where Teller and the League have already been. What we need to discern to stop them is where they're going to strike next. Or where they are now. Their home base.

I sigh and settle in to wait for the others to join us. Bloggler said to make ourselves at home. She fusses with her laptop until we're all gathered in her kitchen. Ger comes to stand beside me and we waste a bunch of time recapping what brought us here and listening to Bloggler summarize all the information that she didn't include in the *Supe Report*. Scraps of intel and rumors that she can't prove or back up enough to make them public. It all paints an ominous picture. The League is planning something big. Soon. Something I'm not sure that the Hero Brigade can stop, if Teller has his augmentation ray.

The fate of the city rests on whether we can find Teller and foil his plans, yet again. The League's base of operations isn't a static location. It never has been. That would make it vulnerable to the Brigade. So, we either need to track a villain back to the current lair, or we have to uncover where they'll strike next.

What do they still need to make their device? Some of the basic components are easily obtained or can be fabricated on site. With modern 3-D printing setups so readily available at a consumer level, they could be working just about anywhere.

Anywhere with electricity and enough room for them to gather unobserved. But they'll need whatever South is going to retrieve tonight.

"We need to leverage South." I blurt out the suggestion, only realizing that I'm talking over Streak when she glares at me. Oops. Well, this is too important to get hung up on taking turns to talk. Ger gives my shoulder an encouraging squeeze, he must agree with that assessment.

"So, we stick to South's side?" Streak asks, skeptical. "He might notice that we all suddenly don't dislike him."

"I can do it," Gerald volunteers. "He expects to bring me along on his mission today anyway. I'll go to him with a change of heart. Play up how upset I am that you all turned your backs on me. Try to gain his confidence. Your pop still has those trackers, right?"

"The ones you swallow?" I mime throwing

back a tracker chip. "Yeah. Probably. You want me to go home and raid his lair?"

"Exactly." Gerald agrees. "You raid the lair for what we need, and I'll take care of the rest. Besides, going home is exactly what you'd do if you really believed I'd betrayed you, right?"

"Sure, as long as no one saw us together leaving campus, I suppose that could work." I nod. Gerald is right. Even though I understand why we can't rely on Moddy and Pop to fix this, a part of me still wants to just go to them and spill the entire problem at their feet.

Moddy might be suspicious, but Pop would want to stop Teller as much as I do. And Foxy's tech could help us. Well, borrowing tech from his lair is the next best option. It will be like he is helping under the radar.

The upshot of doing things this way is that when I eventually tell my parents that I'm not an H class, that I've been lying to them for years and all I'll ever be is a sidekick, I'll at least be able to tell them I stopped a big villain plot despite my shortcomings. This time will be different, not a fluke of being in the wrong place at the right time. This time, we've got solid intel and a plan and Teller will regret coming after me and mine. He won't be in a position to hurt anyone else after this. If we can pull it off. We have to.

"If anyone asks, we'll spread the story that Zap came to us after you two fought about last night." Cinder turns to address Gerald. "Gust, we'll say you followed them to try to explain, Zap didn't want to hear it, but you were determined to make them see your side. We took Zap home to their folks and convinced you to go cool off."

"That could work." Gerald nods.

"It will have to." Streak rubs her hands together, like she is ready to get to work on this flimsy plan. "So, Bloggler stays here and keeps looking for any new tips about what Teller might have planned once they have the device assembled. Meanwhile, we get the goods from Zap's place to monitor whatever South has planned for tonight. Zap stays with the parents to throw off any suspicion from the rest of South's crew. Cinder and I will stick around to console them. Gust, you can get back to campus on your own once we get you geared up?"

"Yeah, there's a metro stop not too far from Ig's place. I'll manage."

The others hash out the rest of the plan once Gerald and I outline what Foxy's tech resources will give us to work with. Short answer, plenty. It's not for nothing that Pop is always dabbling in the latest technologies.

I can't help a certain satisfaction that our plan

targets South as well as Teller. He extorted Gerald to drag us into this mess. It only seems fitting that we would use him to get into the villain base and stop Teller before he goes too far.

CHAPTER 25

Gerald

Iggy and I have perfected the trick for getting into Foxy's lair. We aren't supposed to play there, or technically even know about the secret door in Iggy's parent's basement, but their Pop has always been indulgent about letting us use whatever we find amongst his tech gadgets. He's a giant softie, despite his villain-adjacent supe persona.

I ride with the others to Ig's folks' place, but they have me wait in the car while Iggy gets what we need. A big confrontation about what I've done will only delay us. And I'm not ready to see how much I've disappointed two people who have been like a second set of parents to me since I was in diapers.

It's a long, boring wait. When Iggy eventually slinks back out to the car, I wish I'd gone inside with them. They look wrecked.

They hand me the tracker and a few other goodies I recognize from previous childish exploits.

"Here. They want me to stay with them for the weekend. Possibly longer."

"But what about classes?"

Iggy shrugs, defeated. "Pop suggested commuting. He could drop me off and pick me up each day. Moddy wants to go to the dean of residence services and have my room assignment changed to a single."

"No."

"That's what I said. They're mad, Ger. Really mad. Moddy said you betrayed us all."

"I'm sorry."

Ig shakes their head. "Don't apologize. You made stupid choices, but you didn't betray us. And your heart was in the right place."

"That doesn't matter. I was part of the distraction that let Teller grab vital components for his ray uncontested. If it weren't for B keeping track of all the recent villain activity, we'd be completely clueless right now. And as it stands, my crappy choices mean no one will take our warnings seriously."

Iggy sighs heavily. "Yeah. That's true. I tried to bring up the ray. What we saw at the warehouse. Moddy didn't want to hear it. Pop is talking to them, trying to help them cool off. That's how I slipped into the lair for this stuff. He'll notice it's missing. So we should act fast."

"I know." I can't tear my gaze away from Iggy, though. They look as worried and determined as I feel. This is it. We're really taking on the League. Like true heroes, this is something out of my fondest daydreams. Except, unlike in all of my fantasies about this day, my best friend won't be standing beside me. And I won't be standing with the good guys. It doesn't matter that I'm planning to go all in with the League in name only to infiltrate their base before they can complete their plans. I'll still be standing on their side while wearing the super suit and villain moniker they chose for me. This is our best bet to stop Teller, but it goes against everything I want to be. And it's dangerous. The League does not take kindly to betrayal. No one does.

I can't stand the idea of going off to do this, not to mention the possibility of not coming back, without telling Iggy how I really feel. I want to taste their lips, at least once before... well, just before. There's no point dwelling on what might happen. One moment at a time is all I can manage.

I lean across the console toward Iggy. They blink at me. This isn't some romantic movie where they lean in to meet me and sparks fly and the music swells.

"What are you doing?" Iggy asks, cocking their head to the side and eyeing my face for clues.

I straighten up and rub at my neck, self-conscious as all heck about just assuming they were on the same page as me. "I was going to kiss you. If you want?"

"Oh."

"That's it? Oh?"

"Oh. Um, why?" Iggy rubs their cheeks.

I sigh, reigning in my hurt reaction. It's not Iggy's fault they see things differently. I just need to adjust my expectations and explain where I'm coming from. "Because, Ig. I love you. Not like friends or siblings. Like romantic love. And I don't want to walk away from you and into danger without telling you."

Iggy nods sagely. "Okay. And a kiss is how you thought you'd tell me that?"

"Yeah. I guess."

Iggy nods again, leaning closer to me. "Well, in that case. We should kiss. A lot. Lots of kissing."

"Because you love me, too?" I ask after a

moment to parse what they said and what they meant.

"Yes. Obviously." And then they lean toward me, mouth puckered, head tilted the way I just leaned toward them, their eyes flutter shut, and I meet them halfway. Our noses bump, and then my lips brush theirs, soft and yielding, and I've never wanted anyone more in my life. The tingle of their sparks passes between us. How in the world did I think one kiss would ever be enough? How can I tear myself away from Iggy after getting the barest taste of them?

Their lips part, and their tongue slips into my mouth, stroking over mine. When I push back to reciprocate, they break things off with a little grimace.

"Okay, tongues are weird." They swipe at their mouth.

"Sorry?" I suppress a chuckle.

"Nope. Don't be sorry. Not bad. Just weird, need to get used to it, I think. We should practice that more. Lots more. While we're snuggling in my bed?"

"That sounds perfect, Ig."

"Ger?"

"Yeah?"

"Don't get dead." They cling to me, the hug

awkward over the console.

I'm not about to make promises I might not keep, so I go in for another kiss, caressing their cheek to encourage them to turn their face toward me. Our lips meet again in another gentle give and take instead of saying words we both know I can't guarantee. This time Iggy clutches my face between their hands and more sparks tingle over my skin. I let Iggy lead, our lips pressing together and saying all the things we can't put into words.

"Love you, too," Iggy says when we part. They're still holding my face in their hands. The tight smile they give me looks forced. Their eyes glisten with unshed tears. The sparks are under control, but their hair frizzes from the static. They are too damn cute, gazing at me with open adoration. So I relent and say the platitudes we both need to hear, true or not.

"Hey, this will be okay. It has to be, because I am going to take you on a date." I bluster. "The plan will work, and I'll be fine with you and Cinder and Streak at my back." I pat the pocket where I stuck the surveillance gear Iggy liberated from Foxy's lair. "We've got this."

"Yeah." Iggy jerks a forced nod. "And after this is over, you are taking me on a date. Several dates. With my boyfriend. That's you." Iggy beams at me for a second, then their smile falters. "Or I mean, uh, yeah. Cool, I guess we could go out sometime."

"Sometime, huh?" I repeat, wondering where the logic behind their sudden change in demeanor is. I don't question them calling me their boyfriend. With anyone else I'd just kissed for the first time, that would be a major overreach, but with the person I've had a crush on since before I even understood what the word horny meant? Yeah, it's perfect. I'll gladly be whatever Iggy wants.

"Yeah. You know, whatever, man." Iggy nods solemnly.

"Do you not want to go out? We could just stay in, if you prefer that. Cartoons and chill?" Now I'm confused at the lack of interest and ridiculous dude bro impersonation. Iggy hates dressing up in any kind of formal wear, so that might be the issue?

"I'm playing hard to get, duh." Iggy sighs. "Is it working? This seems pointless. Why would pretending not to want to date you make you want to date me more?"

Their earnest rules following startles a chuckle out of me. The adorable furrow in their brow over the illogic of this social rule makes me want to kiss them again until they relax. I know better than to argue directly against Iggy logic, I rarely win. But since they're already questioning the validity of the concept, I nudge them toward skipping the aloof act.

"You're doing fine. But I think that's an outdated rule and we don't have to apply it."

"Good, I don't want to pretend." They wiggle happily in their seat, their full wattage smile back on display. "I want to date the crap out of you and I don't care who knows it. Oh, and cartoons in bed sounds like a perfect first date."

"I agree, Ig. As soon as we don't have Teller's doom ray hanging over our heads, we'll do it."

Iggy nods again. "Cartoons in bed with my boyfriend. I like it. And we can do more kissing, right?"

"Right. More kissing, and more than kissing, if you want. Um, if I'm your boyfriend now, does that make you my themfriend?"

Iggy nods. "Yes. Themfriend is fine."

By mutual accord, we both lean in for another chaste kiss. A physical I-love-you. And then Streak is knocking on the car window and Iggy has to go back inside to deal with their parents while I throw back the swallowable tracker chip coded to the app on Iggy's phone, and catch a bus back to campus to set our plans in motion.

CHAPTER 26

Iggy

Streak is silent as we walk back inside. That silence stretches until I can't take it any more. I need to break it. Get what happened out in the air where it can be real.

"I kissed him," I admit, because I need to tell someone that everything has changed in my world.

"I saw." Streak nods.

"He said he'd be my boyfriend."

"I wondered when you two would figure that out."

"Huh?"

Streak crosses her arms over her chest and snorts, giving me some major side-eye. "It's obvious that you two have been in love for ages.

You're like Cin and me. Meant to be. Gust is wild about you, and you think he hung the stars." She shrugs. "I was more surprised when he said you weren't together than I am to hear that you are. Too bad we've got a villain to stop so you two can't act on it yet."

"Yeah," I agree, uncomfortable at the thought of what acting on it might entail in Streak's book. I consider asking, but I decide not to. "He promised me a date. After."

"Yeah, Zap, after. We're all going out to celebrate after." She opens the door to my parent's place for me and gestures for me to go first.

Cinder is waiting in the living room and she fills the anxious quiet with chatter that I think she means to reassure me, but it just sounds like empty platitudes. I focus on obsessively refreshing the app that I registered Gerald's surveillance chip to before I gave it to him. He knows how to activate the tracker when he's ready to start the mission. We've played with Pop's toys before. I know he must not have even gotten back to campus yet and it will probably be awhile before we can actually do anything, but I can't help checking.

"Everything will be fine, you'll see," Cinder pats my hands and I jerk away. She apologizes and continues to spew platitudes. I tune her out after that. I can't focus on anything but Gerald right now. He's on the metro, headed back to campus and into the arms of the enemy.

Streak and Cinder try to cheer me up, both of them sticking by my side even after my folks come back from discussing the situation. Pop offers me a hug, which I decline. It's not rational, but I don't want to erase the feel of Gerald's arms around me in the car before he left.

My parents have gotten good about accepting when I'm not in the mood for physical affection, so he shrugs and offers me his hand to squeeze instead. I let him offer that much comfort; it's easier to give them what they need sometimes.

Moddy seems calmer for having discussed the situation. "I'm making grilled cheese and tomato soup. We'll eat before I have to leave for the Brigade meeting with the city council this afternoon." Their tight smile rings false, but that's my favorite meal, so I'm pretty sure they aren't mad at me. Even if they are banging around the kitchen like the pots and pans are at fault for the League of Villains recruiting my best friend.

No, Moddy isn't mad at me; Gerald is another issue entirely. It might take a lot for them to forgive him. Something like stopping Teller from taking over the city. I snort at the unfunny thought. It's not really my parents' reactions that have me down, though. I'm terrified of what comes next.

As the child of two supes, I'm no stranger to worrying about the people I love while they go charging into danger. Moddy with the Toronto Hero Brigade and Pop off on his own missions. Ger and I have spent many a sleepover cuddled together, sharing a silent fear that one or more of our parents might not come back from whatever it is they're doing. It's worse without him to cling to through the fear. Not that I love Gerald more than my parents, but it's different.

And part of the fear might be knowing that he's depending on me to have his back. Me. With my weak little sparks. They're practically a parlor trick, and that's what Gerald is depending on as a safety net. Well, okay, not really my powers. He's got more than enough sparks of his own. What he needs is the kid who grew up watching Foxy's antics and grew so enamored of the tech that I learned how to use it. I can be Gerald's backup. And more than that, I've got Cinder and Streak to help. We can be a team. Gerald is right, we can do this.

Gerald still hasn't activated his tracker by the time we finish eating the food Moddy makes for us. I keep refreshing my phone, hoping he'll pop up and I'll be able to see that he's safe. Silly thought, of course he's safe. The real danger won't be until he approaches the league for whatever comes next.

"Ignatius?" Pop using my full name makes me wince. I must have been off in my own little world and missed the first several times he tried to get my attention.

"Yes?"

"What's so fascinating on your phone?" Moddy gestures at the device.

"Nothing." I turn off the screen and flip it face down, as if that will hide it somehow.

"He isn't going to message you, sweetheart." Moddy puts their hand over the back of mine. I know they mean for the touch to be comforting, but it isn't. It makes my stomach churn with nerves that they are comforting me because they don't trust Gerald anymore. I hate this entire situation and I don't know how to handle it. Except that I don't think I can stay here and pretend not to care or worry about him. I can't lie to my parents and I can't sit around doing nothing and not knowing what is going on with our plan. I jerk my hand free and spew out excuses so I can focus on something other than Moddy's hurt frown.

"I should go back to campus and get my books. Need to study. And you're busy with your meeting later," I explain as I abruptly stand from the table.

"We can take you back, and you can stay in our room for a while if you want to stay on campus." Cinder exchanges a glance with her girlfriend as she makes the offer. I can't tell what that look is meant to convey, but Streak shrugs and nods.

"Are you certain you have to leave already, Iggy?" Moddy fusses. "You and Pop could check out the art festival in Dundas Square while I'm meeting with the mayor. Get your mind off things."

They don't offer to skip the big meeting with the city leadership. Not that I expected them to; a hero has to put the needs of the many before comforting their adult child over a broken heart. That's probably not fair. Pop will be around if I need my folks to get through Gerald's supposed betrayal, which I don't. I'm not actually upset about Moddy going to the meeting, just aware that I'd have the right to be, because that's the sort of prioritizing that would upset Gerald on my behalf.

"Give them space, dear." Pop gives Moddy's arm a comforting pat.

"Of course, whatever you need, Ignatius." Moddy still seems unimpressed at the entire situation, but I don't know how to fix that, so I don't try.

"We should go before it gets too late. Need to study. Thanks for lunch, Moddy." I duck my head and sidle toward the door.

"Of course, any time." Moddy stands to see us out of the house. "It was nice to meet your new friends. I'll call you tomorrow in case you change your mind about staying here for a while."

I nod woodenly. "Thanks. Bye."

Cinder and Streak thank my parents, and they all exchange the social niceties before we leave. Thanks for the meal. Nice to meet you. Come back anytime. Blah, blah, blah. None of it means anything. It's just the awkward bits you have to say for reasons I don't care to understand, even if it's not true. We eventually make it to the car and I ride in the backseat, still refreshing the app way too often, like everything depends on it.

CHAPTER 27

Gerald

"What do you want?" South demands as he flings open his door. After spending the morning trying to make plans without vital information, I was too anxious to wait for his summons to whatever nefarious deeds he's got on the roster for today. He gives me a suspicious once-over.

"Can I come inside?" I ignore his question and move to step past him without waiting for his reply. I hold up the bag from last night with our villain super suits still inside it.

"Why?" South stops me with a hand on my chest. He grabs the bag from me and tosses it into a chair with his other hand.

I glance down at where he is touching me, as if I don't care in the least about the implicit threat of having his hands on me, his power a blink away from freezing me. I can give as good as I get in a fight against him, and he knows it. "We need to talk."

South snorts. "Oh, do we? I thought you already had a partner?" He relaxes his stance and lets me into his room, though. "What do we have to discuss?"

"How you and Teller have been holding out on me. Or the fact Zap and my friends won't talk to me after our little stunt last night. They figured out we were a distraction from the main event. So, since you've forced my hand, I'm all in on this. I want the perks to go with it. A cut of whatever we're doing." I shove past South, letting my shoulder bump into his with more force than necessary.

I take in the room to avoid looking at him. Same tiny square with side-by-side closets next to the door, identical to the one I share with Iggy. The furniture layout is a little different, with both beds lofted near the ceiling instead of just one. It's also much sloppier, books and laundry scattered on every surface. South's roommate isn't here.

"What perks?" South shuts the door and saunters over to lean against his desk, arms crossed over his chest as he eyes me.

I gesture vaguely. "You tell me, fam. I saw the League hit a jewelry store and a medical supply place last night while we were keeping the Brigade busy. What's my cut for putting my ass on the line and burning bridges with my family?"

South barks out a laugh. "Oh, that's right, your folks work with the enemy, huh? Toss you out over it, did they?"

No, they hadn't. All three of them had blown up my phone with disappointed messages demanding an explanation, but they're still my parents. Both of my dads work with Foxy, so it's not like they would actually disown me over turning to super villainy. I don't think so, anyway. But there's being a villain like Foxy, who works for causes he believes in, and then there's joining the League and preying on the innocent. Foxy is more like a modern Robin Hood than a true villain. My folks won't ever approve of putting NPs at risk, which our little display last night could have done if it got out of hand.

"Let's just say they weren't pleased." I clench my fists and focus on the prize. This is about protecting the non-powered masses who Teller is planning to harm with his ray. I can play whatever role is necessary to stop the League.

"I just bet they weren't." South snorts, but he

straightens up and uncrosses his arms. "Want a drink? I've got beer and pop." He turns toward a stash of cans under his desk, giving me his back. That gesture tells me he might actually trust me. At least enough not to be on his guard with me. Good.

"Pop is fine. Got root beer?"

"Just cola."

I grimace, but nod. "That works."

South grabs a can and tosses it to me; frost forms around his hand where he touches it. Of course the guy doesn't bother with a fridge when he can just cool his beverages with a touch. I catch the icy cold can and pop it open, raising it toward him in salute. "Thanks."

"Uh, huh." He chills a pop for himself and cracks it open. "So, did you come here to discuss terms, or what? Because in the eyes of every supe who saw you last night, not to mention the Loser Brigade, the League owns you now, Whirlwind. It's a bit late to be negotiating anything."

"I set my terms when you recruited me. You leave my family alone."

South waves that away. "Sure, what do you honestly think we want with a powerless legacy kid? Bug Zapper isn't worth the effort of recruiting them. Teller knows how pathetic they are and we aren't about to use them for anything other than leverage. True to their moniker, they're just bait to lure in the real powers in their orbit."

I want to punch him for that. But Iggy can show them all just how wrong they are without me going all overprotective macho asshole mode here. Those protective impulses running rampant got me into this mess. I need to put them aside if I want to get us out of it.

"A deal is a deal. No more using Zap at all. They get left out of all of this. So they can live a normal life. I'm all yours now. A full member of the team. With a name and a super suit and everything. In return, I expect my cut of whatever profits the League reaps from having my help."

"Ah, such a noble sacrifice." South rolls his eyes. "Figured you were more like us than you cared to admit. You can talk to Teller about getting your cut when we meet up for the next League assembly."

"And when is that?" I press.

"Whenever Teller gets in touch with us." South shrugs like it's no big deal. "You'll be informed. In the meantime, like I told you last night, we've got another mission. I was going to have the boys back me up on this, but you'll be useful, too. Plus, it will give you a chance to prove your loyalty before we meet with Teller."

"I saved your ass last night, didn't I?" I flash him a cocky grin.

South raises his brow at me. "Sure, and that's why I'm trusting you to tag along tonight."

"So, what exactly are we doing tonight?" I ask, trying not to let my hope about ending this threat so quickly give me away. If he notices the way I perk up, he must attribute it to enthusiasm for the plan.

"Yeah, Tell's got big plans for this city. And that's just the start. But we've got to move fast, before the Brigade puts the pieces together and stops him."

"What pieces?"

"You'll see. Teller will give you as much information as you need to do your part. I'm not about to spill the beans without Tell's say so. Come on, let's suit up and collect Gill and Pugsly. I'll explain your role on the way to the site."

I expected the League to move fast, but this is sooner than I'd hoped to put our plan in motion. Guess pulling South's ass out of the fire last night worked out better than I could have imagined.

Perfect. Now I just need to discreetly activate my tracker for Iggy and the others to get in on the action. Easier said than done with South scrutinizing my every move as he pulls both balled up suits from the bag I brought along. He tosses me mine.We both change into our villain attire.

Once we're dressed, we leave his room to meet up with the others. I expect that we'll be driving somewhere to collect whatever other items Teller needs for his augmentation ray.

Instead, we walk across campus toward the science labs.

"Gill, get the car and meet us out back." South waves flippantly toward his car as we stroll past the resident lot where it's parked.

"Wait, where are we going?" I demand, not quite stopping, but unease is creeping in. The plan was for my friends to track us and have time to meet up before we did anything. If Gill is meeting us wherever we're going, then our target is on campus. Or at least, in walking distance. Too close. Too soon. I might be flying solo tonight.

Okay. I can make that work. I still need to activate the tracker, but not while South seems annoyed, and both Pugsly and Gill are eyeing me with suspicious resentment.

"They've got what we need in the science labs. Teller had a little chat with my research advisor about ordering special supplies. Relax, this will be child's play." South claps me on the back. "Back alley, like we discussed, Gill, go." He tosses the sidekick his keys.

Gill catches them, salutes and trots off to do his boss's bidding, like a good little hench. And I fall into step with the other two for the rest of the walk to the labs. We pass a few other students, but not a ton. It's Saturday, so most of them have better things to do than hang around near the class buildings when they could be enjoying their social lives.

There's a frisbee game on the green outside the library, lots of powers on display there. Our villain costumes garner some attention, lots of whispered comments behind hands. South and Pugsly stare straight ahead and stride toward our goal as if it doesn't even register that most of campus has to have heard about last night's game and know that we're in league with the League.

Not that anything will come of it. The school won't interfere in our extracurriculars as long as we make a nominal effort to keep our supe personas separate from our student identities. That's, like, the golden rule among supes. We keep the polite fiction of a bit of spandex and an alias obscuring a true identity as something sacrosanct.

No one gets in our way and we walk around to the side of the building. We use a side door where there isn't anyone around. South lets us in with a swipe of his student ID card. "I'm a TA for Dr. Rittenhouse. All hours' access has its perks," South comments as he tucks away the card. The three of us make our way up to the third floor biochem labs. Just because we're a superhero university, doesn't mean we don't have strong STEM programs too. Plenty of supes dabble in tech to augment their abilities. Or just to have fun toys for their arsenal. We stop outside the supply room next to the smallest lab on the top floor. It's one that's restricted to faculty and their hand-selected student research teams.

South grins at me. "You stand guard. Let us know if we get any company. Pugsly, you're up —we need to get the nitrogen canister down to the rear exit for Gill to collect us. Think you can manage that?"

"Piece of cake, boss." Pugsly rolls his shoulders, cracks his knuckles, and strides into the storage room. He plucks up the canister like it weighs nothing, turns and heads for the stairs. I glance pointedly at the safety warnings plastered on the wall about using appropriate PPE for this sort of thing. South snorts.

"Relax, Whirlwind, it's not like it can actually hurt us. Pugs can carry anything so long as he doesn't stop. I can keep things cold enough that we don't have to worry about the nitrogen boiling or exploding, and you've got the wind at your beck and call. If there's a leak, you just snap your fingers and we've got instant high-power ventilation."

Exploding. Great, that wasn't even something I had considered when I hesitated. I'll sure as shit be thinking about it now. And how does South expect me to know when we need my ventilation services? I take a deep breath, square my shoulders, and follow South down to his car. Gill is tapping impatiently at the wheel, and Pugsly is already maneuvering the purloined cylinder into the trunk. It barely fits upright and I have visions of them tipping it and spilling liquid nitrogen and whatever it is keeping in a deep freeze all over the trunk.

"This would be easier if we could lay them down," Gill grumbles.

"And if we wanted to lose half the contents and end up with the containers exploding, or asphyxiating us while we drive, we could do that. Get on with it and stop with the whining." South gestures sharply at his cronies.

"Yeah, yeah, I'm doing it. There. All secure, do your thing, boss man." Pugsly gestures to the canister packed into the trunk with a blanket wedged around it and bungee cables securing it in place to keep it from moving while we drive.

"Hmm. We'll see how this goes. The Dewars are well insulated, at least." South steps up, touches the trunk and frost blooms over the entire array with a crackling sound. South grimaces. "I can only sink so much heat and negative two hundred Celsius is no joke. Might have to ride in the back and keep a hand on the cylinder to maintain the temp. We should hurry."

"Yeah, don't have to tell me twice. Come on, noob." Pugsly thumps me on the back and propels me toward the back seat. I end up wedged between Pugsly and South while Gill drives. Not ideal. They have me pushing air out of the trunk so that if the nitrogen leaks out back there, it won't fill the cab. Ah, the joys of transporting something dangerous when you can't sense it. Still, I'm pretty sure the positive pressure I've got going between the cab, the trunk and the outside will keep any air flow going out rather than in, where it will just mix with the outside air to disperse harmlessly.

I'm still a wreck about transporting dangerous chemicals we have no business messing around with. Cryogenically frozen action heroes from the movies keep flashing through my mind. I always wanted to be immortalized as a hero, but not like that. Shudder.

The drive to a run-down building near the

outskirts of downtown is nerve-wracking as hell. I reach into my pocket and fumble with my phone to activate the tracker. The feedback buzz of my phone seems too loud in the cramped backseat. South gives me an annoyed glance and snaps at me to turn it to silent. The others exchange banter at first, but South snarls at them to shut up and let us concentrate, so that dries up fast. A fact for which I'm thankful. I hope the tracker going live gets my friends' attention. I'm having second thoughts about approaching South and moving up our timeline, but it's too late to change anything now.

It isn't until we arrive at our destination, and one of Vespula's minions who I only vaguely recognize opens the loading bay doors to let us park out of sight, that I truly begin to worry that I'm in way over my head. It's another several fraught moments before I end up herded into a holding room to wait alone for the others. They still don't trust me, that much is clear. While I wait to see what the League has planned next, I pace and try not to consider what I'll do if they decide not to risk letting me out of here. That fear proves short-lived when Teller enters the room, flanked by South and Vespula.

"Arctic Blast tells me you've finally seen the light?" Teller looks down his long nose at me. It takes a second to remember that he's using South's League moniker.

"Yeah. I mean, I've always kind of questioned why NPs expect us to bend over backwards to use our powers to benefit them. But last night, at the stadium, it was freeing to let loose. Just *be* a supe without apologizing for it. And then the Brigade attacked us over it. For what? Disrupting their propaganda show? Screw that! Arty could have gotten hurt if I wasn't there to catch him, all because they don't want other supes to hear your message? It's a waste." I can't decide whether Teller believes my sincerity, but South scowls at the nickname, so that's a win in my book.

"Hm, yes. Quite. So, let's see you put your powers where your words are. I have several minions at work replicating the modified spore samples you and Arctic Blast acquired from the university today. Wind dispersal is ideal for such a tool, so I will require your assistance when we are ready to deploy the agent."

"Agent?" I repeat the word blankly. "What agent?"

I thought we were taking the liquid nitrogen for the ray. To use as a coolant. In all our plans, we figured they would need a serious cooling system for something that draws as much power as the original specs for the ray required. Then again, that might have been a foolish assumption, considering that Teller has South to keep things chill. I didn't sign up to kill anyone, or spread some sort of freaky airborne bioweapon. Geez.

Teller gives me a sympathetic smile, but his eyes are gloating. "Agent X. It's a semi-synthetic Entheogenic compound derived from the bio-engineered fungal samples Arctic Blast acquired for us. Known to make subjects more susceptible to psychic suggestion. Dr. Rittenhouse at the university has been working on a more stable inhaled preparation of the agent. To help his patients overcome addiction, anxiety, and other conditions where psychic suggestion has proven effective."

"I see." I swallow hard. He's not only got all the parts for his augmentation ray, he's also got some sort of inhalable drug to make his victims more susceptible to his powers. Awesome.

"I'm not sure that you do, but you will soon. Come along calmly, all three of you, we have no time to waste." Teller turns away with an airy follow-me gesture. He's humming some song about everything going his way as I fall into step behind South and Vespula, powerless to ignore the simple command in his voice.

So much for the villain saving his strength for the big reveal. Now that Teller has given me a direct command, I can't even seem to feel the panic I know should be pulsing through me at being a dupe in his plans. That at least might alert Iggy and the others that something is amiss here. If they followed the tracker. And if they're close enough to pick up the biometric readings that it sends out. Well, I can hope they are nearby and that they can stop me before I make everything so much worse.

CHAPTER 28

Iggy

We're halfway back to campus when Gerald's tracker goes live. My phone buzzes with the alert, making me jump and give a startled squawk. Cinder turns in her seat to look at me.

"Everything okay back there?" she asks.

"Yeah. Ger is on the move. I mean Gust." I enlarge the map to full screen and try to puzzle out where Gerald might be heading.

"He must be with South. I guess they are making their move fast. Like we hoped." Cinder observes, still craning around to watch me. Her scrutiny makes me twitchy and I fidget, wiggling my toes in my shoes to let the squirmy sensation out in as subtle a way as I can.

"Excellent. Let's see where we're headed."

Streak reaches back for my phone without taking her eyes off the road. I reluctantly pass her the device. My lifeline to Gerald.

"Let me do that. Just because you can flash us out of trouble doesn't mean you need to be reckless at the wheel, babe." Cinder takes my phone from her and clips it into the holder on the dash. Her comment soothes some of my nerves. It's a timely reminder that Streak is a badass chronomancer. My powers might not be all that impressive, but between Streak, Cinder, and Gerald, we are more than a match for South and his pals. I convince myself of that as Streak swerves across multiple lanes of traffic to swing off the 401 and grab the Don Valley Parkway back toward North York. Where South and Gerald appear to be making their move. Her erratic driving makes my stomach lurch. But at least that gives me something other than my nerves to focus on while she follows the tracker to my best friend so that we can provide the backup I desperately hope he won't need.

I'm not sure whether I'm sick with nerves or from Streak's driving by the time we pull up a few blocks from where Gerald's tracking chip shows he stopped moving. There's been no change in position for several minutes, so the nondescript shuttered factory where he stopped appears to be the target. Unless they are hankering for a burrito and some cheap bread? The factory sits between a bakery's outlet store and a strip of fast-food joints and NTs do all sorts of weird shit, so I won't put that possibility past South.

If I was a super villain, I might send my villainous minions out to do my shopping for me. No dealing with stores and it puts the supes under me in their place. Totally logical, right? So that probably isn't what they're here for. The problem is, I can't think what they might actually want with this place. What is it with the League and derelict buildings?

Oh. Oh shit. What if this isn't a job that South brought Gerald along for? What if this is a meeting with his boss?

"Um. You two?" I interrupt Cinder and Streak speculating.

"Yeah, Zap?" Cinder angles herself toward me.

"Just, uh, what do you suppose they might need from an empty bread factory?" Nerves have me rubbing my face and rocking in my seat.

"Is that what this is?" Streak sniffs the air. "Whatever they're baking smells divine."

"Focus, babe. Mission first, carbs after," Cinder teases.

"No, pretty sure you carb load before the mission, just like any other team sports." Streak shoots back.

"We just had sandwiches," I point out, because, duh.

"Yes, what they said." Cinder nods. "We already did the team carb loading. Now we're doing the clandestine surveillance to have Gust's back."

"Oh, right. Never was any good at behind-the-scenes support, was I?" She flashes us a cheeky grin as she unfastens her seatbelt and reaches for my phone, removing it from the dash holder. "Catch, Zap. You two stick here." She tosses the phone to me. I fumble catching it.

"Don't," Cinder groans, reaching for her partner to stop her. But of course she's too late, because Streak can manipulate time. Which she must have done to go from sitting in the driver's seat and sounding bored to out of sight, over the fence, and around the building in the time I take to catch my phone and open up the app that picks up the signal from the vital stats monitor integrated into the tracker I gave Gerald. We're in range to get biometrics data now. Good. His stats load in real time.

Cinder sighs. "I knew she was going to do that."

"Did you give her a tracker, too?" I ask, not looking up from checking Gerald's vital signs. It's a relief to see that he's okay. He seems calm.

Heart rate and pulse both imply that, at most, he's taking a leisurely stroll. Huh. I'd expect him to be more alert whether this is a mission or a meeting with Teller. Oh well, Ger always was brave. "If you have the serial number, I can sync up with Streak's stats, too." I offer without looking up at Cinder. I can still scan for the signal if she didn't record the number, but it will be harder to isolate and pair the device that way. Hopefully, she has it.

"Um, no. I didn't think to do that," Cinder admits. "Give her a tracker, I mean."

"Next time you should." I roll my eyes. NTs make no sense. If she knew Streak was going to run off into the fray, she should have planned ahead. Like I did. Gerald's heart rate spikes for a second, but then he goes back to his usual baseline. Something must have startled him. Something that wasn't actually a threat, judging from his quick return to baseline. He's fine.

Watching the numbers on the screen, I can understand why Streak was too antsy to just sit around waiting to see how the situation develops. Anything could be happening in there while we're out here observing a building facade and a contextless monitor.

"Oh, hey, check this out." Cinder sits up in her seat, waving her phone around like she just got a message or something. "B says she got a hit on our search."

"Huh?" I'm still too focused on what may or may not be going on with Gerald to concentrate on distractions.

"For potential ray targets where Teller might intend to use his new toy," Cinder explains patiently.

"Oh. Right. What is it?" I ask without looking away from my screen, aware this might be important but still preoccupied.

"There's an indie art festival in Dundas Square this weekend."

I blink and dart a glance up to see if she is teasing me. "What? You mean the one Moddy mentioned?"

Cinder sighs and rubs at her temples, but she keeps her tone calm. "Yeah. Shit, why didn't we see that sooner? The plaza right beside city hall. With streets blocked off all around for pedestrian use only, and a bunch of vendors selling mouthwatering street foods slathered in deliciousness."

"You like carnival food?" I ask. From the way she is describing it, she should have had another sandwich at lunch earlier. Maybe we can hit up the burrito place after all. I'm not hungry, but I do like their salsa.

"Not the point, Zap. The point is that loads of people will be there. And this event has a permit for thousands of guests. They're expecting a huge turnout, right outside city hall. During their emergency meeting with the Hero Brigade's leadership about addressing the escalation in villain activity over the past few months."

"Oh." I consider a moment. "Ohhhh. That's probably not good. If he uses his ray on a giant crowd and then sets them loose on the city council, there's no telling what might happen."

"Exactly."

"So. What do we do?"

Cinder rubs at her temples again and makes a frustrated, low sound. "Suit up and get Streak back here. Then we go set up a watch at the festival, in case they act today. It should be too soon, if they still need more materials to scale up the size of the ray to control enough people to pose an obvious threat, right?"

"Right." I nod. "Unless they found a way to amp up the power with the smaller prototype that they already have enough juice to run."

Cinder groans. "Text your man to see if he can talk. Then we go get Streak in case you're right about them having everything they need. This might be a decoy site if they don't trust Gust."

"Sure." I'm already typing out a message to Gerald. Cinder pulls two balled-up student super suits out of the car's console. I ignore her wriggling into hers in the front seat while I type. We're in the far corner of the bakery outlet's lot, as far from other cars as possible, so the odds of anyone looking in are low.

Zap: Hey. Call me if you can. I'm worried about you.

There, that should be vague enough not to arouse suspicion if South or anyone intercepts it. I hope. I don't want to blow Ger's cover, but that's the sort of thing someone might say after a fight, right? It seems reasonable enough. I already hit send, so too late to second guess it.

Cinder nudges the second suit into my hands with a pointed look. I reluctantly pull the tight stretchy material on over my leggings and remove my t-shirt to pull on the long sleeves. Super suits suck. I always feel too exposed in the skintight material, but they are better than a trip to the hospital from getting hit by another supe's powers.

There still isn't a response when I finish changing. I stare at my phone, tug some wrinkles out of the irritating, clingy fabric. I refresh the message thread with Gerald, willing it to at least switch status to read. Or even better, for the little dots showing that Ger is typing a reply to appear. They don't.

I tab back over to the tracking app. Maybe his stats will reveal when he's read it. Yeah, because seeing my name on his phone is going to make his heart race? Silly. His vitals all remain within normal limits.

Cinder opens her door. "Come on, let's fetch my wayward hero before we miss the show. And you might want to give your moddy a heads up about the meeting with the city council, if you think they'd listen. Can't hurt to have backup if it all hits the fan."

"Good idea." I shoot off a text to my message thread with my parents, then pocket my phone and scramble to follow Cinder across the gravel parking lot, past the bustling bakery outlet with its deal-hunting shoppers, and to the chain-link fence surrounding the empty building where the tracker shows Gerald's location. My phone buzzes in my pocket as Cinder scales the fence with the practiced moves I've seen her use in our sessions in the skills training rooms on campus. I check the screen, hoping it's a message from Gerald. No such luck.

Moddy: In a meeting, I can't talk.

That's her auto-reply. So I got the tip too late for it to matter.

Pop: They're already on alert, Zap. The League has been active enough lately that they aren't taking anything for granted. Try not to worry.

Pop's empty reassurances only make me feel like my parents are brushing me off as an over-concerned kid instead of a colleague in training. Even if he *did* use my hero moniker. Guess it's just me and my friends, like we thought from the start.

There's also a notification from the tracker app. I tab over to check it. Gerald's moving again. Away from us. Huh, well, his vitals are still normal. It's possible that means they're done doing whatever it is they came here for. All the more reason to collect Streak and get to the site of the potential attack.

Everything about this makes me nervous. And nerves always bring my sparks to the surface. That will make climbing a metal fence all kinds of fun, as the steel calls to the electricity within me. I ball my hands into fists and try to psyche myself up to just do it.

"You coming?" Cinder hisses at me from the other side of the fence.

"Yeah. Sorry." I wiggle my fingers and toes to ground myself. The sparks fizzle to a lower intensity. I scramble over the fence. Sure enough, more power jolts out of me and dances over the metal in blue-white arcs that look more impressive than they really are.

It's not like it hurts me, but it draws a bit of attention from a couple of young kids leaving the bakery and getting loaded into a minivan by their frazzled looking parents. All excited about "lightning coming out of that guy's hands", the kid squeals and points at me.

I tense up, cringing at both the misgendering and potential confrontation if they decide to go all Good Samaritan about Cinder and me hopping the fence. Neither parent spares a glance our way, though. They avert their eyes quickly at the sight of the sparks still dancing over the metal lattice behind me.

I overhear them scolding the kids. "Remember how we talked about the League marking their territory with snake fangs, dear? When we see that picture, like on the building next door, it's best for those without powers to mind our own business or call the Brigade's tip line. We're just here to get your favorite croissants, remember?" The side door rumbles closed and the adults make a point of not looking our way as they get into the van and pull out of the parking lot.

That's a lucky break for us, though I know Moddy would have strong words about everyday citizens living in fear of the League to the point they routinely lecture their kids to keep their heads down around supes.

"Reel in the charge, Zap," Cinder chides me, snapping me out of my thoughts. Right, we need to put our mission first.

"Sorry, right behind you. Gust is on the move, heading away from us." I hold up the phone. Cinder glances at the screen, nods, then leads the way around the building to an out of the way back door that looks rusty with disuse.

She tries the knob, to no avail. I place a hand near the door jamb, trying to detect any electronic mechanism that I can short out, but there isn't one. That would be too simple, I guess.

Low-tech locks are more of an obstacle. Still, when your powers are weak, you've got to learn how best to apply them. Ever since the moment I thought I'd have to leave Doctor Lewis to burn, I've been working on opening locks with my powers. It doesn't take too much charge to create a miniscule localized magnetic field. At least, no more charge than I can easily command.

What I lack in strength I can make up for with precision control. After a moment of poking at the lock with my powers, I can sense the way my charge wants to leap into the metal of the mechanism. From mapping out the lock with my powers, it's just a matter of winding the charge into a tight coil that generates a magnetic field in just the right spot to tug on the lock's internal mechanism into alignment and bam—instant key. The door clicks free and I nudge it open with a gentle push.

"Nice. Didn't know you could do that." Cinder claps a hand on my shoulder in approval. I shrug away from her touch, skin prickling at the uninvited closeness. "Sorry, Zap. Good work, though." She pulls her hand back and shoots me a thumbs up instead. I huff out a breath, relieved that she seems not to be upset about my foibles and I didn't even have to remind her. That makes things less awkward.

I flash her a tight smile. "Let's get in there and collect our heroes."

She returns a genuine grin and the two of us make our way down a dimly lit, narrow corridor. The glow of the emergency exit sign casts everything in shades of red. It's eerie. The echoes of distant voices, clangs, and thumps carry down the hall. Someone curses. Someone else laughs. It all makes me hyperaware of the tight press of my super suit against my skin. I want to peel the fabric off and rub away the touch of it and of this musty place.

The old building reeks of dank and decay. A fine layer of dust coats the floor, undisturbed until Cinder and I pass. Great, we're leaving a trail of footprints for an observant villain to follow. Also, that means Streak didn't come through here, wherever she is now. As if the locked door isn't enough of a clue that we aren't on the right path.

Still, we continue to creep along the hallway until we reach a juncture where it spills into another, wider one. This hallway is lit with a flickering fluorescent bulb and the dust is more disturbed. Hopefully, no one will notice Cinder's and my trail if they happen past here.

"Which way?" I whisper, glancing anxiously around. I'm sparking again, but she doesn't comment on that, just raises a finger to her lips in a cautionary gesture. Right. We don't want to attract attention. I cut my eyes toward our footprints meaningfully. Hell of a lot of good our silence will do when we might as well have scrawled "intruders were here" across the floor.

Cinder glances at the trail we left in the dust,

then sends her fireball licking along the floor with a flick of her wrist. The flames devour the dust, erasing the evidence of our passage before dissipating. It leaves an acrid burning stench behind, but it's not any worse than the stale air in here was before.

Cinder winks at me, then leads the way toward the low tones of a hushed conversation carrying from one end of the hall. My heart trips to a faster beat at the thought it might be Gerald talking, but no, he was moving in the other direction when I checked the app.

Sure enough, when we creep up to the closed door, the voices coming from within are familiar, but they aren't my best friend. It's Streak and someone I've mostly heard screaming hoarsely for help in an abandoned building, much like this one. Poor Doctor Lewis must be freaking out after how his last encounter with Teller went. Speaking of whom, it never hurts to take extra precautions. While the hallway is still empty, I flick on my noise-canceling headphones and gesture for Cinder to do the same with the spare pair she borrowed from my folks' place. The press of a button should fill our auditory channels with music and drown out anything Teller says. Years of observation have shown that you have to hear his commands for the full compulsion to take effect. It's a shame this trick wasn't an option for Gerald if he's going to convince the baddies he's all in on their side.

Once Cinder and I are both as protected as we can be, Cinder eases the unlocked door open. She must recognize that Streak is in there, too.

Except, when the door opens, the scene inside is nothing like I expected. I blink in shock at the sight of the doctor unharmed and unbound, busily assembling his device. The only person being held under threat in there is Streak. Blot and Pugsly have her arms pinned behind her back, not allowing her to move enough to engage her powers and escape their clutches. Blot is struggling to wrestle her into a pair of power dampening cuffs that might stop her from blurring out of the room even if they give her an opening.

"Streak!" Cinder calls to her girlfriend, immediately drawing all eyes to us. Gill whips a ball of water toward her. If she gets drenched, then her fireball will be out of commission, at least in any meaningful form.

It's telling that none of the henches seem the least bit concerned about my powers. They must all know what a fraud I am. Well, even a small charge can make a big difference when applied correctly.

Too bad I'm still not quite over the fact that Lewis seems to be helping them of his own volition. The doctor didn't seem like he was a willing participant in their work. I don't get it. "Doc?"

He doesn't even glance up, muttering to himself as he assembles the final few parts laid across his work bench into the device we're here to stop. Too late. My heart sinks. We're too late.

The doctor is moving like he's in a dream. An automaton stripped of free will. His blank expression and the fine tremor in his hands remind me of the utter powerlessness of being under Teller's control.

That thought makes it all clear. He's already under a compulsion. Which means Teller must be certain of his success here if he is willing to dole out so much of himself to see the augmentation ray completed today.

My mouth goes dry, palms sweaty. Teller must be nearby to maintain the compulsion. We are so screwed.

"So glad you could join us." The voice that haunts my nightmares purrs from behind me. I spin to face him, slapping a hand up to trigger the music that drowns out that hypnotic voice.

It isn't Teller standing behind me that makes me shiver in fear. No, he's there too, and that would normally be enough. But what really has my pulse jumping is seeing Gerald standing behind the villain in his Whirlwind guise, face a blank mask as he backs up the bad guys. Not so much as a flicker of recognition or concern in that beloved face when our eyes meet.

CHAPTER 29

Gerald

Teller's powers are stronger than I suspected. No wonder this freaked Iggy out so much when it happened to them. It's not even the fact that I can't seem to fight the compulsion to follow along mutely and obey the man. No. It's that the part of me that even wants to, fades to something small and distant. Unreachable.

Resistance to Teller's command is as impossible to me as shooting lightning from their fingertips is to the typical NP. Not even an idle imagining. Iggy and my eyes meet, and that withered desire to fight sparks inside me. I want to respond. To refuse Teller. To do anything that isn't standing behind him while he threatens my Iggy.

An eternity seems to pass as I remain unable

to tear my gaze from Iggy's face. The generic face mask of their student super suit frames their features, and I want to kiss away their fear and worry. Ridiculous, but I'm frozen in that moment of desperation to connect with them.

As our gazes lock, Iggy forcing themself to meet my eyes in a gesture I know they find as uncomfortable as being stabbed with needles under most circumstances. All hell breaks loose around us. A whoosh of flames flies toward the table covered in the remaining parts of the mostly assembled augmentation ray.

Doctor Lewis screams, clutching the assembled weapon to his chest, before dropping it with a howl of pain. The casing must be hot from the fire.

That, or the terror of the flames breaks him out of whatever trancelike state he was in when we entered the room. He starts to scream, and even after Gill douses the flames in a torrent of water, the doctor doesn't stop babbling in terror, or trying to get to the ray.

Streak breaks away from her captors when they turn their startled gazes toward the commotion. And in a blink, she's gone from the room. But not before she grabs the shrieking civilian. Doctor Lewis's shrill cries echo back toward us in a weirdly distorted howl as Streak flashes them ahead in bursts of accelerated time.

Chronomancy is weird.

Cinder wastes no time making good on her girlfriend's retreat. She grabs Iggy with one hand and calls up another fireball to hover over the other in a threat to ward us off.

"Stop them!" Teller commands. But Cinder isn't listening to him. She drags Iggy down the hallway behind her and the two of them flee, while her fireball fills the space between us and their escape route, buying them time to run after Streak.

Everyone remaining in the room turns toward Cinder's retreating form. Teller's obedient minions, one and all. In unison, we fling our powers into the effort of recapturing the interlopers. Except there's some tiny part of me jarred loose. Enough to realize that I can't run, but I can help without disobeying. My wind howls down the hallway toward us, strong enough to slow Cinder's running strides by a fraction, but more importantly, it stokes Cinder's wall of fire into a conflagration that we can't get around in time to stop their escape.

That's all I manage before the iron will of Teller's command clamps around me, killing the wind. It hurts to disobey, even in such a small way. My muscles cramp and I get light-headed to the point of falling on my ass. Teller glowers at me. Gill throws water at the fire licking along the walls. South sucks the heat out of the blaze, frost icing along the floor in fractals. At the center, though, Cinder's fire continues to burn bright enough to cut off pursuit just long enough for the sounds of my friends' pounding footsteps and the doctor's yells to fade.

Iggy and the others are getting away. If I had control of my body, I'd smile at that. At least until Teller picks up the undamaged augmentation ray, looks it over and smiles approvingly. "Let them go, we have what we need."

The others stand down, South and Gill tamping out the last of the flames. The others fall into place around Teller, peering at the ray in his hands. I don't have the strength to get up from where I'm cowering on the ground.

"Hm," Teller tinkers with the machine, snaps the side panel into place, and aims the barrel right at me. "Time for a test. I'm not taking any more chances with you, Whirlwind. I need you to disperse Agent X once we are in position. Obey me."

Bright light obliterates my field of vision as the crushing weight of defeat settles over me and Teller's new command roots into my psyche.

CHAPTER 30

Iggy

The drive to downtown passes in a blur that owes nothing to Streak's powers. She's sitting in the back with the rescued doctor. Cinder is the one driving while I quietly lose it over Gerald just standing there behind Teller with his other lackeys. Under his control and using his wind to hinder our escape.

We're not in great shape to be taking on Teller. Streak seems exhausted from her daring rescue, slumped in the backseat after using time hops to get the doctor out of danger. Cinder says that extending Streak's chronomancy to include another person more than doubles the effort required, especially when the person in question is panicking and fighting her every step of the way.

Doctor Lewis is a blubbering mess behind me.

He thanked us before lapsing into muttering about the device and how he needs to finish it. Having experienced the crawling need to obey when Teller uses his powers on a person, I don't doubt that he's still under the compulsion to finish the augmentation ray. Poor guy. It should wear off soon. Time and distance from Teller usually speed up that process. Except the doctor seems just as firmly under the villain's spell now as when we first walked in on him obediently assembling the device.

It's troubling that Teller seems to have found another way to increase his mind control over his minions. He's gotten stronger, even without the ray that we had to leave behind in our wild flight from the factory. I shudder to think how strong he'll be with the device at his disposal.

Cinder calls up Bloggler to relay what we've learned. We try to find a safe place to drop off Doctor Lewis. I'm worried that if we leave him alone, he'll follow his compulsion right back into Teller's clutches.

If anyone has a way to reverse Teller's commands, it would be the Brigade. Moddy's cell is still giving me their auto-reply, though. I try calling Gerald's mom, Eloise, but her phone goes straight to voicemail and her box is full. No shock there, considering most of the supe community saw her son turn villain last night.

Not that they all knew Whirlwind was Gust, but enough people will suspect to make his family's weekend miserable. Her phone must have been ringing off the hook all day. I don't have any other way of contacting the Brigade.

Pop might have something in his lab that could help. If this is a long-term effect, he has to, because Teller has Gerald under his sway, too. If whatever he did to the doctor is permanent, then Gerald is... well, that doesn't bear contemplating.

I can't accept that Gerald is Teller's permanent puppet. Or that Teller might have the League poised to take control over the giant throngs of people supporting the arts on what promises to be one of the last weekends of nice weather this fall.

The aroma of fried food fills the air as we approach the festival. I've been to similar events in the past. I'm used to smaller gatherings that consist of a few stalls in a parking lot near a strip mall. This one is bigger than those. A lot bigger. And more crowded. Several downtown streets are closed to vehicles. We wend our way through heavy traffic. Every moment that passes, the urgency to act grows. Cinder has to circle around detours to find a parking garage several blocks away that has room for us.

It's too late to find a secure place to leave the doctor. We can't risk taking the time to secure him when it might mean leaving the festival open to attack. Besides, he's so intent on getting back to Teller and finishing the device that he could easily hurt himself or others if we let him loose.

Cinder finds an empty spot in the crowded parking structure. That seems to rouse Streak from her lethargy.

"Go time?" she asks.

"Yeah. I think this might be worse than we suspected. The event looks packed." Cinder says, checking something on her phone.

I pull up the tracking app and see that Gerald is moving slowly toward downtown. Toward us. His vital signs remain eerily stable, all things considered. He's under Teller's control. I convince myself that's the only reason he is doing the villain's bidding, but it's hard to accept.

"The device must be ready in time. We have to bring it downtown," Doctor Lewis mutters.

"Yes, that's where we're going." Streak pats the man's hand. He flinches.

"I must finish my work." The man curls in on himself, looking utterly wretched. "My life's purpose."

"You will, doc," Streak assures him. "You'll finish your life's work just fine. Can you tell us what happened to you at the factory?"

He shakes his head. "Nothing else matters. Finish the device for the grand finale. He wants it ready today. So much to do, so little time."

"What grand finale?" Streak presses.

"It's going to be a special display." Doctor Lewis waves his hands in the air. "Proof of concept. I..." he trails off, shaking his head in defeat. His fists clench. "Can't. Can't disobey. Must return to him. Finish my work. Help me?" He turns a pleading expression on us. I'm uncertain if he's asking us to help him escape Teller's control or to help him return and finish his work. My companions choose to interpret his plea as the former. Having spoken to the man prior to his recapture by the League, I suspect that's what he would want if Teller hadn't compromised his free will.

"Of course," Cinder assures him. "We'll help you. For now, come with us and we'll go find the ray." Streak and Cinder each take one of the doctor's arms and he stumbles along between them, docile, but still muttering under his breath about finishing the device. I trail after the trio as they make their way along the crowded streets. Following on their heels means I don't have to waste energy shoving through the throngs and getting constantly more on edge with every accidental brush and bump.

We join the stream of pedestrians meandering toward the streets filled with others enjoying the festival. We aren't the only ones in super suits. I recognize several fellow students among the crowd.

Local shops have their goods set up on their sidewalks. Food trucks and stalls offering everything from ribs to fries to cookies, vendors of various wares, the flyers tacked up to every post even mention a small midway with rides for children. We walk several blocks following the flow of traffic and our noses toward our destination. The acrid smokiness of roasting meat, sickly sweet confections, and the carnival aroma of hot oil combine to make my eyes water and nose twitch with all the conflicting scents. Art installations occupy most of the space around the square. And it is packed with people. The crowds rub every nerve I have raw, but there isn't a choice to avoid it. We have a job to do.

This is worse than I imagined when Bloggler sent us confirmation that this is the most likely target for Teller to attack. So much worse. All these unsuspecting NPs are gathered here. Families, students, young and old, they are all at risk. The Brigade's emergency meeting with the town council is too tempting a target for Teller to pass up. That much is obvious.

There are Brigade heroes in their super suits

watching over the event, but not many, and none of them are the big names. I spot a pair of mid-level heroes that Moddy has worked with in the past, chowing down at one of the long trestle tables set up for people to enjoy their food stall purchases. Others are wandering around with giant roast turkey legs and other food items.

Lustra is the biggest name I recognize. She is performing illusions for a gaggle of wide-eyed kids and their families near the entry to the festival area. If Teller shows up like we expect— well, someone has to stop him before it comes to that.

Except we're already too late to stop it from happening. Didn't I see that first-hand? Teller is stronger than I remember him ever being before. Somehow, he's strong enough to control an entire room of supes for an extended command. Strong enough that Dr. Lewis is still under his control to the point of mindless obedience. Much longer than the few minutes Teller's compulsions usually last when they go against the target's natural inclinations.

This is a disaster in the making. I doubt she'll believe me, but I have to try raising an alert with Lustra. Surely her rivalry with Moddy won't overshadow a warning from me, right? Not when her job today is keeping everyone here safe?

"Lustra?" I force myself to blurt her name, eyes focused just past her shoulder. This entire situation is exhausting, draining me faster than a kid sucking back a sugary soda. But I have to try. I ball up my hands into fists, squeezing until the borderline painful clench is enough to distract from the pins and needles squirming of having to interrupt her and look at her and figure out how to convince her she should listen to me. A kid she watched grow up. This is hopeless.

"Yes? Want an autograph, kid?" Lustra turns toward me, and recognition turns her tone from the bored greetings she's got for all the NP families gathered around her to something else entirely. "What are you doing here?"

"Teller is going to attack the festival," I say. And yeah, there's a chance he might have another target in mind. But I don't think so, and expressing any doubt will only make it easier for Lustra to ignore my warning.

"We are aware of the increased League activity in the city over the past several weeks and we've prepared accordingly, in cooperation with the event organizers. The higher-ups already ordered enhanced supe presence after their little stunt last night. Relax, enjoy the arts and let us do our job, Ignatius. I'll let Balantin know you're around when they get out of the Brigade meeting with the mayor. I'm sure they'll tell you the same thing."

"That's not…" I protest, but Lustra has already turned her attention back to a new knot of admiring fans.

"Don't waste your breath with that one, Zap." Streak grips my elbow in a firm grasp that bothers me less than all the casual little brushes of getting jostled in the crowd to pull me away. This entire situation is annoying, but I'm more irritated at Lustra dismissing my warning than Streak interfering. I follow along behind her and Cinder as we wend our way through the masses, with the doctor still between them, still mumbling wretchedly about how he must get back and finish his work.

"We need to scout out the most likely spot for Teller to set up shop," Cinder observes.

"Easy." I tap my headphones. "He'll strike wherever they have the sound system. He needs people to hear him for the compulsion to take hold. It's auditory and mental."

That little-known tidbit about Teller is something I learned thanks to Pop for studying the quirks of various heroes. He's got an analytical mind like that. Part of what makes his approach to incorporating tech into his hero persona so unique is that he draws inspiration from all sorts of weird sources. The thumping beat of music blares over loudspeakers designed to drown out a boisterous audience.

So that makes it easy to pinpoint where we need to focus. I turn toward the loudest noise. I hate raucous venues like this. The closer we get to the speakers, the more the vibrations seem to rattle me right down to my bones and burrow into my head like thousands of tiny ice picks. I can ignore it for a while, not like I have a choice. We just have to stop Teller. I can get through whatever it takes to manage that and get Gerald back from his clutches. I have to. Hopefully, my headphone batteries are up to blocking everything out for as long as this takes. I can't spare the energy to keep topping up the charge if our plan is going to work.

We spend a tense half hour that seems like an eternity scouting the area. Cinder and Streak discuss potential evacuation plans for the gathered NPs in hushed whispers. I have little to contribute and all my nerves are raw from overstimulation. We find a vantage point far enough from the central stage that the vibrations from the speakers don't entirely feel like they'll rattle my teeth right out of my skull. It will have to do, since it offers a good view of the stage and the crowds while giving us some space to act.

It might be a moot point, since there's still no

sign of Teller, at first. Gerald's vital signs blip an alert once, but it's just a tiny spike in pulse and BP before he returns to baseline. But that isn't reassuring, considering how he was behaving at the factory. They still seem to be headed toward us, though not in a car.

We shepherd the doctor around the crowded festival area until Bloggler meets us and cajoles him into leaving with her. She lures him off with the promise that she'll take him to finish his work. I don't question how she intends to deal with him when she reveals she isn't returning him to the abandoned factory. I've been saving my headphone batteries for the main event, so the stress and noise have me on edge, a constant strain on my attention.

Streak asks what Bloggler has in mind.

"Cherry coke, of course." Bloggler winks at us and passes the doctor a bottle of soda. "A bit of REM sleep will do him a world of good. With any luck, when he wakes up, he'll return to himself. Ta ta."

"We'll be in touch to collect him," Streak insists. Bloggler waves that away.

"Don't you worry, I'll keep our new friend out of dangerous hands until someone competent can get a new safe house for him. I might know just the people for the job, too."

She gives Cinder air kisses that make Streak scowl, then leaves with the doctor trailing along in her wake.

"Cherry coke?" I repeat, not sure what that gross combination of flavors has to do with falling asleep.

Streak rolls her eyes. "She's going to drug him."

"Benadryl in his coke," Cinder elaborates. "My parents used to give it to my brother and me when we went on road trips to visit relatives as kids. She thought it was hilarious."

"Is that safe?" I ask, uncomfortable with the idea of someone putting something in my drink without telling me. Like what South did to Gerald. It seems wrong.

"They sell it as an over-the-counter sleep aid." Streak shrugs. "If he runs off into the middle of whatever Teller has planned, he's likely to get hurt. Much as it pains me to agree with B, it's probably the best option to keep him safe. And sleep seems to lessen the effects of telepathic compulsion in general, so there's that."

"And if we get really lucky, the League won't be able to finish their doomsday device without his help." Cinder holds Streak's hand. I don't share her optimism about today ending in an anticlimax.

Sure enough, that's when the tracker shows Gerald's movement increasing as his blinking icon on the tracking app puts on a burst of speed and closes the remaining distance to the festival. Cinder sighs and Streak cackles.

"Well, babe, doesn't look like we're getting lucky today."

"Guess we've got a villain attack to stop. With no backup. So, let's review the plan." Cinder gestures toward the crowds around us and we scramble to get into position. At least Bloggler should have time to get the doctor clear of the square. The last thing we need is him interfering.

CHAPTER 31

Gerald

When I blink back to myself, I'm standing at the center of a crowd. Pugsly and Blot are still gripping my arms, even though I've been docile as a lamb since Teller put his whammy on me back at the old factory.

I don't bother fighting their hold, even though it wouldn't technically break my compulsion to do so. Teller only told me to obey him. Any attempt to run now would be a waste of effort without some plan to make good on my escape.

I've lost all recall of the trip here in a hazy fog. Like zoning out on the walk to school. Retracing a familiar route on autopilot the morning after pulling an all nighter and blinking back to awareness at my locker with no solid memory of going from home to school. Only this isn't a matter of engrained routine. This is more like there's a missing chunk of time from whatever Teller did to me.

From the moment of his command to obey to this moment here, I don't know what he asked me to do. Or if I've already done what he wanted. It's terrifying not knowing what he might have used me for during that blank space. It makes me sick to my stomach and reminds me of having a fever. Shaky and out of control.

I try to distract myself by taking in the situation. We're on a raised platform. No, that's not quite right. It's a temporary stage festooned in sound and lighting equipment. Like they have at music festivals.

Teller is standing near the front of the stage. Vespula and South are with him as he addresses his audience using a microphone that projects his voice across the entire crowded expanse where several city blocks are closed for some sort of festival.

As I take in my surroundings, I recognize where we are from various hero-related media appearances. Dundas Square. And it's packed with people. Thousands of pedestrians are gathering around the stage, riveted to Teller's every word. That's not good.

Did he already unleash the poison he wanted

my help to disperse? Is it too late to stop him? If the effects his augmentation ray had on me are anything to go by, no one standing in range will be able to resist his commands once he uses it, even without my help.

"That's right. Gather round, one and all," Teller beckons everyone closer. I'm not sure if he's putting a sliver of his power into the words, but I lean closer, hanging on his every word. Impossible to know if that's the lingering effects of his earlier command, or something new. "You'll want to hear this." His voice is full of ominous promise as he lifts his arms and beams around at the gathering throng. His smile borders on sinister as he glances at those of us gathered behind him. Or that might just be recent events coloring my view of him. Either way, his gaze chills me.

"Release the Agent X." Teller flicks his wrist in a dismissive wave. Vespula dons a gas mask, increasing her resemblance to her wasp namesake. She launches into the air. Her shining black and yellow costume catches the light in a bright warning to any who see her that she isn't to be trifled with. Her sting is worse than her bite and she's fast as heck on the wing. Of course, any supe with flight powers is vulnerable to the whims of the wind. I could bat her out of the sky without breaking a sweat. *If* I was in control of my actions. As things stand, I can barely call up a puff of air to cool the anxiety roiling through me.

I watch in horror as Vespula flits forward, winging up above the crowd. She's got a large container strapped to her back and in place of her usual dart guns, she wields a wand connecting to the canister of Agent X. It reminds me of someone spraying herbicide. At a crowd of innocent bystanders. The queasy nausea in the pit of my stomach only grows as I watch, helpless under Teller's compulsion.

When all of this was hypothetical, I thought I'd know what to do to stop the League. That I would somehow triumph with the power of good, and just shake off Teller's control to be a hero. I never imagined that I'd be taking the role of double agent anywhere near this far. I steel myself for what I know comes next.

Vespula hovers above the thick crowd, joined by several other flying League supes. Villains. Teller must have called in every villain under his command for this.

Wonderful. Whoever Teller charged with replicating the drug must have known what they were doing to accomplish their task in mere hours. Or have had a superpowered knack for the work. I wouldn't have thought it was possible to have enough of the agent to dose the entire sea of people gathered around us, considering the small size of the sample they took out of cryopreservation. Yet, here we are. Is it my imagination, or can I really hear the ominous click of a mechanism ticking open and the hissing release of pressurized gas from the canisters held high above the gathering?

"Make sure everyone in range gets a good dose of that, Whirlwind," Teller instructs. The command grips me again, sinking claws into my mind just as strong as when he first laid his compulsion on me. I have a physical need, an insatiable hunger, for carrying out his orders. The wind leaps to my command at a thought. At least my abilities are as strong as ever. I'm not sure that it's the ideal outcome, but my powers are still my own, no matter what else Teller tried to take from me.

They aren't currently listening to my panicked desire to disperse the agent far from this crowded square on a strong updraft, but the wind is still there for me. If I can figure out how to free myself from the compulsion before it's too late, then I can stop this. Too bad Iggy isn't here to try true love's kiss to break the wicked spell. This is no time to be thinking about making out with my favorite person, though. I have to stop what Teller has put in motion.

A little gust twirls around my hand, flattening out when it reaches the villains disseminating the Agent X. In short order, the wind is tugging at clothing and creating echoing feedback as it buffets the mic in Teller's hands.

"Control it, Whirlwind. You are better than this."

I am, and the compulsion tightens around me since he knows I'm trying to circumvent his will.

"Blow the spores into the crowd, now." Teller growls the command at me. He levels the ray at me again and a fresh wallop of his power has me suggestible as hell. The wind howls and a shimmering cloud of fine particles fills the air, drifting down toward the crowd. The playful breeze that was tugging at my hands kicks up, and without my volition, I lift a hand to direct the breath of air into a strong downburst, propelling the particles far and wide and down toward the rapt onlookers.

Teller turns his attention to his victims, adjusting the ray and aiming it at them. The pulse of power through the weapon as it powers up calls to the electrical side of my abilities, letting me feel it discharging as I watch helplessly from my front-row seat, trapped by his commands. "Behold!" Teller gestures upward and the festival goers turn their faces upward in unison. That command isn't directed at me, or rather, in my case, he wants me to see what he's about to do, if he cares at all about me beyond my momentary usefulness. It's utterly eerie to watch all those rapt, upturned faces.

"Breathe it in," Teller demands. Thousands of innocent bystanders breathe in as one. My wind whips their hair and clothing around them. Propels the particles toward their lungs. Some cough or have other involuntary reactions to the dank, earthy scent of the agent, but most only do exactly as they are told, breathing deep, and falling more under Teller's spell.

I notice his control over me relaxing, now that I've served my purpose. I let the wind die away, considering if I can force the agent back out of their lungs without harming them, now that I've regained some semblance of control. No. Too risky.

The crowd remains riveted on Teller. All of them stand eerily silent as they await his next command. The villain brandishes his weapon toward his newly minted minions. Just like that, he has thousands of innocents awaiting his command.

My heart sinks. Too late. I'm too late.

CHAPTER 32

Iggy

I have to hand it to them, Teller and his cronies arrive in style. If they weren't here to carry out some sort of nightmare scenario bent on violating the free will of every person present, I might admire their flair.

As it stands, I do my best not to draw their attention, cowering in the shadows next to the stage as Gill and South, dressed as Arctic Blast, work in tandem to glide Teller and the unflighted members of his entourage in from above on a rippling floe of ice. Gerald standing there with the bad guys makes my heart ache. It isn't supposed to be like this.

Vespula and several other League members fly to either side, flanking the rest of the party in defensive positions. They seem prepared for resistance from the Brigade, but their unconventional arrival catches the nearest heroes unaware. You'd think they'd expect the bad guys to bypass the more secure perimeter by dropping into the middle of the square unannounced. But then, flight powers aren't the most common.

A quick-thinking member of the event staff snatches up a microphone and tries to get the crowds to remain calm and disperse in an orderly evacuation. I don't hear the rest of his attempt at controlling the situation because I flick on the music in my noise-canceling headphones to drown out anything Teller might say. He can't compel me if I can't hear him. He might be able to force his thoughts into my head, but it's his compulsions that I truly fear, so I'm not taking any chances. I'll just have to bide my time and wait for the signal from the others to act. Until the eleventh hour, I've held out hope one of the established heroes would show up to save the day, but it doesn't happen.

By the time Lustra and the other professional heroes set to guard the festival react, Pugsly has subdued the event organizer who was frantically trying to direct a calm and orderly evacuation. The milling crowds impede Lustra and the Brigade's efforts to intervene. Teller takes the mic from Pugsly, and any chance of removing his potential victims from the scene before he can act evaporates.

I don't hear what he's saying over the beat of the music in my headphones, but I see the reactions. The crowd moves in unison like something out of a horror flick. Lustra gets caught up in the compulsion along with those she is here to defend.

Gerald goes rigid, fighting Teller's command. He can't resist for long; no one can when Teller puts his mind to it. Gerald slumps in defeat as Teller compels him to control the wind. As one, the crowd inhales whatever chemical Teller has his minions spraying on the crowd below. His triumphant expression makes me shudder as he takes aim with the ray and opens his mouth to give his next command.

In my periphery, a fireball glows to life. Cinder lobs it into the air, giving the signal. After a beat, the fire erupts outward as Streak does her thing in spectacular fashion. I'm watching the paradox of a time rewind unfold, but there's no time to analyze it or get lost in the sheer amazement that she can undo the past several seconds of whatever mysterious substance traveling to everyone present's lungs. Streak pulled the substance backward in time, and then Cinder lit it on fire, destroying whatever chemical Teller is using to make the crowd obedient even without his augmentation ray.

I don't have time to marvel at their skill or

seamless teamwork. It's my turn to act, before Teller can use his augmentation ray. I reach for my powers, pulling all the sparks I can muster out of the air and condensing them into a single burst bigger than anything I've attempted before. It's a monumental effort, but I can't hold back if I want this to work. I don't have the strength to make a lightning strike. Lucky for me, I don't need raw power, just control. Enough control to take all that static energy, and force the amplitude to follow a damped sine wave pattern until it gives off a pulse that will disrupt any nearby electronics.

Just as I'm about to release the pulse and destroy the augmentation ray for good, a familiar figure rushes the stage. Dr. Lewis charges toward his goal, heedless of danger, intent only on fulfilling the letter of Teller's earlier command. He throws himself past the assembled villains and henchpeople in a surprising show of agility, and makes a grab for the ray.

Teller aims it straight at the doctor. Considering how addled he already is, I'm not sure what another concentrated dose of Teller's coercion might do to the man. It could cause permanent damage, if it hasn't already. There's no time to think or gather more energy to push into my attack. I have to act now. The pulse seems to detonate in my ears with a dull pop as my favorite headphones succumb first.

The huge speakers mounted to the stage above me also die in a horrific feedback screech as I destroy them with my localized EM pulse. As expected, every electronic device in my range is a casualty of what I've done. Even my phone's special shielding might not be enough to protect it at this close of a range. I can accept the loss, if it means saving the doctor and protecting all the innocent NPs gathered around the stage from Teller's control. There is no room for second-guessing. It takes every ounce of my strength to defy physics and contain the damage to the stage's immediate vicinity.

Drained now that I've completed my role, I slump down to sit. My head spins dizzily from the effort that one act cost me. But the dazed looks on the faces of the people crowded around the stage are transforming into panic, proving that they are no longer under Teller's spell. This isn't over yet.

All around me, shocked silence lasts for a heartbeat. Then the crowd snaps out of their haze and everything erupts into chaos as NPs flee to safety. Up on the stage, the villains under Teller's command scramble into action, some trying to salvage their plans, others scattering to flee the fallout before the Brigade arrives in force.

There are event staff with megaphones that

must have been outside my blast radius, directing everyone away from the stage and trying to turn the terrified mob into an orderly evacuation. But they aren't a mindless horde intent on storming city hall, so that still seems like a win to me.

It worked. Our wild plan actually worked.

I focus on the stage, wanting to catch the moment Teller realizes he failed and make sure the doctor is alright. Teller appears to be trying to get the ray to work, screaming something that is drowned out in the chaos and noise. He slaps the ray's outer casing, as though that might bring it back to life. I fried the wretched thing, though. Just like anything else with a circuit board. Teller throws the junked weapon at its inventor, his expression a portrait of thwarted rage as he turns to flee. Lewis cradles the ruined device to his chest like a child clutching a doll. He appears dazed, but unharmed.

Teller gestures for the others to retreat, waving Vespula toward him. She launches through the air, scooping Teller up under the arms to go with her. Before she gets more than a meter off the ground with him, Gerald springs forward, propelled by the wind into a superhuman leap. His hands dance with electricity as he tackles the League's ringleaders to the ground, sending a thousand volts into them both and knocking them unconscious like a human stun gun. There's no hiding that. Everyone will know Gerald's got electric elemental control now. But considering what we just did, maybe I'm not as weak as I thought. My powers might just work a little outside the box, like the rest of me. I'm okay with that.

Of course, that's when the Brigade finally reaches the stage to round up the bad guys and get them all secured with power dampening cuffs and loaded up to be transferred to secure supe holding.

Cinder and Streak stagger over to join me where I'm still resting amongst the destroyed sound equipment. Between pushing my powers to the extreme and the strain of a day spent navigating the festival, I'm more exhausted than I've ever been. But together we make our way to join Gerald behind the stage.

There's a tense moment where Lustra tries to bundle Gerald away with the League villains, since he was standing on the stage with Teller and used his powers as part of the attack. I bristle at her, acting as though we didn't do her job for her.

Before things can escalate, Balantin intervenes. I'm not sure when they arrived, but it must have been in time to see Ger's spectacular take-down. They remind everyone that Gust was the one who apprehended the villain responsible for coordinating not only this attack, but the entire recent supervillain related crime spree the Brigade has been struggling to contain.

I breathe a sigh of relief then. Moddy is going to forgive Gerald and everything will be alright. Lustra reluctantly releases Gerald, and he staggers into my arms where I cling to his solid presence, letting him block out all the noise and rock me side to side until some of my equilibrium returns. It's enough that I can face whatever comes next. Moddy gives us a minute of calm before they have to put on their Balantin hat again and usher all of us into City Hall to debrief.

CHAPTER 33

Gerald

I t takes ages to wrap up the aftermath of foiling a villain attack. The Brigade and city council sure change their tune fast now that the League plot Iggy tried to warn them about almost succeeded. In the time it takes for the Brigade to sweep in and detain the members of the League who were present, we transform from being a bunch of pesky kids to ignore, to being key witnesses, questioned for hours.

The long interviews, repeated over and over with various important personages, continue until I'm ready to drop from exhaustion. Iggy gave up trying not to openly stim ages ago. Their moddy steps in as soon as they finish escorting Teller and the others to supe holding. Balantin easily talks the inquisition into thanking Iggy, Cinder and Streak for their efforts to save the day. Then the three of them get bundled off to a quiet room with a nice cup of cocoa. Perks of having family connections.

Perks I don't share for once. My part in the attack prevents me from joining in that reprieve. And being questioned by an angry and overprotective Balantin after my perceived betrayal of their kid is not an experience I hope to ever repeat.

Still, I answer their questions honestly, as confirmed by Valor, a supe with telepathy that lets her function as a human lie detector. Even Balantin seems mollified when they finish questioning me solo. The Brigade lets me loose with a grudging apology for detaining me for so long, and an appointment to follow up with them about testifying against Teller when his case gets tried.

When my questioners finally allow me to see Iggy and the others, Iggy runs to me. They hug me so hard it squeezes the breath from my lungs. Then they kiss me right there in front of their moddy and our friends. Not any tame peck on the lips, either. Iggy doesn't do halfway.

They cup my face in their hands and devour me, for all the world like we've been kissing all our lives instead of only sharing this level of intimacy once before. Earlier today. It almost seems like this morning was a lifetime ago after everything that's happened. But Iggy's kisses are everything.

They don't stop when their moddy clears their throat pointedly. Streak wolf-whistling doesn't phase them either. I flip her off behind Iggy's back for that. But I eventually pull away before either of us gets carried away and forgets we have an audience. I still hold their hand after, unwilling to stop touching now that we're reunited.

On the walk back to Streak's car, the others fill me in on everything that's happened while I was getting interrogated. The Brigade seized the destroyed augmentation ray after another telepath helped the shell-shocked doctor shake free from the vestiges of Teller's compulsion. Cinder tells us that her ex lost track of Doctor Lewis in the commotion of the villains' arrival. He's now with the Brigade so they can place him in protective custody again. Hopefully, it will prove more secure this time. If not, Bloggler has promised to ask her connections about protecting him from further villainous interference.

Streak mentions overhearing lower level Brigade supes discussing a cleanup crew sent to the League's factory to confiscate any remaining samples of Agent X and the ray plans. They hope to stop anyone trying to replicate the ray or any similar devices. Talk about an uphill battle.

Once tech like that gets out, it's hard to keep it contained. But that's a problem for the future.

Iggy and I hold hands as we walk to the parking garage, and it is liberating to be free of any secrets. Iggy knows just how I feel about them, and with this simple gesture, I can let the entire world see that Iggy is my partner. We hurry past the mostly deserted festival that ended well before the scheduled time, thanks to the League's attack. That's a sobering sight.

It's late as we head back to campus. My thigh presses against Iggy's in the back of Streak's car. Iggy nestles their head against my shoulder and promptly falls asleep. We exchange groggy goodnights with Cinder and Streak before we part ways at our dorm. Then Iggy and I navigate the stairs up to our room while awkwardly clinging to each other, with Iggy still half-asleep. And now we're finally alone in our room.

Iggy tugs me wordlessly to their bed. I don't resist being pulled down on top of them, pressing them into the soft bedding. We kiss and cuddle and fall asleep with our mouths lazily moving together and our bodies tangled together. There might not be anything in the world better than falling asleep with the person I love next to me.

Except maybe waking up in the wee hours of the morning to Iggy rocking their hips against my ass. They have their leg thrown over my thigh and their hand caresses my face in the same firm strokes they prefer.

"Mm. You up, Ger?" Iggy whispers near my ear.

"I am now," I agree, amused. I capture the hand they are stroking my cheek with and turn it to kiss Iggy's palm. They giggle and squirm, grinding their dick between my ass cheeks. "Feels like I'm not the only thing that's up."

"Yep." Iggy rocks their erection against my ass with more intent. "My dick's up too. Is yours?"

"Yeah, Ig, feel for yourself." I arch to grant them better access. They reach around to palm my answering erection. I groan as I grind against their hand, and then back onto their dick. It's amazing to know I can have this with Iggy. "Do you want to fuck me, Ignatius?" I put it as bluntly as possible, trying not to leave room for them to worry about what I mean.

"Mhm," Iggy moans as they continue to stroke my dick and rock against my ass. "How do you want to do it?" They gasp out the question between thrusts.

"Tonight? Let's rub off on each other. Frottage," I say.

We're both too tired and horny to deal with penetration, but someday I want them inside me.

It's a fantasy I denied myself for a long time. One I thought I shouldn't want early in my transition, when I let stereotypes guide who I should be as a man. But I enjoy getting fucked. Or at least, when I play with sex toys, that's the fastest way for me to get off, and no, that says nothing about my masculinity.

It helps that I could get into a private clinic for my metoidioplasty the summer before my senior year of high school, not long after my 18th birthday. Having the genitals that fit with my self-image makes it easier to look at sex as an affirming act instead of something dysphoria-inducing. I still haven't found the right person to share it with, though. Or rather, I hadn't gotten up the courage to ask them for this until now.

And sure, my dick isn't that big and my balls are purely decorative, but they're mine. I can get erections, I dribble pre-cum when I'm really turned on courtesy of my Skene's glands, and I can have sex with Iggy without worrying about what's between my legs.

Sex got so much better after I healed from my surgery and I could jerk myself off just like any other guy. Iggy's warm palm slides past my waistband and wraps around my straining dick. I buck into their grasp. Iggy squeezes me tight. Their thumb rubs over the sensitive head of my cock, smearing the drops of moisture gathering there along my entire length. Their touch elevates pleasure to another level.

"Oh, fuck, Ig. That's so good," I groan, caught between the sensations of the hard erection pressing into my ass and their hand on my cock. Iggy kisses my neck.

"How about this?" They shift their grip to fondle my balls. The gentle roll and tug sends pleasure arcing along my nerves and I take a moment to realize that some of the sparks are literal. Tiny tingling buzzes of their powers dancing over my skin are like soda fizz, adding another layer of sensation and making it even more real that I have Iggy's hands on me. That thought alone has me teetering on the cusp of orgasm.

"So, good." I grind against their groin with more urgency and crane my head around for a kiss. "Need you to kiss me, Iggy."

"Then you should turn around so I can reach your mouth." They pull their hand out of my pants, wiping the wetness off on their sheets. The abrupt interruption cools my ardor and helps me back down from the edge of coming. I take the opportunity to wriggle out of my pants and boxers and toss them aside to deal with later. Iggy follows my lead so that we're both lying naked in their bed, taking in each other's bodies as lovers for the first time.

I've caught glimpses of them naked before. We crawled around in diapers together as babies, and ran naked through a backyard sprinkler on hot summer days as little kids. So it's not like this is completely new, at least in principle. I distinctly remember a shared oatmeal bath after a misadventure with a hornet nest when we were in grade two. That was one of the first times I comprehended our bodies had a glaring major difference. Over our years of friendship, I've seen them in swimwear, or just a pair of boxers, and a few times even stark naked.

This differs from all the other times I've looked at them. It's the first time I have their full permission to admire their body sexually and that changes everything. I want to take my time relearning every inch of them. How they like to be touched, where to kiss and stroke and lick. And where to avoid. How they look when they come, the way their dick feels in my hand, my mouth, my ass. I want them to lay me bare and make me feel things I've never experienced with anyone else.

Iggy swallows hard, eyes roaming hungrily over my body, reflecting similar thoughts to mine. "I love you, Gerald." They reach across the gap between our bodies and touch my face, drawing me toward them. We roll onto our sides, face to face and Iggy presses our foreheads together, eyes closed, then smooshes our noses together, too.

"Love you right back, Ig. What do you want to do first?" I nuzzle into their hand on my cheek and return the gesture in kind, keeping my touches firm, the way they prefer. Light touches make them squirm in a not fun way and I want this to be good for both of us.

"Kiss you until my jaws ache. And I want to rub our cocks together, make you come and cover you in my cum." They wriggle closer to me until our groins meet in a wet glide of hard dicks. Mine isn't as large as theirs, but it still feels incredible to rub along their length.

"Oh, fuck, Ig, yeah." I grind against their erection. "I want that, too. Want to kiss you and love you, and make you come. I want to fuck our cocks together until it seems like you're a part of me."

Iggy kisses me hard. I wrap a hand around our dicks.

"We can do that, like swap body fluids. If you want. I haven't been with anyone else. I mean, it might be kind of sticky and gross, but if you want to try it, we can," Iggy babbles.

I kiss them to get them to stop. "Yeah. Me neither."

"But you dated loads of people in high school." Iggy frowns at me, hips stilling as they process that information.

"Dated, sure." I pause my stroking and shrug like it's no big deal. This is one of those times when I'm glad Iggy doesn't expect eye contact when we talk. I've never really had to share my sexual history with someone before, and I don't want it to change anything between us. "Didn't sleep with any of them. You know until my hysto I was terrified that if I looked at a cis guy wrong I'd end up preggers, and before my meta I was too uncomfortable with my own body to even consider sharing it with anyone else. Most I ever did was kissing and a little heavy petting. And I got a full blood panel before the operation, so, yeah, all negative. Besides, I was kind of hung up on my bestie, so sleeping with someone else never happened."

"You wanted me all along?" Iggy sounds incredulous.

"Yeah, Ig. I've wanted you forever." I give them a chaste kiss. Iggy deepens it. We lose the thread of conversation for a while, our bodies coming together as we kiss. Chest to chest, we rub our dicks together with every writhing movement we make, arms wrapped around each other, leaving no space between us. For the moment, all coherent thoughts vanish in the rising tide of lust.

I wish we could stay like this forever, kissing until we're lost in rediscovering each other in this new light. Drunk on pleasure. Iggy's fingers glide along our lengths, joining with mine. They gather pre-cum from their dick before tracing their slippery fingers back past my balls and along my perineum to my hole. They press against the tight pucker. I moan into their mouth and bear down, inviting the touch.

Iggy pauses our kissing long enough to ask, "You can't get pregnant anymore, right? You got those bits removed?"

"Yep." I stifle a chuckle and refrain from pointing out that I wasn't ever going to get knocked up with ass babies regardless, and they would have stroked their fingers over it just now if the other option was still there. Ig won't find that funny. And the only reason they are asking something they already know the answer to is that they know just how much the idea terrified me. They were the person I sobbed to when I was twelve, extremely fuzzy on how reproduction worked, and convinced I was going to get pregnant after I kissed my first boyfriend.

"So, we can just fuck, right? Nothing between us?" Iggy works their fingers inside of my body and thrusts our stiff cocks together. Heat and friction meld with their tingling, electric fingers to make it all unbearably good.

"Yes," I agree, stroking our dicks harder. "You can come all over my junk," I urge them.

"I, ungh, you're so tight. Is this okay, Gerald? Want me in here?" Iggy wriggles their fingers past my rim.

"You have no idea." I moan as they rub over a particularly sensitive spot. Sticking toys up there got even better post-op. Not only am I more sensitive now, it also made it easier to find just the right angle to make anal awesome. And now Iggy is pressing on me just right and their dick feels beyond perfect against mine. Literal electricity dances over us both in tingling shards of pleasure. "So good, gonna come, Ig," I warn them. "Next time you can fuck me with your dick instead of your fingers."

Iggy doubles down, stroking me with little static discharges and thrusting our dicks together. I can't even wrap my head around how lucky I am to be here, exploring this wonderful new world of sensation with my best friend. The person I love.

I can't hold out much longer, and I don't try, just lock my mouth to Iggy's and buck out my release in their embrace. Iggy does the same, kissing me like it's the air we need and nothing else matters. The warm spill of their cum coats us both and I don't bother trying to hold back, grinding against them until long after I've come. Until I'm too sensitive to do anything but hold them close. Iggy eventually gets up to grab a washcloth and wipe up the sticky mess, but we find our way back into each other's arms when they climb back into bed with me. After today, I don't think there is a power on earth that can keep us apart for long.

CHAPTER 34

Iggy

T he week after the attack drags past in a muddle of exhausting tasks we have to deal with. The usual class stuff isn't so bad, but everyone on campus knows about what happened. Supe-related gossip always spreads like wildfire, and since Whirlwind being instrumental in stopping the League happened the day after his big debut as a villain, that seems to be all anyone can talk about.

Too many people saw what happened at both events to deny that Gust is Whirlwind. Everywhere we go on campus, we have to dodge all kinds of well-meaning attention from our peers. Bloggler at least spins the story to clarify that Gerald was never a willing recruit for the League. She does an entire piece on him for the *Supe Report.* I'm not sure how much her endorsement helps, considering the blog's reputation, but it's a gracious gesture. My folks apologized to Gerald, at least. And his family is proud of how he handled the Teller situation. So the people who count aren't holding it against him.

One of the best results of the entire debacle for me is that South and his gang are keeping a low profile now that their roles as Teller's pawns are an open secret. They swore they joined the League under duress and made some sort of plea bargain for a reduced sentence that amounts to community service for their role with Teller's plot. I don't know how involved they really were, but they haven't harassed me at all since the incident.

The other day, when I had to see a prof to clarify something about an assignment, South even stepped aside to let me have the elevator in the Nutter building. He didn't even crowd in after me like he would have before, despite the two of us being the only ones waiting at the time. He just nodded in acknowledgement and told me he'd wait for the next one. Almost like he cared about not trying to intimidate me after the way he treated me before. We aren't friends, but he isn't going out of his way to harass me anymore. It's a change for the better.

On top of our newfound popularity, we keep having to answer questions about the League attack and what we knew and when we knew it. If the Brigade, including Moddy, had just listened and taken us seriously when we told them about Teller's augmentation ray plans last spring, none of this would have ever escalated so far that the city is facing a class action lawsuit from the families affected by Teller's Agent X attack. That's going to be an expensive settlement.

Not to mention the civil suit from Doctor Lewis of the Brigade failing to protect him. It's bad enough that he got kidnapped once. The second abduction while he was posing as Nathan Steele doesn't make our local heroes look good at all. After a tip from Bloggler, a supe agency from out west swooped in to recruit the doctor with promises of providing a new identity, housing at a secure compound and funding to further his work with their technical team. He accepted. Which, good for him, but without him around for the city and the Brigade to nag with their endless questions, my friends and I keep having to provide what little information we have about what happened over and over.

I am not looking forward to having to testify when and if Teller's case gets to court. Filling out the deposition paperwork was stressful enough. It was emotionally draining to relive some of the worst moments of my life. And I know it was worse for Ger in a lot of ways, being powerless to disobey Teller's commands. Even thinking about it makes my skin crawl.

Gerald hasn't spent a single night in his own dorm bed since the incident. I've always been a cuddler when it comes to him, so waking up with Gerald wrapped around me every morning is pretty much the perfect start to my day. And he seems to take comfort in it too. That, and it makes it easier to fool around and help him get back to sleep when he wakes up with bad dreams. Orgasms seem to be effective at clearing his mind. And I have zero objections to that.

We've mostly stuck with rubbing off on each other and exchanging blow jobs over the past week. Classes and dealing with the aftermath of getting dragged into the League's nefarious plots have been beyond exhausting, so that was all either of us had the energy for in the evenings.

Now that it's finally Friday night, we have nowhere to be tomorrow. Which means we have all the time in the world to exchange pleasure. And, not for the first time this week, I'm staring at the food on my tray and daydreaming about sex with Gerald instead of paying attention to our friends. The cafeteria is overstimulating as all heck, so I tend to zone out during meal times. I need to replace my ruined headphones ASAP. I catch bits and pieces of my friends' conversation. Something about Streak wanting to host a sex toy party to get Gerald to loosen up? Pun intended, whatever that's supposed to mean. I go back to picking at my food.

"Sleeping," Gerald says with a low laugh that draws my attention to him. "I don't know about you all, but I am exhausted. Right, Ig?" He nudges me to give a response, but I didn't catch the question.

"Huh?" I glance around at the others, then back to my mashed potatoes, channeling the nerves at tuning into the too loud, too bright cafeteria into carefully smoothing my glob of mashed potatoes into a perfect circle.

"I asked if you had exciting weekend plans," Cinder repeats patiently.

"Mhm," I hum, smiling at the thought of what we are going to do tonight when we get home. "Big plans. Not sure on the details yet, though."

"Oh, yeah?" Streak asks, propping her chin on her hand. "Do tell."

"We're going to try anal," I reply with a shrug, since she asked and all. Cinder and Streak aren't exactly quiet about what they get up to in bed, so I figure it's okay to share with them. They were just talking about sex toys, after all. "Gerald still hasn't decided if he wants to top first or bottom, though." I don't really care either way, I just want to see what all the fuss is about.

"Oh, my god, Iggy. TMI," Gerald groans. He does that embarrassed thing where he looks all around to see who overheard. I doubt anyone cares. Why would they?

Streak chortles and elbows Gerald in the ribs. Cinder covers her smile with her hand. So I guess discussing our sex life at dinner is off limits. Good to know. I was just excited about it and everyone expects couples to fuck, so I don't see why we shouldn't be able to have a frank discussion about it. Besides, Cinder asked if we had any fun weekend plans. Pretty sure we're supposed to be all sex-drunk on each other a week into our sexual relationship, right? That's what all the shows I've seen portray as normal behavior. NTs are weird. How is this any different from Streak and Cinder mentioning that they are spending their night screwing each other so we couldn't play video games last night?

"What? It's just sex, Ger. We're dating. Everyone is going to assume that means we're fucking now. Right?" I ask, rocking a bit in my seat at the faux pas. I hate reading social situations wrong. This is why I avoid people most of the time.

Gerald drops his face into his hands. "That *so* isn't the point, Ig."

"Then what is?" I ask, smashing my perfect

round blob of potatoes in irritation. I'll have to start over now, but that's okay. It will give me something to focus on while the others finish their meal. "Streak showed me the new vibrating glittery dildo she got in the mail last week. How is this different?"

"It's not, but your boyfriend is a prude." Streak gives Gerald a playful shove.

"Boundaries, Zap," Cinder suggests. "It's great that you both got your heads out of your asses about bumping uglies, but we do not need a play-by-play of the details if it makes Gust uncomfortable to share."

"But it's okay for you to talk about sticking our anatomy into asses?" I grumble. Yep, it's official; social interactions make no sense. I wish someone would just write out a rulebook with all the nonsensical unwritten rules they expect me to follow, so that crap like this never happened. Oh well. I guess it makes sense to ask Gerald how much he is comfortable with other people knowing about our sex life.

"Figuratively is fine, literally, not so much," Gerald explains. "Anyway," he changes the subject, thankfully. He gathers his stuff to leave and puts his napkin on his tray. I perk up, not at all hungry when going home means getting to be with him. "On that note, we're going to go get our weekend started. We'll see you two tomorrow.

Ready, Ig?"

I glance up and he winks at me. Yep, I'm done eating. The potatoes taste like the cardboard stuff that comes in a box anyway, so it's not like I'm planning to actually eat it. I scramble to my feet to leave with my boyfriend. As we exit the crowded, noisy dining hall, he leans in close to whisper into my ear. "To answer your question from before, I plan to bottom first, Ignatius. I want you to bury your delectable dick so deep inside me I can feel you for days."

He nips my earlobe between his teeth, a gesture that somehow sends pleasure shooting straight to my dick. Or maybe it's the mental image of being inside of him. And that sexy growl more than makes up for the tickle of his breath on my neck. The hard scrape of his teeth helps override the shivery brush of air on my skin. My dick is very on board with his plan. We should be home now so we can do that. I lose control of my sparks and they dance over my arms in shivery swarms.

"Home. Now." I grab his arm and drag Gerald back to our dorm to have my wicked way with him. Or something. He laughs at my eagerness, but he picks up his pace, too. We stumble into our room and I don't even try to keep my hands off him, alternating kissing with tugging at his clothing in an uncoordinated effort to remove it.

Gerald eventually grabs my wrists and smiles at me. "Slow down, Ig, we've got all night."

"Yeah, but I'm horny now." I roll my hips against him, pressing my hardness into him. Gerald chuckles. "I can tell. Let me go clean up first, okay? Why don't you get comfortable in here?"

"You mean like strip and wait for you in bed?" I ask, to be sure I'm on the right page. At least I know what he means about cleaning up. I read about how to prep for this. It's one reason we agreed to wait until the weekend. Prepping sounds messy and unpleasant and I'm glad Gerald volunteered to be the one doing it first, because ick.

"Yeah, Ig, that's what I mean." Gerald rummages around in his closet for his shower stuff. He kisses me on his way out of the room. I flop down on the bed to wait. And wait. Gerald has been in the washroom for ages. I idly stroke my dick to stay hard. My bedding smells like sex and his body wash. Weird that I like it, but it's a reminder that Ger has been sleeping here with me. That he's all mine and I associate the smells with being held close to him after we come. Perfect bliss.

Gerald finally comes back into the room, wearing nothing but a towel slung low on his hips, and I prop myself up to take in his toned chest. I almost want to pinch myself to be sure this is real. He's everything I want.

Gerald struts right to the bed. He whips off the towel and drapes it over the back of his desk chair. I reach out to trace the fuzzy trail of hair leading from his navel to his perky little dick. My mouth waters at the thought of having him in it. I want him so badly. I roll out of the bed and kneel in front of him.

"Can I suck you?" I ask. His erection is centimeters from my mouth and I know the hot wash of my breath over the sensitive flesh has to be driving him wild.

"Do it." Gerald buries his fingers in my hair and tugs me toward him.

His other hand grips the base of his cock to aim it toward me. I lick a broad stripe over the smooth head. He gasps and moans, bucking forward. Mm, I love the slick slide of his dick past my lips, the way he fits on my tongue, a perfect mouthful. The taste of him, clean from the shower. And I love the low moan he makes as I give him pleasure that no one else has.

I'm the only one who gets to share this intimate piece of him. He's mine and I'm his and I can share all of me with him. Even the little tingling sparks I allow to dance from my tongue along his shaft. Static prickling between us, like pop rocks, making him thrust and moan and grip my hair tighter, not quite pulling, but gripping me in an effort to keep a tenuous grasp on his control. He tastes like sex now. Musky arousal flavoring the smooth flesh I'm sucking and licking.

"Shit, Ig. That's... ngh... Ig." His body tenses, and he pushes in as deep as he can get, his neatly trimmed pubes mashed against my face in a scratchy counterpoint to the smoothness of his flesh. His pleas trail off into wordless moans. I reel in my powers and let him ride out the wave of pleasure before I ease off his cock.

"Did you come?" I ask, wiping my hand over my lips as he catches his breath.

"Yeah, Ig." He drops down to sit on the bed.

"Can you come again?" I ask, climbing up to sit beside him.

Gerald laughs and leans over to kiss me, tender and sweet. "I might need a minute to recharge first. But I still want you to fuck me."

"Okay. Good." I climb onto his lap, straddling him for more kisses. "Because I want to fuck your brains out, Ger. Want to feel you come on my cock." He groans into my mouth and I grind against his belly until I'm smearing him in pre-cum and I have no control over the sparks tingling on our skin.

"Mm." Gerald kisses me once more, then shoves at my shoulders. "Okay, let me up so I can assume the position."

"Which position?" I ask, standing to let him adjust.

"Doggy style, I like it from behind like this, better angle." Gerald gets up on all fours, legs far enough apart that I can see his balls sway between his thighs as he wiggles his ass in my direction.

"Perfect." I stand behind him, so close that my achingly hard dick bumps against his ass. I am so on board with this plan. My first time making love to him like this will be way more fun if I'm not focused on whether he expects me to gaze lovingly into his eyes and then overthinking where to look or if it's okay to close my eyes. I've pretty much worked out that we can just get lost in kissing when we frot, but this is new and I don't need more details to worry about.

Gerald reaches back to hand me our bottle of lube. "Here, I already put some in there, but a bit more never hurt anything."

"Okay." I dab out a glob of the cool gel and slick it over my dick. "Is it okay to cum inside you?"

"Yeah, Ig. More than okay. I want it. Want to

have a piece of you inside me after we're done."

Okay then, for some reason, things that might normally sound gross are hot when we're talking about having sex. Weird. Not going to focus on that now. I want to be inside him already.

"Yeah?" My voice is all breathy with lust and I nudge my glans against his rim, pressing into him.

"Yeah." Gerald rocks back against me, bearing down on my dick. I lean into the resistance until his pucker softens and I slide inside. "Fuck me, Iggy."

I can't tell if that's an exclamation or a command, but either way, I'm not inclined to do anything else. He feels incredible. Tight heat envelops me, inviting me into his body. I thrust all the way inside of him, wishing we could stay like this forever. Always joined at a primal level that obviates the need for any communication beyond the way our bodies fit together.

I pull back and thrust in again. Gerald moves to meet me. We repeat the motions a few times, finding the angle and rhythm that works best. And then I hit just the right spot and Gerald gasps, arching his back and grinding his ass against me.

"More, Ig, fuck me right there." He reaches back to tug at my thigh, encouraging me to move. So I thrust into him faster.

"Harder, Ig," Gerald pleads, and I give him all I've got, listening to his keening moans and trying to stave off my orgasm long enough to let him come first. He asks for more, and I'm right on the edge. I don't think I can fuck him any harder, but I can send a jolt of static electricity right into the nerves he's begging me to pound.

My electricity, jolting along my shaft, sends tingling pleasure straight to my balls as it flows into him. The extra little spark is enough to make him come undone; a burst of wind pummels me forward, plastering me against his back, driving me deep inside of him and holding me there while I pump out my orgasm and give him everything I've got.

It seems to last forever, pleasure rolling over me in waves, Gerald's wind swaying me against his body. I thrust into him, shallow little rolls of my hips so I don't have to pull away. I never want to leave the warm embrace of his body. Eventually I have to ease out, though. My dick is getting too soft to stay inside him and he gives a whimpery little whine at the loss that makes me feel amazing. Like I'm awesome at sex and he wants me in him as much as I want to be there. He wants this moment to last.

"I love you, Gerald," I say, pressing a kiss to his bare shoulder.

"Mm. Love you too. Pretty sure you just fucked my brains out." Gerald collapses onto his belly on the bed.

"Yeah?" I stand, uncertain what to do now.

"Yeah. Snuggle me?" Gerald reaches for me, his wind nudging me closer.

"After we clean up." I might like the comforting smell of us, but that doesn't mean I relish sleeping in a wet spot.

Gerald grumbles a protest. I ignore him and reach for his damp towel from the shower earlier and wipe us both clean. Then I slide a dry towel under his ass in case he leaks, and curl up around him so we can cuddle together with one of our shows playing on my phone. We fall back into our usual bedtime routine and knowing that sex didn't change who we fundamentally are to each other makes everything even more perfect.

EPILOGUE

4 years later

Iggy

Graduation day comes too soon. Gerald and I moved out of our dorm room for our last semester at university. Now we live in a cramped little one bedroom condo that our folks and a hefty signing bonus from the Toronto Hero Brigade are helping us to finance. It's tiny, but the two of us are making it into a home.

The day we're supposed to get our diplomas, with all due pomp and circumstance, dawns with overcast skies. I spent most of the morning putting off getting ready by reading the *Supe Report*. Bloggler's doing her usual series of profiles on the latest crop of heroes to graduate from Super Universities this Spring.

The most recent one is about Ciaran, a European Super U grad, helping to recapture the escaped supervillain, Lady Diamond. Huh. Guess Gerald and I aren't the only students to have had a memorable college experience to put on our job applications. I finish reading the article and run out of time to procrastinate as the sound of running water stops in the next room. Gerald is finished with his shower.

Our cozy room with my blanket nest piled in the middle of the mattress calms my nerves. I love being here, in our shared space. The formal attire hanging ominously in the front of the closet is an invader here. Symbolic of the intrusive outside world and its demands. I stand and face down the new suit. It's probably the most comfortable one I've ever worn, but that's not saying much.

Most formal shirt fabric is scratchy and too stiff, the buttons too fiddly and the gaps let in random puffs of air if I stand wrong. Ties are too tight and flop around distractingly or drag into stuff if you don't pay attention to them. The jackets are too heavy most of the time, too, but that's formal wear for you. Ger helped me find a softer shirt and a clip-on bowtie that doesn't choke me or dangle weirdly, at least. And this particular suit is in a summer weight fabric that doesn't hang too heavily on my shoulders and breathes better than most. And a suit's layers of discomfort are better than wearing a dress.

I hate the irritating brush of excess fabric draped over my body, shifting and swirling with every tiny movement. It feels like something is crawling all over me on the rare occasions I've worn them in the past. Too bad, because I like the idea of mixing up my wardrobe with more femme-coded stuff. But in practice, I'm all about the comfort and the most I push the envelope on my gender presentation is when I wear my favorite faded pink and purple narwhal hoodie.

I got the suit because Ger thought it would be cool if we matched under our caps and gowns. I'd have just ignored the school's suggestion of formal wear under our robes if this wasn't important to Gerald. But he's really excited about dressing up and taking pictures and a fancy dinner with our families, so I figure I can cope with a few hours of discomfort to make him smile at me the way he beamed when we tried the penguin suits on at the store. That was my choice. And I'm cursing it as I stand in our bedroom staring down the darn clothing. There's something off about Gerald's suit. It's hanging crooked. I tug it straight and it seems heavier than mine. Weird. I won't dwell on that.

It's not just the outfit that has me out of sorts. It is still sinking in that we're finished with school now. I'm not ready to give up my comfortable routines. The vast lists of unknowns that are ahead terrify me and I've spent most of the past semester trying to work out how I might deal with any number of situations that Gerald assures me are unlikely, at best.

I'm pretty sure there is a non-zero chance of getting forcibly recruited to a villain organization. It happened to him once, it could happen again. And that's just one of the many terrible potential futures that have kept me up late at night pondering what life might look like after graduation.

I thought about applying to graduate school, just to put off this transition away from the familiar life of a student. Not out of any great love of academics or a particular subject. More because school is safe. I know how it all works and what is expected. And if I'm a stuffy academic, no one will expect me to be some sort of witty conversationalist. If I make a career in academia, I won't be the only professor who finds eye contact uncomfortable and I could get lost in my interests without it being a problem.

Except that Gerald signed on with the Brigade. As Gust, after the Whirlwind debacle, he's been a bit more humble, but he's still determined to be the big hero racing into danger to save the day. The only way that I am going to be able to deal with him out there on the front lines of defending our city from the League, and any other villains who pop up to cause havoc, is if I'm right there at his side. Where I belong. His sidekick. Or partner. Whatever title he prefers. I don't care, not as long as it means I can be the one who has his back. We make a pretty outstanding team.

"Hey, change of plans." Gerald leans into our bedroom and holds up his phone with a cheesy grin on his face. "Guess they need us again."

"Yeah?" I turn my back on the suit, glad of the reprieve.

"Yep. It's time to bring the storm." He strikes a ridiculous hero pose and winks at me like some giant cliche come to life. I lean in to kiss him, because I don't care how corny he is; I love this guy.

"That one's a keeper," I comment as I reach past the formal wear for the matched pair of super suits hanging behind it. The designs are new, now that we're fully trained heroes. The patterns come straight from the Brigade's marketing team. They have a thing for branding. Our hero suits complement each other. Gust is swirling blues, grays, and muted purples that evoke a hurricane and mine is all jagged lines in the same color palette, with lighter highlights to form lighting strikes. Together, we look sort of like an abstract rendition of an electrical storm.

"Yeah? I think it's my best catchphrase yet." Gerald nods and reaches for his super suit to get changed.

"Better than 'feel the charge'," I agree. "And 'zap attack', 'race the wind', or 'every storm needs a rainbow'."

"Hey, I liked that last one," Gerald protests. I roll my eyes at him.

"There's no rule that we even need a catchphrase," I remind him. Again.

"It's implied. Anyway, we've got one now."

We pull on the stretchy fabric. I've gotten used to the way it hugs my body over the years of training, and the newest models are even nicer than the ones we used as students. The Brigade's designers have the latest tech, so my custom Zap costume is softer, more supple and more breathable than the student super suits we wore at school.

"Are you ready?" Gerald eyes me.

"Yeah, I'm ready." Not even that worried about our first official mission as full heroes now that it appears to be about to start. Or the fact we're probably going to miss our graduation. I went last year to support Streak and Cinder and it was miserable. The super ball stadium where they set up the stage for everyone to march was loud, hot, too bright, and overcrowded. The graduates were all flashing their powers in celebratory displays that only made the entire experience even more overwhelming.

I bolted to Ger's car to unwind after our friends got their diplomas. I'm not looking forward to sitting in the sea of students who make up my graduating class. I'm mostly doing it because it's something I want to share with Gerald and it will make our parents happy. Well, they'll understand if we miss it working for the Brigade.

"Great—we should probably bring our graduation stuff, in case we get done with the mission in time for the ceremony." Gerald shuffles past me into the narrow area between the bed and the closet. He reaches for the suits and graduation gowns, bundling everything we need over his arm.

"Is it bad that I hope we miss it?" I ask.

"No, I'd wonder what you did with my Iggy if you were excited about the ceremony. It'll be over before you know it, though, and then dinner at the Keg." Gerald kisses my cheek as he scoots past me with our stuff.

"True." I perk up at the mention of the steakhouse. It's fun to go out and enjoy a fancy meal. The booths there always seem more private than a lot of places. The lights are lower too. So it's not as jarring to my senses as most restaurants.

As Geralds squeezes past me, something falls out of the pile of clothing in his arms, bounces off my foot, and rolls under the bed. Gerald groans, tosses everything onto our messy bed, and drops to his knees to retrieve the item. It must have gone pretty far. Gerald leans over more, lifting his delectable ass into the air. Damn, my boyfriend is sexy in his tight new super suit.

"What's that?" I ask, eyes glued to his flexing glutes while he searches for whatever he dropped.

Gerald sighs, gusting out his breath and using his powers to retrieve the item that rolled out of reach. He turns toward me, raising up halfway to standing so he's facing me, still on one knee. I try to read his expression. Not upset. Is he nervous? Weird.

"I was planning to do this after we got our diplomas. Hence the nice suits..." Gerald fumbles with the little box in his hands and doesn't move to stand. "Ignatius, you're my best friend. You're the spark in my storm and I want you to be my partner for life." He holds up the open box with a thin black band nestled inside. "Will you marry me?"

I freeze. Overwhelmed doesn't even begin to cover it. The silence stretches as I figure out how to react to this. I've never gotten a marriage proposal before, and I want this to fit the scripts I'm pretty sure Gerald had in his head. Am I supposed to jump his bones? Kiss him? Squeal and grab the ring like some rom-com heroine?

I don't know the correct response. So I just stare at the ring like it might bite me. Damn, this is so *not* the moment he had planned, and the pressure not to fuck it up or disappoint my love swells in my chest. But then I glance up to his face, the worry creasing his brow. I have to say something. I open my mouth and shake my head, tug at my ears, hoping that if I can calm down, I can find the right answer.

"Ig? It's okay if you say no." Gerald stands. He tosses the ring on the bed and opens his arms to me, a gesture he often uses when offering me a hug if I want it. I do, but I have to fix this first. I shake my head again, more emphatically.

"Oh, hell, no," I snap, reaching for the box. Gerald wilts and I puzzle out why. Oh. "I mean yes, I'll marry you. And hell no, I am not saying no to you, Gerald. I am going to marry the fuck out of you. Partners forever. But like, maybe we can just go to city hall and sign the papers, because I don't want a big party where we're the center of attention. So, yes to marriage, but no to a traditional wedding."

"Sounds perfect, Iggy. Anything you want. Always." Gerald wiggles his fingers, inviting me into his embrace and I give him the hug he wants, planting a kiss on his lips. It's fun to feel him up with our super suits on. I appreciate the illicit appeal of kissing him in our work getup, our faces obscured by the attached masks. It's hot on a whole new level.

Gerald's phone rings with the song he assigned to our Brigade handler. We both groan at the interruption and pull apart with reluctance. They ought to give our handler the moniker Buzzkill. It looks like we don't have time for a celebratory quickie for the road. I am definitely adding fucking my betrothed in his super suit to my list of fantasy fodder, though. I gather up our stuff to leave while Gerald handles the call.

"Duty calls. We need to get to Mississauga to handle Vespula's latest schemes. Looks like she's organized some sort of robbery at a medical supply company," Gerald gives a succinct recap of our first official assignment now that we're certified as fully trained superheroes.

"Guess we're off to save the city." I shrug. The chatter at Brigade HQ for the past several months is that Vespula has been working on a new allergen-free formula for her poison darts that has a faster onset.

An unfortunate incident last year ended with a teenaged hostage almost dying at a League affiliated bank robbery due to an allergy to an additive in Vespula's darts. Normally I'd be all for a villain fixing the problem and making herself less of a risk to public safety. Unfortunately, word on the street is that she also took the change in formula as a chance to find a compound that is harmless to most NPs, but that supes are more likely to metabolize into a potent neurotoxin that can knock us out of commission for several agonizing days. Or worse, depending on the dose. So stopping her from acquiring the tightly controlled chemicals she needs to produce the new formula is a top priority.

I'm surprisingly calm about our first official call out as full members of the Brigade. Probably because we've been doing missions with other heroes all semester as interns. I have an idea what to expect, and I know that with Gerald by my side, we can handle anything life has to throw at us. "Guess we can figure out wedding plans later."

"Sure." Gerald nods, flashing me a cocky grin as he gathers up our graduation clothing to bring along with us. "We'll hash it out over dinner. If we hurry, we might still make it to campus in time to get our diplomas. Come on, Ig." Gerald gestures for me to follow him, then he throws back over his shoulder, "It's time to bring the storm!"

***

Thanks for reading Super U: Rising Storm. If you enjoyed it, be sure to leave a review at www.amzn.com/B09FDJJ227.

For more adventures with different heroes in training at Super Universities around the world, check out the other books set in the Super U universe.

Each of the five books can stand alone, but there are plenty of heros to discover. https://www.amazon.com/gp/product/B09G2X6SQY

ABOUT THE AUTHOR

Alex Silver (he/them) grew up mostly in Northern Maine and is now living in Canada with one spouse, two kids, and a lovebird. Alex is a trans guy who started writing fiction as a child and never stopped. Although there were detours through assisting on a farm and being a pharmacist along the way.

Visit me online at:

http://alexsilverauthor.wordpress.com/

Join my Facebook group at:

https://www.facebook.com/groups/alexsalcove

Follow me on BookBub at:

https://www.bookbub.com/profile/alex-silver

Sign up for my newsletter for a free short story at: https://landing.mailerlite.com/webforms/landing/i2w6l7

And as always, consider leaving a review on Amazon or Goodreads if you enjoyed this book, reviews are of vital importance to independent authors, thanks!

Other Works By Alex Silver

Shift Work

Omegaverse MPreg Romance

Papa Bear (M/X)
Squirrel Trouble (M/M) (expanded edition)
Trash Panda (M/M)

Summer of Adventures

Kinky Contemporary Romance

Dungeon Master (M/M)
Knotty Boy (M/M)
Service Call (M/M)
Picture Perfect (M/M)
Puppy Love (F/X)
Stud Muffin (M/M/M)

Table Topped

Contemporary Romance

Roll for Initiative (M/M) Book 1
Charisma Check (M/M) Book 2
Saving Throw (M/X) Book 3
Plus One Bonus (M/X) Book 4
Dump Stat (F/F) Book 5
Party of Three (M/M/X) Book 6

Hauntastic Haunts

M/M Paranormal Romance

Dan's Hauntastic Haunts Investigates:

Goodman Dairy (*Book 1*)
Hawk Lake (*Book 2*)
Ivarsson School (*Book 3*)
Joliet Asylum (*Book 4*)

Free download links to the shorts are available in my FB group: https://www.facebook.com/groups/alexsalcove
Drew's Haunted Hangout (*A Hauntastic Haunts Short Story 1*)
Rafael's Haunted Halloween (*A Hauntastic Haunts Short Story 2*)
Lee's Haunted Holiday (*A Hauntastic Haunts Short Story 3*)

Psions of SPIRE
Urban Fantasy

Shelter (M/M) Novella 0.5
Bright Spark (MMMM) Book 1
Bold Move (MMMM) Novella 1.5
Keen Sense (M/M) Book 2
Weak Link (M/M) Novella 2.5
Quick Fire (M/X) Book 3
Clear Sight (M/M) Book 4
New Look (M/M) Novella 4.5

A SPIREverse daddy kink standalone
New Ground (M/M/X)

Shared Universe Series

Super U - Superhero Romance
Super U: Rising Storm (M/X)

Final Days - Zombie Romance
The Willows (M/M GNC)

Anthologies

Listen: The Sound of Fear
Haunt (M/M trans gothic horror)

Fix the World
Upgrade (gay trans cyberpunk)

www.ingramcontent.com/pod-product-compliance
Lightning Source LLC
Chambersburg PA
CBHW051529250626
47156CB00001B/286

* 9 781777 678678 *